Eden

Words of the King Series: Volume 1

P.S. LaRose

Renaissance Publishers
A division of The Renaissance Group
Irvine, California

Published by Renaissance Publishers
A Division of The Renaissance Group
9 Cortona, Irvine, CA 92614

Printed in the United States of America

ISBN: 979-8-88831-128-8

Cover Photos

Landscape: Anna Grist

Sword: Hundankbar at Pixabay

Cover design by Anna Grist, Serendipimoose Designs

Publication date 2022

I will open my mouth in a parable:
I will utter dark sayings of old:
Which we have heard and known,
and our fathers have told us.
We will not hide them from our children,
shewing to the generation to come
the praises of the King, and his strength,
and his wonderful works that he hath done.
For he established a testimony in Kaleo,
and appointed a law in Shammah,
which he commanded our fathers,
that they should make them known to their children:
That the generation to come might know them,
even the children which should be born;
who should arise and declare them to their children:
That they might set their hope in the King,
and not forget the works of the King,
but keep his commandments:

1

*"And then he will send out his chyail
and gather his Eklektos from the four winds,
from the ends of all worlds to the ends of the heavens."*

Eden rolled her hazel green eyes and shifted uncomfortably in the stiff-backed chair, realizing it was her teammates that were going to keep her out of the fire academy this year.

"You really need to work on your leadership and teamwork abilities." her examiner was saying. "You can't let someone try and take the load by themselves, you saw the result of that. You can't berate and shout at another for struggling, you need to learn to encourage and help them. Your angry shouting caused more problems for your team." Eden assumed he was trying to look sympathetic as he leaned across his desk, "I know that I will see you here next year, but right now, we feel that you need some experience working as a team. Maybe join a sports club or something where you can work on those skills, and if you get a job as a paramedic that will definitely help. Your firehouse is the most important team and family you will ever be a part of you cannot do this job alone or on your own terms," He stood, obviously ending the meeting. "I look forward to seeing you next year," his smile seemed insincere to Eden at that moment as she blinked in shock at the outcome of this day.

Eden moved mechanically towards the door. She didn't slam it or hit walls or yell. She just walked silently down the hall. She had been training for years for this moment, focused on this and had fully expected to succeed. The fact that she failed because of other's shortcomings was incredibly. She pushed open the front door and headed to the car that was idling in the parking lot. Her adopted father, Ian, must have seen the look on her face so he didn't ask anything when she got in.

"Hey, we got lucky, and Heather's folks called and said we can use the cottage this week, so we're going to go up tonight," he moved to a totally unrelated topic for which Eden was thankful. "If you want to pack when we get home, we can leave just after supper."

Eden nodded absently, thinking the quiet of the cottage might be good right now. "You're only twenty, there's lots of years to come," he said softly as he pulled the car onto the road.

Ian and Heather were being pretty good about the whole failing thing, Eden thought. Though she had over-heard worried conversations when she had come home, mostly wondering how she'll deal with this set back to her plan. Will she snap, or maybe it will be good for her, or what if she shuts down. They were always worried about her, she had always been different, didn't like socializing with other kids, seemed distant to most people, but she was driven. She had made it through her schooling for a paramedic but was always focused on becoming a firefighter. Eden just shrugged off their worries and ignored the comments and went on as if nothing had changed. She kept working out, kept studying, and never told them what had actually caused her to fail. She knew Ian thought it was the physical tests because she seemed overly obsessed now with working out. She'd spent each day at the cottage either running, biking, or swimming for miles.

In truth, Eden was going over every word that the examiner had said to her and finding all the problems with them. She concluded that if she'd just been in a different group she'd be studying in the academy right now. Her inability to do anything about this though, was what was really making her angry. If she thought long on it she usually got flustered and upset and then couldn't stand to be around the rest of the family. In fact, the kids were driving her mad.

At the moment she was trying to ignore them as they yelled from the dock below wanting her to come and swim with them.

"Eden said not now," Heather yelled down at them, "so stop bothering all our neighbors and be quiet," her voice gave a hint of frustration. Eden felt a little bad about that. She knew they cared about her, but she never knew how to interact or talk to them. She just never felt like she fit in, even though she'd been with them since her parents had died when she was four.

"Sorry Heather," she had never been able to call them mom and dad, "I'm going to go for a bike, then they can't call me," she averted her eyes as she spoke and headed over to the shed for her mountain bike.

"Okay honey, but remember supper will be in an hour, don't forget to be back," Heather smiled at her, but Eden was sure she could detect a sense of relief in her as she watched Eden get her bike.

Eden pulled her dark brown hair off her shoulders and up into a ponytail, snapped her helmet on, then hopped on and started up the hillside. There were several good trails in the area; none were really hard core, but good for a serious workout at least. She was quickly sweating as she worked to get up another hillside. The rocks were slippery after an early sprinkling of rain and it was hard to keep her tires on the track. Inevitably in these conditions, just over the ridge, she wiped out on some loose stones and tumbled ungracefully off her bike and into the bushes on the side of the trail.

She lay there for a few minutes looking dejectedly at her bike. It seemed uninjured itself, but Eden could feel the blood running down her leg from a good-sized scrape. She wiped it off with the sleeve of her t-shirt but could tell she needed to get a bandage. "The one time I forget my first aid kit," She grumbled, trying to decide if she could go on further. She really didn't want to go back already and have to deal with Heather who would be worried about the cut.

Just then an ear-piercing scream erupted from the woods behind her. Eden leapt to her feet, startled. The sound sent fear trickling through her. All the horrors of what could have happened in the woods were flashing through her mind. A bear, some other animal, some stalker in the woods, broken bones…

The scream came again, and now it had some urgency in its tone. Eden grabbed the heavy metal lock off her bike and rushed into the woods in search of the voice. She realized the lock wasn't going to do her much good in any of the situations she'd thought of by now, but it seemed irresponsible to go into an unknown problem with absolutely nothing. She crashed through the underbrush and was rewarded with countless scrapes from brambles and low hanging branches. She paused and waited for another cry, before going on, wanting to be sure of her direction. Following the voice, the trees began thinning and she could see someone standing ahead of her.

The noise she was making alerted this person to her presence, making them turn to her and she came face to face with an old woman. Eden stopped on the spot when she saw her. She was your classic grandmother, complete with curlers in her hair, old sundress, glasses on her nose, and even slippers. But the woman's face was contorted in fear. "Oh please help!" she gasped.

Eden approached her, still confused by her appearance, "What's wrong?" she asked.

"It's my grandson, he jumped off this cliff into the lake and he seemed fine, but then as he was swimming he went under water and hasn't come back up," her voice cracked from age and fear.

"Does he always jump from here?" Eden asked, going to the edge and examining the water below. It wasn't too high, maybe a thirty foot drop.

"Oh yes, all our kids do, it's quite deep…I just don't know what's happened!" she started to sob. "Please, help him," she thrust her hand out towards the water.

"Okay, okay," Eden removed her shoes and socks and the helmet she had forgotten she had on. "You'll have to point me to where you last saw him once I'm in the water okay?" she waited for the grandmother's nod then turned to the edge again. She knew it was not smart to jump into unknown waters from a height, maybe there were rocks and that's what had injured the boy, but her innate desire to be the hero took over and with a deep breath, she hurtled herself off the cliffside.

As she struck the water she was instantly refreshed from her bike ride, its cold penetrating her skin. She enjoyed it for a second, then struck out to swim back to the surface, relieved that there were in fact no rocks under her.

However, fear gripped her at that moment. As she started to try and swim up, something was sucking her down below. She felt like she was caught in some incredibly strong undertow. But there was no current here, she didn't understand what was going on, but her lungs understood that they needed air, or they were going to burst.

Frantic she thrashed out, trying desperately to fight against this pull and get to the surface. The more she struggled the further down she was pulled. Her mind was rolling over everything she had ever heard of about being caught in an undertow, but none of it seemed to fit with what was happening to her. She was now being spun in circles like a whirlpool, faster and faster until she was so dizzy she gave up her fight for the surface. As soon as she relaxed, she was pulled straight down with incredible force. Having lost all of her equilibrium, she started to black out, unsure which way was up, she felt herself hurtling forward until just as suddenly as that scream had come in the woods, she was shot out of the surface of the water to land in the shallows of a sandy beach.

Eden dug her fingers into the sand and spit water out as she pulled herself further onto shore. She gasped for air, and lay heaving half in and half out of the water. She had yet to open her eyes, she was only concerned about getting more and more oxygen into her lungs.

When her breathing had slowed slightly she heard a little 'hem hem,' of someone clearing their throat for her attention. It was then that she opened her eyes. She saw the lake beside her, and a great stretch of sand. Quite a bit further down the beach, large boulders jutted out into the water, and the tree line rose behind them. She shook her head a bit, blinked and rolled onto her back. She could not figure out where she was. Surely she'd known every last bit of beach on Lake

Kushog, she'd been exploring it for years. Then she heard the 'hem hem,' again behind her. Leaning up on her elbow, she turned her head.

Standing about ten feet away from her was the sternest looking woman she had ever seen. She stood only about five feet tall, but the scowl on her face would have frightened anyone. She had the appearance of a very angry teacher. She even had the glasses on the end of her nose to fit the description. However, her clothes did not work with the picture. She was wearing a billowing white blouse, like you would see in old pirate movies. Her pants were simple brown trousers, tight at the ankle and her hair was caught up in a flowing, magenta scarf, one reddish blonde strand fell down her cheek and added to the whole mystery of her look. Eden also noticed a ring with a huge black stone on her right hand. It was large and ornate, and somehow seemed an extension of this woman.

For a third time this woman did her little 'hem hem,' and her eyebrows rose slightly, suggesting she was waiting for Eden to get up. Eden struggled to her feet, still disoriented from the spinning and completely at a loss for what had just happened. She could see no sign of the cliff she'd jumped off and no clue where the grandmother had gone.

Seeing her standing the woman spoke, "Now, it is time we are off," she turned on her heel and started towards a thin line of trees behind them.

"Excuse me," Eden called, stumbling a bit as she followed. "Excuse me," she called again, but the woman simply continued walking. "Hey," she yelled this time, angry at the woman's silence. She tried to look stern herself but failed as her knees buckled slightly and she had to grab a tree for support.

"You will not speak to me in that tone," the woman turned on her with green eyes flashing and scarf whipping around with her apparently angry as well.

"I'm sorry, but you weren't answering me," Eden responded, refusing to be frightened.

"I will answer all your questions in due time, but you will have to wait until we are somewhere safe. You will meet the King and after you have spoken with him, I will answer the questions you might have," she enunciated each word with a sharp tongue, obviously annoyed at having someone not listen to her. "Now come, and quietly," she instructed, spinning again on her heel so that her scarf swung again behind her and Eden noticed some streaks of grey in her hair.

She glanced back at the beach, then at the receding view of this woman's back. Totally unsure of what was going on, but with no other explanation available, she shakily followed behind, grabbing trees to keep her steady as she tried to catch up, all the time wondering what she had gotten herself into

2

*"To the Eklektos exile of Perelandra, Thulcandra, Chalawan, Avior and
Baten Kaitos according to the foreknowledge
of the King."*

They walked in silence and soon came to a small dirt roadway.
Eden had recovered her balance and was trying to piece everything
together. She didn't dare ask another question, but she was struggling
to work out the puzzle of the last twenty minutes. The most difficult
question that she was facing was where on earth was she? She was
positive that she'd never seen this part of the lake before, she knew
every inch and was very aware of all that surrounded her biking trails.
"And the cliff was nowhere in sight?" she muttered to herself,
continually shaking her head and going back over the images of the
beach she had found herself on.

Suddenly she realized that her guide had stopped. She came up
a step or two behind her and stopped as well. She seemed to be waiting
for something and looking anxiously down a dirt road. Eden followed
her gaze, but the trees closed in around the road just ten feet away, so
there was not much to see. Eden hoped that perhaps now this woman
might explain a few things to her, but her hopes were soon dashed as
her guide did speak, but said, "Ah, here they come."

Eden was sure this woman was a bit off, especially because she
could neither see nor hear the signs of anyone else's approach.
However, just as she was reassuring herself of her own sanity, out of
nowhere four horses galloped into view and came to a screeching halt
in front of them. Two young men sat on the front horses, they were
dressed similar to the woman, with billowing shirts and plain brown
pants, but at their sides hung swords. Only the hilts were showing, but

the elaborate engravings suggested these men's importance to someone. She was just close enough to see a great lion engraved on the one sword, its mouth open in a silent roar and its paws up to attack. The same insignia was also blazoned on the halter of the horses and the sides of their saddles.

The horses themselves were incredible animals. Eden had ridden several times at summer camps, but the horses there did not have anywhere near the magnificence of these. They stood with their sides heaving as if they had been running hard for hours, yet their heads never dropped, they held them aloft and ears alert as if they too were on watch. All four were solid black, and the sweat from their run gleamed in the sunshine.

"Hurry up," the woman's voice broke her concentration.

"What?" Eden responded, realizing that her guide had mounted one of the two horses the men had been leading and was awaiting her.

"Get on the horse, we have far to ride," she sighed, as if she felt that Eden should have some idea what was expected of her.

"But…" she began, and with a quick look at her guide's furrowed brow she shut her mouth and grabbed the saddle horn of the last horse and swung herself up. Her mount took an anxious step as she settled herself, and threw her head around to look at this obviously inexperienced rider that dared to sit on her. "Is she going to throw me?" she asked worriedly, eyeing the horse as much as it was eyeing her. She secured her feet in the stirrups that were set exactly for her five foot five inch frame, she noted.

"What? Ruach has never thrown so much as a child," one of the men turned offended, "she is the most experienced war horse we have, she may not like you, but if she is told to carry you, carry you she will, until her death – or yours," he replied ominously.

"War horse?" Eden exclaimed, only slightly reassured by this man's comments. "What war am I going to?" she gripped the reigns tighter, and squeezed her knees into the horse's back. Just then, she heard what sounded like a branch cracking underneath a boot to their left. The other three must have heard it too because all of their eyes focused there, and the two men had their hands on the hilts of their swords.

"We are not going to war, I have already told you we are going to see the King," her guide sighed again turning back to face her, obviously exasperated. "Come, we have wasted too much time out here in the open," and she kicked her horse into the lead.

Eden barely had time to prepare herself before Ruach took off after the woman. She assumed that her horse's name must mean something to do with speed, as it seemed they were flying over the ground. She was not certain if the men were following or not, she was so desperately trying to hold on and not to scream as they flew around corners and jumped over logs that she did not dare to glance behind her for a second. All her concentration was rooted on the horse's mane in front of her.

She was not sure how long they had ridden for, but the sun was beginning to drop behind the trees as they came into a clearing. Now, rather than being surrounded by trees, they were galloping through farmers' fields. Occasionally there were small cottages with thatched roofs on the lands, and then she saw directly in front of them a huge walled city. She did not have much time to observe it, but the walls seemed to be made of cut stone, nothing overtly ornate, but well maintained. There were what appeared to be guards on the tops of the walls, and she could see inside that there was obviously a palace of some sort. As they drew nearer, the gates swung outward for them and they quickly passed beneath the walls. Eden noticed that here too were engravings of the lion as on her escorts' swords, and she thought she noticed several engravings of sheep or lambs.

Their horses only slowed slightly as they weaved through the streets, but they were certainly the focus of everyone else's attention. Eden dared to glance around her now that their speed had ceased to be breakneck and she noticed that there were some farmers here, as well as soldiers and what were perhaps groups of students. The earthy smell of animals and soil was strong. It was strange, she felt that she had gone back in time to the Middle Ages.

They came to a jarring halt in what appeared to be the courtyard of the palace she had seen from the road. In the centre was a tall marble fountain of the same great lion. The palace itself did not seem gaudy, but made of elaborate stone work. Its walls loomed over the courtyard with only small slits for windows. The front gate was at the base of a huge tower that was topped with a battlement with several guards patrolling. Its size dwarfed the rest of the palace that stretched out lengthwise, and was not more than two stories high. Scattered throughout the courtyard were also several tall leafy trees. They stole away the hardness of the stone and made the palace inviting. It certainly did not suggest war in anyway. Granted, there were patrolling guards, but several were lounging by the stables, others were talking and laughing in groups around the courtyard or clustered by fires, and farmers and regular citizens seemed to be mingled in as often as soldiers in the crowd that thronged around the street.

"Come," one of her escorts was standing beside her horse, holding his hand out for her to get down.

"Oh, sorry," she replied, not taking his hand, but sliding out of the stirrups and dropping to the ground on her own. He looked a bit taken aback but recovered quickly and took the reins from Eden leading the horse towards the stable.

"I'm sure she's glad I'm off of her," she muttered to herself, thinking it was really herself that was glad to be off, her legs and bottom had never hurt quite as much as they were right now.

"The King is expecting us," the woman called to her from the steps in front of the palace tower.

Eden paused for a moment. "How is he expecting me?" she wondered aloud, then asked "Shouldn't I change or something?" she gestured to her wrinkled and dirty clothes. She definitely stood out in her running shorts, shoes and athletic t-shirt. Her clothes had dried while riding but had acquired quite a layer of dust from the road making an epic appearance in this new place. She was sure her hair must be standing on end, her olive skin a shade darker with dust and she knew without a doubt that she reeked of horse.

"No, you may never do that," the woman exclaimed, almost upset at what Eden had just suggested.

"I just thought I'm a mess, and we don't usually meet royalty like this you know," Eden tried to justify her words as she followed the woman up the steps.

"We must all face the King just as we are, he must accept us that way or no way," she said cryptically, straining to push open great doors that looked like mahogany and seemed to weigh like stone. The inside was stately, Eden thought. The floor had a thick carpet of deep red running down the centre of it, leading them to a staircase at the far end of the tower. Stones in the walls were stamped with the image of the great Lion, and there were several crests and seals hanging regally on the walls.

The halls were lit with flaming torches that cast frightening shadows on the walls, but as they progressed down the hallway, Eden was struck by the sight of the most magnificent tapestry she had ever seen. It hung just before the stairs and was alive in rich greens, golds, reds and blacks. But what made her stop and stare at it was the scene it depicted. Here was the lamb that she was sure she had seen on some of the soldiers' armour. There was a great battle in the background, and you could see the King's banner in the middle of the fray with the Lion shining on it. But, here in the foreground of the picture, not the front of the battle, was a lamb, perfect and snow white. It stood all alone and was facing a soldier from the opposing army. It seemed to be staring him down and daring him to touch it. The soldier held a shining sword aloft and was about to slay the defenseless lamb, but it was the lamb that held Eden's eye. It stood with a majesty that the lion might possess, it stood with apparent knowledge of some great victory that would come. It was the strangest and most powerful picture that Eden had ever seen.

Suddenly she was aware of the woman standing beside her, not with angry eyes this time, but eyes staring admiringly at the tapestry as well. "This is a picture of our country's darkest day, and yet greatest victory," she said. Eden was sure there was a catch in her throat.

"I don't understand it," Eden said, still gazing at the lamb.

"You will someday," the woman turned her eyes onto Eden and almost looked proud, "I know you will," she turned and beckoned for Eden to follow her and the two began the arduous task of climbing the tower stairs.

As they ascended, they passed several floors. Most of these seemed to contain bedrooms, and there were servants bustling about between them with sheets in their hands or food on platters. One floor about five flights up was a great hall of meeting. Eden was able to glance in the doorway from the stairs as she stopped to catch her breath for a moment. It was a room that even felt serious. A large rectangular table filled most of the space. Around it were richly decorated chairs with a throne at the far end nearest the window. She was sure that noble and mighty things had been decided in that place.

She could not think long; however, as her guide called her on again. Finally, on what she realized was the seventh floor they stopped. She was breathing heavily and was sure that everyone in the tower must be in incredible shape to make the treks up and down these flights, even between one floor there were at least four sets of stairs.

The woman looked at her as she stood with her back to a heavy oak door. "You will meet the King now," she said, "when you enter, walk directly to his throne, drop to one knee and bow your head to him. When he permits you, you may stand to speak to him," she instructed her carefully, but Eden wasn't worried so much about what she was going to do as how she looked to be meeting a King.

"I'm in no shape to be in a building like this, let alone, meeting royalty," she exclaimed, "I've been drowned, air dried by a horse, covered in dust and horse sweat, and now that's all mixed with my own sweat from making my way up these stairs."

The woman actually smiled at her for the first time. "It makes no matter to the King, as I told you, he only wants you to come as you are," with those words she turned and pushed open the doors in front of her with a great sweeping gesture and proclaimed loudly, "your royal

Highness, I present to you the lady Eden," she stepped to one side and bowed her head.

For a second no one moved, and Eden stood frozen to the spot, but her guide glanced at her and whispered a harsh, "go," without moving her head. Her word threw the world back into action for Eden. Fear gripped her insides, which she felt was silly since she didn't even know this King that she was meeting. But as she stared down the room and saw him sitting on a huge golden throne, that had one arm shaped as a lion and the other shaped as a lamb, she was awestruck, and fear took over every part of her body.

It was only some strange mechanism inside that drove her forward, she felt like running the entirely opposite direction. She knew for certain that she was not dressed or prepared for this meeting; and yet the King rose with a wide smile on his face as she progressed down the carpet to him. His eyes were fixed on hers and never wavered but cried out love and acceptance. It seemed that for this moment alone he had been waiting forever. She couldn't even decide what colour his eyes were as with each step they appeared to change. Shecould see an agelessness covered with wisdom and sealed with love. It was the most profound moment of Eden's life. She had never experienced the emotions that were swelling within her.

In one moment, she felt totally ashamed of all that she had ever done or thought, in the next there was relief in acceptance and love, and then fear at the almighty authority and power this man possessed. Finally, as she stopped a few feet in front of the King, she didn't even have to think of what the woman had told her outside, her whole being knew she had to bow to this King and her knees gave way and she fell face down before him.

The world stopped again. All Eden could feel was the carpet pressed deeply against her forehead and her heart pounding inside her chest. In the most tender movement, the King placed his right hand on the back of her head and said, "Eden, arise and stand before me."

As he moved his hand back, Eden was almost pulled to her feet and timidly raised her eyes to again look into his. "Your … your majesty," she stuttered awkwardly, wanting to explain her appearance but knowing inside the situation called for silence.

"I have been waiting for this day for a very long time," he smiled, his mouth revealing itself under a short beard that was spotted with white. "I realize that you really have no idea of all that is happening here so if you will permit me to explain things to you, you will then have a choice in front of you, but you must listen carefully to me," his smile faded and his brow crinkled slightly with concern. "Will you sit with me?" he asked.

Eden had never wanted so much to be with someone before, and it was all she could do not to scream out "Yes," but she tried to remain dignified and said a simple, "Of course your Majesty," she tried to hold in her smile without much success.

"Good," he smiled warmly, "please, sit here on the steps as I instruct you," and he turned to take his seat again on the throne, his hands resting on the heads of the lion and the lamb. Eden sat down on the top step and turned her body to look up at the King, in fact, it was hard to look anywhere other than his eyes.

"Eden, you have been called here," he told her plainly, "you were always meant to live here since the day you were born. I was waiting only for the right time to call you to me," as he spoke, Eden's heart swelled, it seemed impossible, almost crazy what she was hearing, but the spirit within her was shouting out "I know, I knew all along." Every moment of feeling like she didn't fit in at home, wasn't understood, was alone - suddenly all fell into place.

He continued, "my name is Melek, King of Kaleo. You are currently in the fortress Migdal, which is in the city of Shammah, in my kingdom. You have met my servant Moreh twice now," he paused looking to the back of the room where the woman that had led Eden in was still standing, her head slightly bowed towards him.

"Twice?" Eden interrupted without thinking, and then slapped her hands over her mouth, horrified that she'd now offended the King, "Who interrupts a King?" she thought, hating herself.

"Oh, don't worry," he laughed, a deep rolling laugh that caused Eden to smile, "I don't stand on pretense so much, feel free to ask any question of me you wish." His eyes enveloped her right there in a great hug. "Yes, you've met her twice, once on a cliffside in your world, and then again on the beach in Kaleo."

His words sunk in and Eden suddenly recognized her as the grandmother that was so out of place on that cliffside, "I should have seen it," she whispered to herself, "and so there was no drowning boy?" she asked hesitantly aloud.

"Not so much, at least not in your world, there are some drowning people in ours, which is why I have called you now," King Melek's face took on a sad expression, but he came to himself again and focused on Eden. "Many of the people here have come from your world, at one time or another, some I have called, others have been enslaved by Nachash. He is the great enemy of our kingdom. His sole purpose is the destruction of my people and his own reign of domination. But there are others, like Moreh, who have always been here with me, they were born here and most serve me. However, some have rebelled and followed the one, Nachash. It is these that we must deal with constantly, and these which enslave your race," his voice dripped with anger. "You will be taught more on this later, but you have been chosen for a purpose here, one of saving and rescuing should you choose to stay."

"What?" Eden exclaimed, she could not imagine going anywhere else right now, and a fear that she was being sent away swept over her. Her rational mind knew it was ridiculous to feel so at home and at peace in a place she never knew existed earlier today, but as her eyes were opened, this world felt more real than her own.

"Yes, you have the choice," the King now stood and stepped forward to sit beside Eden on the step. He looked her closely in the eye, much more like a father than a king. "I have chosen you, but you must choose me as your king. You can go home, go back to your family and can never be bothered with us again. Or, you can choose to stay, at which point you will leave all you have, all you have done and become in your other home and remain here with me forever." He sighed now, "I realize I have not explained everything to you that you would probably like, but to do so would take years and you would need a greater wisdom than you currently possess. I have to ask you now, based on all I have told you, and all that you have seen to make a decision," he stopped and stood again.

Eden did not even have to think, her heart and spirit was doing all the thinking for her, "I want to stay," she cried, also standing now. King Melek looked at her, his face beaming with delight.

"Are you certain?" he asked again, "you will never be able to go back, and will possibly never see your family again. You are choosing to leave everything for me."

"That's okay," Eden nodded. "They love me, I know that, but they are not my real family, I never fit in there, maybe it's because I always knew I belonged somewhere else, and now I have finally found it!" she was speaking more to herself than to the King, but he again looked pleased with her response.

He nodded, smiling at her and placed his right hand on her shoulder. "Then daughter of Kaleo, I ask that you go through that door on my left," he pointed to the side of his room, "and take off all that was yours from your other home, discard it and put on your new clothes that you will find there. Once you have changed, please return here to me so that I may instruct you further," his right hand directed her a bit, as she stepped away from the throne and made her way over to the door he had pointed out. As she walked, she was sure that she caught a look between Moreh and the King, one that looked pleased with all that had gone on.

The room Eden entered was a small dressing room. One side had mirrors on the walls, and the others were lined with plush couches, covered in soft red velvet. Torches blazed on the walls, and again she could see that the stones were engraved with lions and lambs. On one of the couches lay a pile of clothes and a pair of boots. Eden quickly pulled her own clothes off and discarded them in a basket near the door. This was the first of many wonders that she would experience;

for as soon as they were in the basket there was a great flash of light that caused her to jump back startled. When she opened her eyes again, they were gone. All that remained was the scent of burnt wood, and a little soot at the bottom of the basket. "Well, guess these had better fit," she laughed to herself, shaking her head as she peered into the basket again.

There was a pair of black pants that came down just below her knees and could be tightened there. There was a soft leather belt with a short knife already attached to it. Eden pulled the knife from its sheath and looked at it. The blade was a brilliant silver and engraved with several words that she could not read. Its hilt had a lion engraved in the ivory bone on one side, and the other had the lamb on it. Its butt was also of silver and was polished to a brilliant shine. She sheathed it again and picked up a soft white undershirt, and then a fitted leather jerkin that went over the top. She was amazed at how well everything fit; over the leather shirt, she put on the familiar billowing white blouse that laced up loosely in the front and the arms tightened near the wrist. She flexed her muscles and stretched to be sure she felt comfortable and able to move well in her new clothing. Finally, she sat to slip on the black leather boots that came above her ankles. They were more comfortable than any shoe she had ever worn, and she stood to examine herself in the mirror. "I feel like I'm playing dress up for Halloween or something," she laughed as she looked the part of an old pirate to be sure. "All I'm missing is the eye patch and gold chain,"

Fairly pleased that at least she'd fit in, she flung the three-quarter length brown leather jacket on and headed to the door to return to the King. As she reached for the ornate oak door she paused, her hand almost touching the doorknob.

"What on earth am I doing?" she said out loud. Suddenly, that feeling inside her that was so sure of itself moments ago as she talked with the King became a horrible knot. She rushed over to the basket where her clothes had been and scooped up the pieces of ash in the bottom and stared at them in her open hand. "Have I just ruined my life?" she whispered. All kinds of thoughts were now rushing through her head as she thought that she had thrown away everything she had ever worked for, she had thrown away reality for some dream she was having, for some man she didn't even know. "And how do I know what he is telling me is the truth?" Nausea set in and she began to sweat. "Who is this Nachash, what's all this about slavery and me freeing them?" The unknown held her trapped in that room. It was as if a dark cloud had descended, her mind darkened, and she felt claustrophobic as fears were gripping her on all sides. She did not know what to do. She could not go back out to the king, nor could she stay here. All she wanted to do was to go home, have supper with Heather and Ian like she was supposed to. Eden inched herself further and further away from the door until her back was pressed up against one of the mirrors. She still held her hand out in front of her with the ashes of her clothes on it. Every childhood fear of the dark seemed to be enveloping her, and slowly, she realized, the torches were going out one by one.

Her eyes were huge, both with fear and from trying to see in the dark, when suddenly the door flew open and Moreh rushed into the room sword in hand. A blazing light burst from the blade as she cried out, "Darkness and Light cannot dwell together," her voice echoed in the small room like she was standing on a mountain top. The power of her words swept the room, and a very tangible darkness fled before them. She watched one of the mirrors sucking in the dark until in a great explosion, it burst, sending shards of glass around the room. In that moment, it was done. The torches were lit on the walls, the soft comfort of the room had returned, the only difference from a moment ago was that everything, including Eden and Moreh was covered in tiny fragments of the mirror. Eden stood from where she had taken cover when the mirror exploded and looked closely at Moreh. The woman was still standing as if on guard, her sword at the ready and eyes flashing, the ring on her hand seemed to be pulsing. She took a step towards the mirror, seeming to want to check that it was indeed gone, whatever *it* was.

Nodding she turned towards Eden. "Are you hurt?" she asked, in a firm, but understanding voice.

"I don't think so," Eden took a moment to brush off shards of glass. "What just happened?" When the darkness left so did all her fears, she was no longer worried about her decision, or about having been tricked, but she was utterly confused. She also noticed she still had her hand clenched around the ashes of her old clothes, and quickly opened her palm to wipe them on her pants.

"Nachash is what happened," the King said from the doorway, his eyes roving over the damage to his room. "How did this happen Moreh?" he questioned, for a moment forgetting Eden.

"I told you that I had heard someone on the path as we met the escort, they were gone once we noticed them, but I believe we might have said too much before, at least it is obvious he knows that she is here," she nodded towards Eden. "I am sorry, I should have been more careful."

"Don't apologize Moreh," the King shook his head, "we will need to investigate how he penetrated Migdal though, that is troublesome. I knew that he would find out of Eden's arrival soon enough, but to gain entrance here…" his voice trailed off as he too went over to inspect the mirror. He stared at it for a long time, then ran his hand around the edges. His fingers closed on something that he quickly deposited in his pocket, he turned and put his arm around Eden's shoulders and led her out of the room and back towards his throne.

It was on this walk that Eden really saw the room. There was not just one throne there, but two of equal size and majesty, but the one was set a little to the right of the throne that the King now took. He waved her towards the other throne saying, "You may sit on my son's throne as we talk."

Eden somewhat sheepishly took a seat and tried to be dignified as she turned to the king. He seemed to know what she was thinking and smiled.

"There is much for you to learn, and I want you to learn quickly. I know you are a good student, and you will need that ability to gain much knowledge before you can proceed from this place. Nachash was one of my servants, my second in command after my son, he is now a great enemy and wants nothing to do with my kingdom, except to take from it. He has been interested in you for a long time and is not pleased you have chosen me King. I'm afraid he was trying already to enslave and take you for himself. We must be diligent and that is why you must learn, can you do that?" he asked her, his eyes imploring her to do her best.

"I will," she replied quickly, letting the idea that some unknown enemy was interested in her roll around her mind.

"Good, then I have only one thing further to discuss with you. You have chosen me, and my kingdom. You now have one more choice. After a brief initial service as Chayil there are many things you can choose to do here, you may live your life in relative peace working a trade or agriculture, you may teach, you may do many things. I have told you what I desire for you, and I believe you have always felt a calling on your life to help people, but I need now for you to choose what you shall study here," he paused and Eden quickly cut him off.

"I want to learn to be like her," Eden pointed to Moreh who was standing by the dressing room door watching the two of them. A smirk crept onto her face as she heard Eden's words.

"Well," the King laughed, "you make my instructions much easier. You have chosen well. You will be trained as a Chayil for Kaleo, hopefully becoming Gibbor Chayil and you will serve me with your life. Stand," King Melek himself stood and pointed to the step in front of him for her to stand on.

Eden stepped down and lifted her head to the King.

"My words are life to you, my words are a light to your path, my words are your salvation, your instruction and your peace. Treasure my instruction, listen to my direction and cling to my words. This above all is the key to life." He spoke in the authoritative voice of a king. Gone was his fatherly advice, gone was his protective gaze; instead, they were replaced by power and authority.

He continued,

> "For the King will not abandon His people
> Nor will He forsake His inheritance,
> For judgment will again be righteous
> And all the upright in heart will follow it.
> Who will stand up for me against evildoers?
> Who will take his stand for me against those who do wickedness?"

"I will," Eden said, punching the air with her right arm. As soon as she did it she was unsure why she had responded like that and again felt embarrassed as she let her arm drop back to her side, but she knew deeply in her spirit that what the King asked, she had to do.

Apparently, her response was what had been expected, as both the King and Moreh nodded. The King spoke again, "then you have pledged the pledge of my Chayil, my warriors, you have given yourself in service to me, all of you," he turned and took something off of the small table to his left. He opened his hand to reveal a gleaming blue stone on a thick silver chain. "This is a pala stone," he slipped the necklace over her head. "Keep it on you at all times, as you become ready you will learn to understand the stone.

Moreh will be your instructor, she will prepare you to enter the Chayil training, help you understand this new world and new life you have chosen. You must learn all she has to teach you, and not until she deems you ready will I permit you to serve me outside of these walls," he paused, and waved Moreh over. "Take charge of Eden, she is in your hands now," and with those words he dismissed them.

3

"The King has said,
'I have made a covenant with my Eklektos,
I have sworn to my servant,
I will establish you forever and build you for all generations…'"

The next few hours flew by for Eden. After the King left her with Moreh, she was escorted through the palace and out into what appeared to be some form of a school just to the west of Migdal. As she trailed behind Moreh she tried to get her bearings. There was a great open field in the middle of several rough stone buildings. In the centre was an area marked off into a square by rope, and a group of ten chayil appeared to be going through some form of training drill. However, Eden did not have long to watch them as Moreh rushed her between the buildings to another set of similar structures about thirty feet behind the first. Here Moreh stopped at a worn wooden door marked with the letter 'H.'

"This is your room. I realize it has been a long day for you, one with many changes so tonight you will rest. Your supper will be brought to you shortly, you may get settled here. You will find reading and writing materials at your desk. Your classes will start tomorrow morning, directly following your breakfast, which will also be brought to you," she glanced behind Eden, "back to work," she called.

Eden turned her head to see several other young people scattering at Moreh's rebuke. "As I was saying, after breakfast you shall meet with me, and we shall have some preliminary classes before you join the general population of students. Do not think you can get away with anything but your best with me. You shall be diligent in all your studies, in class and on the field or I will send you to a lesser trainer and find you another vocation to pursue," she was glaring down her nose at Eden at this point, so Eden nodded without responding. "Good," Moreh pushed her glasses up and looked somewhat satisfied. "Your most important task is to learn all that the King has transcribed. His words are life, and you must not depart from them. They must be hidden in your heart, or you will not survive," With those ominous words, she turned on her heel and stalked back across the yard.

As she disappeared between the buildings, Eden sighed and reached for her door. As the iron handle lifted, she wondered how a five-foot-tall woman can stare you down. Entering, she discovered a humble room. The walls were stone, like an old Scottish settlement home, even the floor was made of stone slabs that had been swept clean. On the back wall was a small fireplace, with a warm fire already glowing for her, and a small pile of wood stacked beside it. The bed was nothing extravagant, but it certainly would do the job. It was layered with linen sheets and a course wool blanket. On the remaining wall was a small wooden desk, and like Moreh said, there was a book and writing parchment sitting on its top. Having nothing to unpack, though she did have a small roughly constructed chest of drawers, she decided she might as well rest a moment until her supper arrived.

Eden awoke to banging on her door and someone clearing their throat on the other side. "Hello?" an impatient voice called out.

"I'm coming, sorry," Eden shook herself awake and stumbled to the door, trying to smooth down her hair as she pulled it open. Standing in front of her was a young woman, probably about her age with piercing grey eyes and jet-black hair. She stood just taller than Eden and was very obviously looking her up and down. She was dressed in the same clothes Eden had on, so she assumed she was a fellow student. The girl's nose wrinkled a bit as she pushed the wooden tray she carried to Eden. "I expected someone…" she paused and raised an eyebrow, "…different," she finished. Clearly unimpressed, she turned and stalked back between the barracks.

"Pleased to meet you too," Eden called out after her, as she watched the girl's back. Sniffing to herself at the rudeness she turned back into her room slamming the door. Her supper consisted of a thick vegetable soup, rye bread, some slices of cheese and a glass of grape juice. "Simple, but hearty," she thought as she set the tray down on her desk and began to eat ravenously. As she swallowed a bite, she looked at the wooden utensils and cup. Both appeared to be carved from single pieces of wood, they definitely had more character than her stainless-steel ones back home. "Home" she said out loud. She thought of her world, wherever that was, as home, but it certainly never felt like home, never felt like this. She'd never done anything in her life based on how she felt. She was always such a planner, organized to a fault, and yet she was so confident in this decision, as insane as it was.

She eased herself back in her chair and paused for a minute. She let her eyes rove around the room again. She still didn't really have any idea of what she was getting into. This morning she had simply been training to take that entrance exam again and now here she was in a whole other world. Not your typical day, she chuckled to herself, but something seemed to fit, to be right. She'd never felt this way about anything or any place in her life before. With a shrug, she decided that she'd take the adventure as it came to her. "Even if they need more comfortable chairs," she stood up and plucked a sliver from the leg of her pants.

Sitting back down, she pushed the tray aside and picked up the worn leather-bound book that had been here when she arrived. "What was it Moreh said?" she asked herself aloud, "the King's words are life? Or something like that," she pulled her chair over so that she was sitting by the fire and turned the book over in her hands. There was no title, or publisher on the cover so she flipped it open to the first page. She was surprised to find that it was more of a journal. It was written in someone's handwriting, no mass production or typed font, "What was I expecting, I'm in the Middle Ages," she reminded herself with a grin. Each entry was dated, and it was signed, she squinted her eyes to try and read the signature, "Melek," she wrinkled her forehead at the name.

"That's the King's name," she suddenly realized. "These must be the King's words that Moreh was talking about," she flipped back to the first page, "I don't understand how these are life, but I'm guessing I have to study this."

She started to read the first entry…

> *For the King will not abandon His people*
> *Nor will He forsake His inheritance,*
> *For judgment will again be righteous*
> *And all the upright in heart will follow it.*
> *Who will stand up for me against evildoers?*
> *Who will take his stand for me against those who do*
> *wickedness?*

"That's what he said," Eden's mind went back to the throne room. Interested now, she began to read and re-read the first few journal entries. She was fascinated with the King's obvious desire for his people, for righteousness and judgment. His words, though seemingly written for himself, also had a strange way of being relevant for others to read. They were full of instruction and ethics. He was very clear why being upright was so important, and what would happen to those who were not.

Eden read into the night, at some point slipping into her bed, and finally, exhausted from her day, she fell asleep with the words of her new king lying on her chest.

Again, Eden was startled awake by banging on the door, and this time it was followed by an exasperated sigh on the other side. Struggling up, Eden pulled open the door to be confronted by the same disapproving grey eyes.

"Breakfast," the girl said to her, this time not making eye contact at all but shoving the tray forward.

When Eden took it from her hands, she spun around and practically ran back down the laneway between buildings. Eden watched her go this time, shrugged and went back inside.

Just as she finished up her breakfast, her door flew open and in walked Moreh. With a sweep of her hand the door slammed behind her, but Eden was almost sure she never actually touched the door. Her forehead gave away her thoughts and Moreh addressed her, "You will learn," she said vaguely.

"Now, we have studies to perform before we go any further, and before you can enter into the other students' classes," she pulled her magenta scarf from her head, letting her hair tumble past her shoulders and sat down on the side of Eden's bed. Her eyes moved over the desk, and darted around the room until she found the King's book lying beside the bed. Her lips curled into a slight smile and she began reworking her silver streaked hair back onto her head. "Good, you have been reading it," she said, more a question than statement.

"Yes, I started it last night, it's the King's words that you told me were life, right?" Eden asked, eager to know if her assumptions were correct.

"Yes...,"

"But I don't understand how they are life?" Eden didn't let her finish.

Moreh sighed, annoyed at the interruption. "That you will learn as you grow. No one can explain that to you, it is something that must be experienced," she held up her hand to stop Eden as she had opened her mouth with another question.

"Do – not - interrupt - me – again," she said pointedly. "You may ask questions when I tell you that you may ask questions."

Eden clamped her mouth closed jarring her teeth and winced.

"Good," Moreh stood. "Now we will learn some history and geography. You cannot expect to succeed or compete with other students who have had a lifetime here if you don't even know where you are going or what you are fighting," she pulled out of the pocket of her cloak what appeared to be a slightly oversized pocket watch. Moreh clicked the face open and set it on the table in front of Eden. "Time, I believe that you measure time differently than we do here, so in order for you to get anywhere when you are supposed to you will need to understand ours."

Eden looked down at the watch. Its face was divided into seven, rather than twelve and instead of numbers there were letters. M L T S N V and C. She looked up at Moreh, who seemed to be waiting for her to do something. Eden's eyes darted around the room and came to rest on the parchment and charcoal pencil that lay there. Suddenly understanding she grabbed them and started to copy the watch face. Moreh continued, "this is a sentinel," she gestured to the watch. "You will see one on the side of the tower facing the training yard, most cities have them, and many inns and other establishments, and some people have personal ones like this," she leaned over Eden's notes. "The day is divided into seven watches."

Eden chuckled at the use of the word watch. However, the stern glare from her teacher convinced her she should keep her thoughts to herself. "The sentinel is based off the moons. You can read the time of day by looking to the sky. The morning moon is Hora and the star Alcar travels around it in the same way the hand on the sentinel moves. In the evening Brev rises and the star Leo travels around it," Moreh took Eden's pencil and quickly sketched the moons. "The first watch is Matin, followed by Laud, then Terce, Sext, None, Vesper and finally Compline," Moreh seemed satisfied with Eden's notes, and apparently felt no other explanation was needed, as she pulled a large parchment out of her own satchel.

Eden shook her head at the thought, "two moons and seven watches, so much for elementary school science," but she didn't have much time to consider this as Moreh lay her parchment out, which was actually a large map of Kaleo and started to lecture.

Moreh pointed out where Eden had arrived, and the route they took back to Migdal. She pointed out strongholds of the King as well as their enemy Nachash. She didn't explain much there yet, but drew Eden's attention to where his strongholds lay, where there had been attacks on the Kings' people and lands, and that in fact, all the lands were the King's and that Nachash had rebelled somehow and taken over various areas, in particular Gavaah to the south.

"You must have this map memorized, you need to know every forest, every pathway, every field and road," she turned from the map to face Eden. "If you do not learn this, you will not be able to be used as you have desired and serve with me," she stressed this point and Eden nodded, staring intently at the map. She had always been good at transposing things quickly from screens and textbooks in school, and all the while that Moreh had been teaching she had been sketching the same maps complete with rivers, paths, roads and more on her paper.

Moreh glanced down at her notes and smiled, "you are doing well," she turned back to the parchment, "Remember, these are the known ways, I am sure there are other paths and trails hidden to the eye out there, some still to be made. But you will only find those through your actions when you are out in the field,"

Eden made a note and nodded. She was determined to learn all and find every possible route in and around this country.

"Am I permitted to leave my room as I study today?" she asked, cringing that perhaps she was not supposed to speak.

Moreh turned and seemed to be estimating why she had asked this question. She nodded slightly to herself then and answered, "yes but beware not to leave the city limits," she drew her finger around the area that encompassed Shammah's borders on the map. "You are not given the right to go beyond these bounds and do not test me or the King on this," she glared down at her student. Eden quickly nodded her agreement.

"Good, now we go on to history," And with a sweep of her hand, she had the maps away. Moreh moved to the bed and sat down. "You must take good notes as I shall simply lecture you on our history and tradition here in Kaleo."

Moreh spent several hours instructing Eden on the customs, sayings, traditions and expectations that are a part of Kaleo. It seemed a huge list, and while she was speaking Eden attempted to prioritize what she should learn first. Things that pertained to royal appearances and dinning etiquette she left for last, but was very concerned about rites of battle, creeds and such. But finally Moreh got to something interesting. They had both been eating some lunch that had been delivered earlier. The teacher took a sip of her drink and then continued.

"Now for Nachash," she sighed, and immediately Eden's ears perked up and she focused all her attention onto Moreh and off her notes.

Moreh saw her interest and seemed wary of it, but she continued, "King Melek has explained to you that people from your world are called here. The King has always been the one who calls, and to do so he has used an ancient artifact called the 'drawing rod'. This rod, when wielded by the King, can allow him to speak to a person's heart and draw them here to Kaleo," she paused for effect, "sadly, this rod was lost to us years ago."

"Lost? How?" Eden scribbled notes as she watched her teacher's face drift off towards some memory.

"How is not important, but it has cost many lives," she almost growled the words, "Nachash was the second in command here, and in his rebellion and flight he took the rod with him."

"But you said only the King can call someone right? So, it should be okay?" Eden tried to understand the problem.

"No, only the King can use it properly. Another one who is also powerful could use the rod, but never to call someone, only to enslave them. Instead of speaking to their hearts, it speaks to their passions and emotions. It gives a false sense of power and pleasure. Nachash has used this countless times since stealing it and has enslaved hundreds, even thousands," Moreh sighed again.

"So, they are all lost? Is there no hope? Is that what he wanted to do to me?" Eden peppered her teacher with questions, having forgotten her paper and notes.

"No," Moreh paused again, carefully considering her words. "No, there is hope, we can free them, that is the greatest purpose for which I and my fellow Gibbor Chayil serve. And no, again to your last question – that is not what he wanted with you."

She looked into Eden's eyes, this time with sympathy. "He wanted you dead."

4

*'For deceivers will arise and perform signs
and wonders to lead them astray,
and if possible, even the Eklektos.'*

With that ringing pronouncement, Moreh decided that there had been enough teaching for the day and packed up her things and left without answering any of Eden's queries into this grim fact about Nachash.

Eden sat down on her bed again as she watched the door close. 'Who leaves after saying something like that?' she thought shaking her head in disbelief. Her mind was reeling from all the information she had tried to absorb, then this statement – she felt a bit fried. She ran her hands through her hair wishing she knew where to get a shower, then flipped open her notebook.

Her eyes ran over the maps she had sketched. She figured she might as well focus on Migdal since that was one location she was actually allowed to investigate. The castle itself was a seven walled structure, with seven pillars being the focal point in the architecture. There were only three games out of the castle the horse gate on the South Side, the Soldiers gate on the North and the King's gate on the East. The home of the King was the Tower that Eden had first entered. The buildings directly attached, branched off in a T shape and held dining rooms, meeting rooms, guest rooms and the King's quarters. Behind the Tower, to the West of the castle the recruit barracks ringed a large practice yard for their training. Eden was in the back row of barracks she could see now, and the kitchen was to the west of her room, south was the stables, and her classrooms were in the southwest corner. The King's Guard had their barracks to the North, directly beside the soldier's gate.

From here, the rest of Shammah mirrored the castle. The Town was also six sided with the seventh side being the horse pastures bordered by a hillside that dropped down to the river Massah. The city had twelve-foot-thick walls where the Chayil patrolled. There were however, four gates to the city. The main gate faced the East, a small animal gate was off to the north, probably to allow for farmers to bring in their livestock to sell. There was a rear gate to the west, and all the way around on the southwest side was the King's Own gate, where only the King's Chayil, servants and horses could pass through. It was from here the cavalry would enter and exit for their practices and to graze the horses. The people of Shammah lived in twelve subdivisions (Eden couldn't think of a better word) that again ringed the castle. There seemed to be many homes within these subdivisions, and two main roads ran in a circle around the Town with other small streets and alleys connecting them. There were also eight guard houses that stood beside each gate. Outside these walls, for what was another twenty kilometers were the farmlands that were attached to Shammah.

Eden went over and over the maps until she was quite confident in her layout. She assumed that it was the twenty kilometers outside the walls that constituted the city limits she was allowed to explore. "Of course, that could get me in a lot of trouble, but Moreh didn't let me ask any more questions, so she can't get too mad," she mumbled to herself as she stuck her notebook into the back of her pants and threw her coat over top. She slipped her boots on and pulled open her door to see the moon Hora. It must be just after… None. She pulled her notebook back out to check that was the right watch, so she had at least two hours before the sun would start its way down, plenty of time to investigate the area. She quickly strapped her belt and knife on, taking a moment to admire the silver work of the knife again, then slipped out her door.

Not many seemed to be about. Eden had decided to walk inside the castle walls first, so she headed off to the south. Everything was made of stone, again, nothing fancy, but well designed, like old settler homes she knew. Each building had either a lion or lamb engraved on the cornerstone. It was at the first building that Eden discovered why no one was about. She could hear classes going on here. She paused by an open window to listen. There was an instructor teaching the use of the staff for fighting and apparently drawing diagrams for his students. Another was asking questions of geography from lands far away from here, from what Eden could recall of her own class. Finally, another was talking about lambs and how they were slaughtered for food. 'That's a strange class for chayil,' Eden thought.

Just then she heard footsteps coming across the wall of the castle, so she moved on. As she rounded the corner of the building, she saw a guard making rounds. He waved down at her as he passed. She kept going in her circle until she had made her way back to the kitchen that was just beside her own barracks. She had passed at least a dozen guards on the walls, more at the gates and the gates to the Tower. All had noticed her, most waved some pointed her out to others and started whispered conversations. She was put a bit on edge by that, but the normal servants and citizens that were in the courtyard or near the stables seemed to take no notice of her.

She stopped at the kitchens because she had now discovered something that was not on her map. As she had come around the barracks, she had spotted a servant returning from near the outer wall with an empty basket. Intrigued, she waited until the servant had re-entered the kitchens then slipped quietly over to where she had seen her emerge from. There, just behind a large hedge, Eden found a fourth exit from the castle grounds. Granted, it wasn't a very nice exit, but one worth exploring and remembering she thought.

What lay behind the hedge was a small ditch, not much larger than one small person, it dropped about ten feet down, then seemed to have made its way under the walls on a bit of a slope. Suddenly there was a great rushing noise and Eden jumped and pressed her back to the hedge. From under her feet a torrent of water emerged and in essence flushed the garbage that the servant had dumped down the ditch out and under the walls. The water ran for a good five minutes, then slowed to a trickle and finally stopped. "That's a bit ingenious" Eden smiled, examining the pipe that she had not noticed earlier sticking out ever so slightly from the base of the hedge. "Outdoor plumbing," she joked to herself. The pipe was about a foot in diameter, so a lot of water could be poured out if needed, though there certainly wasn't that much just now. "It must be some sort of aqueduct system," she mused.

Eden shrugged and decided she might as well see where this led, and carefully she picked her way down the steep slope of the ditch. Her clothes didn't quite make it safely, and by the time she stood at the base, her sleeves and pants were both wet and dirty. She tried her best to wipe them off, but gave up as she had to do a sort of crab crawl on all fours to get out under the wall anyway. On the other side she could see she wasn't in the best part of town. Not that it looked dangerous, but it certainly smelled bad. "Must be the dump." She screwed her nose up at the scent and quickly got herself out of the ditch.

From the looks of things not many people would come down here, and they certainly tried hard to hide this place. Directly behind Eden was a huge wall of what looked like cedar trees that stood as a guard to the not so pleasant side of life. In a few places were spots of broken branches and faint trails that must have been made by whatever poor servant got the job of dumping the garbage. She glanced back at the ditch again. "Not much actually in here though." She thought and paused a moment, making sure to breathe through her mouth. Then she noticed the burn marks and the soot that lay on the grass there. "They must burn this every once in a while." She guessed. Not being able to stand the smell anymore, she drove through the trees.

Immediately on the other side of this hedge was a bustling town. Women were traipsing back and forth between stores with children in tow, vendors were crying wares from outdoor displays. The occasional chayil wandered through the crowd as well, and some older children ran between the legs of passersby playing an imaginary game.

Eden smiled, with the thought – and smell, of the dump behind her, she felt different. As if this wasn't a dream, as if this was really happening, these were real people here, going about their normal and very real lives. What was now her reality started to sink in and she was intrigued by it.

She spent some time wandering down the streets. She discovered the two main thoroughfares that ran in circles around the town and wandered up and down several of the smaller streets that connected them.

As she rounded the next bend, she found a blacksmith that was just putting away his swords. She stood and watched him for a bit. "See something you like?" he asked smiling as he continued to clean up.

"No," Eden started, not having actually spoken to anyone yet, but she quickly recovered. "I mean, yes," and she pointed to one he had just taken down. "That one is amazing."

It was in fact a beautiful sword. It matched her own knife in its silver work, complete to the silver butt of the grip.

"Ah, a discerning eye you've got miss," the man laughed, "or was it just the shiny color that struck you?"

"No, it matches my knife," she stated flatly, not liking his tone, and she pulled her own out.

The blacksmith's eyes widened. "Well, that's a trinket you've got yourself lass," he rubbed his hands together as he moved to look closer.

Eden pulled the knife back and asked, "did you make that sword?"

"Er, what?" the blacksmith stopped, "Oh, ah no – my apprentice made it." he grumbled, "But let's see that knife of yours."

"Sorry sir we've got to be going now," a young voice spoke up on Eden's right side, and a hand gripped her elbow leading her into the crowd away from the staring blacksmith.

Eden fought her elbow away from the death grip and turned on her escort. "What do you think you're doing?" she asked, as her eyes registered a young girl beside her.

"I was protecting you," the girl said, pushing her blonde hair back out of her face to reveal a beautiful, if studious looking young woman, probably a couple years younger than herself. She was dressed much as Eden was except for the belt and knife.

"And who says I need protecting?" Eden was annoyed that this stranger had interrupted her chance to get some answers, even if he had been a bit creepy, she had wanted to see if the blacksmith knew what the words on her knife meant.

"It was obvious," the girl drawled and rolled her deep brown eyes.

"What?" Eden was indignant but quickly was interrupted again.

"Obviously you don't know what you have there on your side or else you wouldn't be going and showing it to anyone you don't know and trust," the girl started to walk again, "my name is Nasah, I'm training in the castle too and I know who you are."

"What?" Eden asked, jogging to catch up to Nasah. "Who am I?" she demanded.

"You're this great eklektos!" she replied, not jealously or angrily, just as a matter of fact.

"Excuse me?" Eden asked again, having no idea what she had just said.

"Eklektos, you know - special servant of the King and all that good stuff," she picked up an apple as she passed a stand and tossed a coin to the vendor.

"Ekleck…?" Eden tried to say the word, "no one told me anything about that," and she stopped and sat down on a barrel of something.

Nasah stopped too and came back to stand in front of Eden. "Eklektos," she repeated slowly. "Well, they probably didn't want to scare you, but I think not telling you is silly – you need to know what other people are thinking. It will keep you safer I think."

"What do you mean, what other people are thinking?" Eden asked, not so annoyed any more.

"Well, I think you will eventually be in my class, and most of our class thinks they have to try and do better than you, you know, you always want to show up the teacher's favorite," Nasah bit into her apple.

"Teacher's favorite, but I'm not even in class yet," she exclaimed. "And why aren't you in class then?"

"Well, all I know is that since yesterday all the masters have been talking quietly to themselves and getting all excited," she shrugged, "we notice that stuff. And for your information our class had early exercises and then a study afternoon."

"Humm," Eden mused, "so do you know something about this knife?" she asked, remembering the first thing Nasah said.

"Sure, anyone does who reads," she looked down, "but of course that's not very many people, but in any case, those knives are only given to those in the Gibbor Chayil, like our masters. No one gets one before they've even had classes and none of them have the writing that I'm pretty sure your's has," she took another bite, "may I see it?"

"Sure," Eden pulled it out, and handed it to the girl.

"Wow, it's just like the drawings," she stood with wide eyes as she turned it over.

"Can you read it?" Eden asked excited.

"Well, no, but I know what the symbols mean because I've read their translation before," she chewed her piece of apple, "they are an old deep power that says, 'rightly dividing the truth.' They say this knife has some ability that only the proper owner can use," she paused again and looked harder at the knife, "I'd think that it would be something along the line of knowing the truth of some situation, place or saying maybe, maybe even people," Nasah seemed excited again, "I can't believe I'm holding this in my hand, I read about it when I was a child."

Just then a trumpet rang out and Nasah started, glancing up on the wall behind them. "Come on, we have to get back inside before they close the gates, that's the evening trumpet for vesper," she handed the knife back to Eden and waved her to follow. "Come on, you can't be late. There are curfews and even us recruits can't break them," she hurried along through the crowd with Eden trailing after.

They soon found their way to the gates and slipped inside. Nasah slowed her pace now and they both headed past the stables and back to the barracks. "It's never good to go past the King's Guard, they just are always uptight and are more likely to question you than let you pass. Suspicious bunch they are," she explained.

"Thanks for helping me, Nasah, I appreciate it, you seem pretty smart," Eden smiled at her new friend she wasn't used to having friends.

"Compared to you at the moment," she laughed, but seemed a bit embarrassed, "Well not everyone thinks that being smart is a good thing, I'm probably the youngest recruit by at least four years, in fact you're pretty young too. My older brother is even in my class, and he hates that I'm here," she mumbled.

"I'm sure he doesn't…"

"Oh, he does, trust me – you'll see," Nasah nodded her head, "but I have to go, and you'll probably have food in your room by now. It was nice meeting you, hopefully I'll see you soon in class," she waved and ran off to the kitchens.

Eden smiled, and slowly made her way back to her room mulling over everything Nasah had told her.

5

*"For the sake of the faith of the King's Eklektos
and their knowledge of the truth
which accords with perfection."*

Eden spent the next several days with Moreh going over more geography, more customs, more etiquette, more names – it felt never ending, but Eden was a fast learner, and it was paying off. Moreh seemed more and more pleased each day she spent with Eden. Eden was just as pleased as she spent each evening wandering out through the town and the outside pastures. She had found a beautiful spot to watch the sun set just on the west side of the King's pasture. Over the past week Ruach had started to come out to Eden when she would go out there, sniffing her and eventually starting to butt her head up to Eden looking for a scratch. It was a little difficult to get back to the gates after the sun set before she was shut out, but the guards on the horse gate were nice. They had been interested in Eden's stories from her world, and they too seemed to have heard of these rumors that she was special or something. Not all the guards were nice to her, some were harder on her than other recruits she'd seen coming and going, but these guys that worked with the horses seemed a different breed and they usually would look the other way if she was late.

It had been a week since she had arrived in Kaleo, and she was thrilled that today would be her first day in class with the other recruits. Moreh had said she had progressed faster than she had expected so she was letting her join the class. They were to begin sword fighting today so Moreh felt that she'd learn better with a class than on her own. "You realize that some of these recruits will have been playing with swords since birth, you will be at a disadvantage," she furrowed her brow as she sized Eden up.

"I know, I'm ready," Eden tried to look mature and serious, but she was leaping inside. "I'm dying for some other company," she said, then gasped, "I don't mean that…"

Moreh waved her hand and glared at her, though her eyes seemed to laugh. "I'll try not to be offended," she said. "Fine, since my company is so painful for you, you may join the class tomorrow, on the practice field by the third watch – this means you will be doing everything with your class, food, breaks, everything – I cannot protect you there," she cocked her head to one side.

"I know, I'm ready," Eden insisted, not able to keep the smile down this time.

Moreh nodded, "I will be watching," she swept her scarf and herself out the door.

Eden hardly slept and was up early in the morning, dressing and fussing with her belt, tying her hair back in various ways then running around her room to see what the best for fighting was. She was nervous too; she wasn't sure what to expect when she joined the class. "Maybe they'll be nice, like the guards by the horse gate," she tried to be hopeful. "Or maybe not," she thought again of what Nasah had said. She certainly didn't feel very special at the moment, it was like grade nine all over again. Finally, opening her door to look at the sentinel that faced the barracks, she decided it was close enough to Terce that she grabbed her cloak and headed out to the practice field.

She was not the only one there early, the girl who had brought her food that first day was also there. She glanced up as Eden approached, and promptly sniffed and turned her back to her. "Great reception there," Eden muttered to herself. Slowly others joined the group, some looked like they had been fighting warriors for years, others looked like they might die if someone pointed a sword at them. There were guys and girls, the oldest looking about twenty-seven and the youngest looked like Nasah. It was with a strange sense of relief that Nasah first came over to Eden when she arrived.

"So, they are letting you in the class now," she exclaimed genuinely excited for her.

"I guess, but I'm kind of nervous," Eden admitted.

"Oh, don't worry, none of us have had any of this training yet, though some would like you to think they had," she nodded towards Eden's nemesis.

"What's her name?" Eden asked, as she watched the girl talk confidently with a group of her friends.

"Parzel," Nasah replied. "She's the best in class. She has been the masters' favourite until they heard you were coming that is."

Eden groaned at that, "no wonder she was so pleasant to me."

"You met her?" Nasah asked surprised.

"She brought me two meals the first day I arrived," she nodded

"Oh yeah, I remember. She made some comment about you not being so amazing when the masters had told us you'd be joining our class," Nasah recalled. "They said she must learn to put others first and sent her with your food," she smiled. "You should have seen the angry look on her face."

"I think I did," Eden laughed, "I guess I have my work cut out for me," she shrugged and turned to some of the other students.

Nasah told her names and described them as Eden asked. Suddenly, one guy managed to trip on the rack of swords knocking it over in a huge crash. "…and that would be my brother, Shephel," Nasah sighed.

Eden stifled a laugh as he clumsily got back up and tried to fix his mess but was brushed aside by a master who had just entered the field.

"Yah, he's – well - I still love the guy," she concluded.

Eden had been about to reply when the master who had just entered turned to address the class.

"I am Master Petros, and I will be your swords-master," he picked up a short sword and began walking around the ring of students twirling it in his hand. He was not necessarily commanding in appearance, but his ability to move the sword so expertly and not appear to even notice made you want to avoid eye contact.

"You will listen to everything I have to say. You will do everything I tell you to do and the first time that you question me you will be excused from these studies and can join your family at home," his words were very matter of fact and Eden wondered what they'd do with her, returning her to her family would be a bit of a challenge.

"This will be your most difficult class and I am responsible to make sure that once the King sends you out you will not die. I take it very personally when any Chayil I have taught is lost or wounded, you will not disappoint me," he began tossing the sword and catching it as he spoke. "I will drill you mercilessly, I will make you cry," he spoke into the face of a girl who looked like she might faint. "I will make you want to go home," this time he addressed Shephel who looked like he was about to be sick, "and I will not lose a moment of sleep over it," he spun and hurled the sword into a pole that stood on the northwest corner of the practice field. This achieved the result that he wanted as everyone gasped, and students in the direction of his throw were now picking themselves up off the ground. He smiled, "you will learn that your sword is a part of you, it is an extension of yourself and it will never go where you do not want it to," he drew himself up to his full height which might have just been six feet, his broad shoulders squared up and his jaw jutted out. He tied a black scarf around his forehead, pulling his dark hair back from his eyes. Everyone was now shrinking away from him when Moreh swept into the middle of the class, her head scarf trailing behind her like a faithful servant.

"Thank you Master Petros, for thoroughly horrifying most of our students," she glowered at him.

"Well, I just want them to know," he sputtered but bowed his head giving her the field.

"Alright class, Master Petros and I have divided you into teams. You will train with this team for the remainder of your lessons. You must rely on each other, the worst one on your team must become the best. You will not be evaluated separately; you will be marked as a team. We do not work alone in this kingdom, even I serve with a team – if you cannot deal with this then, as Master Petros informed you," she nodded to him, "you may join your family at any time," her eyes were boring into Eden at this moment, and she could see Parzel laughing behind her. She moved to face Parzel. "The first team will join Master Petros at the pole his sword has made home," she paused for effect, "Shephel, Sela, Nasah, Eden and Parzel," she emphasized the last two names to make her point, never breaking eye contact with Parzel.

Eden's eyes rolled and Parzel simply stood with mouth wide open.

"The second team…" and her voice trailed off as Eden focused on getting herself to the pole without arguing. It didn't help to have Nasah gripping her arm in excitement.

"Great, I get my little sister on my team," Shephel threw up his arms in exasperation. "It's not bad enough that you get in the same year as I do, but now I have to have you with me every day till we graduate," he shook his hands in her face.

"If you graduate young sir," Master Petros emphasized the 'if.' "We chose the teams because of your weaknesses. Find what yours' is and you will find why your sister is still at your heels," he turned to make sure the other teams were coming together.

Eden watched the other students, most not much happier about their new teammates than she was, but no one spoke anything directly to the Masters. Moreh was moving around the groups until finally everyone was divided.

"Alright students," she commanded their attention with a voice much bigger than Eden could have imagined for her. "You are in teams of five and you each have one instructor with you. Please take your swords and give your attention to your instructor."

Eden's group each took up a wooden practice sword from their rack and turned to Master Petros. His lesson was quite boring for the first bit, as he explained the parts of the sword and how to grip it. He demonstrated the perfect balance of a truly magnificent sword (his words). Finally, he said, "alright, move a bit apart and we will go over a few drills."

Eden shook her head, feeling overwhelmed again. She moved as far from Parzel as she could and focused her attention back on Master Petros.

"Let me see your grip," he said and began moving between them, correcting minute little things, muttering things about the hilt and the pommel.

"Shephel, two hands. Your sword is a one and a half grip, you cannot accomplish what you want with only one hand," he slapped his forehead in disgust.

After an age of just holding the swords, Eden finally thought he was going to get to teaching them a drill, but instead he cleared his throat so all the students could hear. "Practice swords away."

The field erupted with groans of dismay as students shuffled to their team's rack and put the swords up. "Hurry up, stop griping and gather around," he called out. All the students pushed into a circle with the Master in the middle.

"Now, there are six basics to sword fighting and only one of them involves a sword," at this comment Eden heard the sighs. The big man Sela, standing beside her muttered, "Great, now we'll never use one," and she smiled agreement with him.

"The basics are breathing, balance, timing, conditioning, mental game and finally equipment," he began to walk around the circle. "If you do not master just one of these basics you will fail. If you master them all, you will be an average warrior."

"What makes an extraordinary warrior?" Parzel interrupted him. Master Petros stopped instantly, looked up to the sky, took a deep breath and replied, "a lack of effort," then he continued to pace and talk.

"What?" Nasah whispered on Eden's other side.

"That doesn't make any sense," Sela agreed.

"Maybe," Eden paused still listening as Petros went on, "Maybe, he means when you can fight without any effort, then you'll be extraordinary."

"Maybe he means that you should be silent when your master is teaching," Moreh's displeased voice broke over them and her hand gripped Eden's shoulder. The three froze and did not utter another sound.

"So today, we work on conditioning," he finally exclaimed. "Your team instructor will take you through a series of events, we will climb the tower, swim the river, run an obstacle course and any other cardiovascular activity your master feels like," he smiled, "remember, if your opponent has one ounce of endurance more you will lose. To your masters," that sent the students scurrying around the practice yard.

They spent the remainder of the day running countless stairs, navigating a maze of obstacles and Eden's favourite (because it took them out of Town boundaries) swimming the river Massah. Never enjoying team sports, Eden had competed as a tri-athelte, and it was paying off. In the end she was pleased with her efforts, only Sela had beaten her in anything. Parzel was usually a close third, and she obviously did not enjoy that position. Nasah always came after her with Shephel bringing up the rear.

As they walked back to the palace Master Petros walked beside Shephel. "Young man, you must put in more effort if you are to succeed in this place," he wasn't being rude or anything, but seemed truly concerned about his performance, "are you sure you want to be a warrior?" he asked shaking his head.

"Yes sir," Shephel answered immediately, "I know I'm not the best, but I have some skills and serving the King like this is the only thing I've ever dreamed of since - " he paused for a moment, "well, since I was little."

"Well, you have passion at least," Master Petros smiled. "You must do some training on your own okay?"

"Yes sir."

"The rest of you well done, get some supper and sleep much, tomorrow is another hard day," he waved them off and headed into the tower, catching up with Moreh as she was going in the gate.

"See you guys tomorrow," Eden called as she started towards her door.

"Hummph," Parzel responded, pushing past her and not saying a word to anyone.

Eden shook her head.

"Good night," Sela called and he and Shephel continued on, Nasah, was already at her own door.

Eden pushed her door open and unceremoniously collapsed on her bed

6

"The King has said, "I have made a covenant
with my Eklektos, I have sworn to my servant,
I will establish you forever
and build you for all generations..."

The next several weeks of classes were much the same. Master Petros had them hold their swords - just hold them. He made them recite the parts of the sword, asking various questions about which was most important? What kind of sword did you want? What length of grip, that sort of thing. For the most part it was deathly boring, and then they had to put the swords up again and start some conditioning. Today, Petros took them out to the river once more and this time he had them dive in, swim to the centre and back, what must have been a hundred times. Each time saw Shephel fall further behind the class until at least Petros was stalking angrily back and forth on the shore. The others were already standing on the bank as Shephel pulled himself up out of the water, clearly exhausted.

"This is ridiculous, is he going to do this until Shephel dies?" Eden muttered under her breath to Nasah. They watched him climb the bank and heard Master Petros' steps behind them. They braced themselves for his angry voice to rip into Shephel, but instead they heard him draw his sword and Parzel gasped, 'he really was going to kill him,' Eden thought, but just as she did, she felt the flat of the sword against her own back and found herself falling headfirst, along with her other teammates, back into the river.

After breaking the surface and shaking the water from their eyes, they all looked up to where their master stood with Shephel beside him. "You will stay exactly where you are, you will not allow yourself to drift with the current," he shouted down angrily.

"What did we do?" Parzel asked Sela beside her.

"What you did, recruit, was fail your teammate," he was practically snarling now. "Do you not recall Master Moreh's words?" he paused, looking disgusted at them. "You are not marked as individuals but as a team. Therefore, you are as weak as your weakest member," he glanced at Shephel, who looked like he wanted to curl up and die on the spot. "You will contemplate what that means for the next hour, longer if you drift." And he pulled Shephel by the arm and the two moved out of sight of the four in the water.

"Great," Eden muttered, "he's weak so we suffer. Why is this always my lot to get a crappy team?"

"Hey, there's four of us here if you hadn't noticed, we all kept up with you oh great one, Don't blame your team." Parzel snapped back at her.

"What's that supposed to mean?" Eden shot her a brutal look, "when have you passed me in the water today?"

"Yeah, it's definitely your bad luck to be on such a bad team," Parzel rolled her eyes as her words dripped sarcasm, "why did we get stuck with such a showboat is a better question? I'd take Shephel any day over you."

"Okay, would you guys just shut up," Nasah yelled at them. "You're wasting your own strength, and I don't even want to think if one of you gets tired and drifts what might happen to the rest of us so - just – shut - up," already out of breath from that statement.

"What do you think Sela?" Parzel asked him.

"What?" he responded, sounding shocked that someone asked him a question.

"Who would you want on your team?" Parzel asked again,

"Uh, I don't know?" he muttered, not making eye contact with Eden.

"Great, another quality teammate with brilliant intellect," she mumbled to herself, and tried to ignore them for the remainder of the hour.

Finally, Petros came back to the bank and waved them in. Each pulled themselves up the slope and collapsed at the top.

"You all have one hour to eat and reflect on why you were out there," he looked at Eden, then Parzel. "And consider if this is where you really want to be," he turned abruptly and walked back towards the palace. Shephel was nowhere in sight, but Parzel set off after him immediately, soon followed by Sela and Nasah. Eden; however, didn't move. She turned and sat watching the river. There were a couple of other teams working further down the bank. She watched some of their drills and tried to forget what her teammates had said, or not said, to her in the water.

"You look tired," a voice spoke behind her.

Eden turned to see a shepherd standing there. He was maybe ten years older than herself, and obviously a farmer in the area. His clothes spoke his profession and were dirty. In his hand was a long shepherd's crook and a small lamb was at his feet.

"Yes, I'm pretty tired," she nodded, pulling her towel over her shoulders, and turning back to the water.

The lamb made its way over to her and nuzzled her elbow. Eden had never really had a lamb that close to her before, but she appreciated its affection and stroked its head.

"He likes you," the shepherd remarked, coming over and sitting on the lamb's other side. The little animal now confused as to who it should go to, its new friend or its master. "He's always been a bit of a loner this one, I was down here pulling him up from the bank where he had wandered off to again," he didn't seem to mind carrying the conversation himself as Eden tried to look uninterested. "I have a farm just back there, but this little one will never stay with the others, always has to be out on his own. I think he thinks he's better than them. He can find the better pasture than what I give him, or where the others are. Causes me all sorts of trouble he does."

Eden looked out the corner of her eye at the shepherd. She was trying to decide if he was making a comment on her behaviour or was just talking about the sheep. He must have heard Petros if he'd been down at the water just now.

"Sheep are funny that way, some are never satisfied with what the shepherd gives them, and they have to go their own way. They don't realize that there is safety in the flock," he rubbed the little lamb's belly and it cuddled into his side. "If this little guy doesn't learn to stay with the flock, I'll have to sell him to the market," he smiled down at the lamb.

"Why?" Eden asked suddenly, startling the shepherd and herself. "You obviously love him."

"Well," he picked the lamb up and looked it in the face. "You see, sheep also follow each other. Before I could come find this guy, I had three others that I also had to bring back that followed him under the fence. If he keeps leading the others astray, he's a danger to the whole flock, so it's better to let him go than to lose the others," he rubbed the lamb's nose. "But you know, I think this one will learn," as he said these words, he had turned his gaze to Eden and she had to look away from his indigo blue eyes felling h could see right through her. There was some familiarity in his face, but as he spoke those words, she knew he was speaking of her and not of his lamb.

He stood, seeing that she seemed to have gotten the message. "Perhaps we will meet again, when this lamb is older."

She could tell he was smiling, but she was too embarrassed to look at him.

"You should eat something before you return to work," and with those words he took the lamb and left.

Eden waited for a few minutes before turning to look after him. What she saw was a small package lying on the stump just to the right of her. She leaned over and found an apple and chunk of cheese wrapped in a soft lamb skin cloth. She smiled to herself and sat back down to watch the river and eat.

Shortly after finishing her food her teammates returned. Everyone was silent, including Eden as they waited for Master Petros. They did not have long to wait as he came storming through the trees. Seeing them all there he started in.

"Alright, I was not planning on this lesson this early, but it seems that you need to learn to trust each other."

He commanded them down the bank right to the water's edge. "Parzel and Eden you will be a pair, Nasah and Sela, and Shephel will be with me."

Eden tried very hard not be discouraged. In reality, Parzel was as good as any of the others now after that conversation in the water.

"Breathing is very important to sword fighting," Petros went on, "you must learn to control your fear, and your mind. If your breathing rushes, then you will be exhausted before you are ever able to fight. Fear in the mind is one of your greatest enemies," he took a deep breath. "One of you will lay on the bank, and the other will hold your head underwater," he stated. They all went wide eyed. "You will start with a count of forty-five, then switch. Eventually you will go as long as I will push you," he motioned them to the water. "Eden, Sela and Shephel, lie down."

The three obeyed, laying on their stomachs, fear in all of their eyes. "Ready? Begin!," he shouted and they thrust their heads in the water.

Eden could feel Parzel's hand on the back of her head. She could just imagine the thoughts going through her mind about holding her head down longer than needed. What if Petros wasn't watching all of them? She was really vulnerable. Eden could feel the fear welling up in her even as her body began to crave oxygen. Suddenly, Parzel pulled her head up and she gasped for air. After several deep breaths, Eden wiped her eyes and looked Parzel in the eye, but she didn't have much time to figure out what she saw there as Petros commanded the others down and she found herself holding Parzel's head. She realized she felt bad about doing this, it was more torture than anything, and at about forty seconds she could see Parzel's body begin to move a bit as she was wanting to bring her head up. "Just five more," she said to encourage her, though she couldn't hear her. As soon as Petros said 'finished', she rushed to pull her up. Parzel looked at her the same way, and Eden knew it now, what Parzel had thought before. It was a mix of guilt for wanting to hold the person down, and yet never wanting to inflict that on even an enemy.

"Good," Petros smiled for the first time that day. "Now we push. You will not know how long you must remain under you will only feel the hold of your partner until I command them to bring you up. I will endanger you, but not hurt you. Trust," he waited till the others were back on their stomachs. "Begin."

Once again, Eden's head was thrust into the cool water. She didn't have the same fear of Parzel, instead she had a fear of herself. What if she lost control? What if she couldn't do it? Again, the fear was rising and she already began to squirm wanting to get some air. But then she felt Parzel's hand on her head, and her other hand had reached in and gripped her shoulder. Her firm grip seemed to say, 'it was okay' and Eden could feel her heart slow and she stopped moving. Instead, she tried to focus on the water, to feel it on her face, feel the pull of the current, even to notice the strength of Parzel's hands, anything to keep her mind occupied. And then, almost as a shock, Parzel pulled her head up.

Eden shook the water from her hair and heard Petros exclaiming, "Well done, that was seventy-five counts. Well done for your first day."

Eden was shocked at the time and turned to Parzel. "Thank you," she said, and Parzel nodded back to her.
"Next," Petros called, and the others settled themselves down.

"Begin." he called again, and Eden held Parzel's head down.

"You will keep them for a count of ninety," Petros stated, "they will have a harder time because they think they know when we will allow them up, so if they are able to count, they will think they know the end, we must make them feel the fear of not knowing," he explained.

"But what if they can't do it?" Shephel asked

"Then you will revive them afterwards," Petros told him matter-of-factly.

"Oh," He muttered and looked in fear at his sister in the water.

Eden could feel Parzel trying to relax, she also knew that she would be the one who would count to know her time, so the difficult time would be coming up.

"Seventy-five," Petros called.

Almost immediately Parzel tried to lift her head, but Eden had to hold her down, hating the feeling, and she could see Parzel start to struggle, so she did what Parzel had done to calm her, and put her other hand in to grab her shoulder. She held her tight, even allowing her arm to pull against her side trying to say, 'it'll be okay.' She realized she said it aloud.

"Pull them up," Petros shouted, and immediately Eden pulled her from the water.

"Ninety," he called, "is everyone okay?" Parzel was gasping for air and leaning heavily on Eden.

"Just try and breathe slowly, you're up now, it'll be fine," Eden pulled her black hair back from her face.

Beside her Sela was looking into Nasah's eyes, "Let me see," Shephel pushed him aside. "Are you okay Nasah?" he asked, making her eyes focus on him.

"Get your bad breath out of my face," she smiled at him and he sighed in relief.

Everyone laughed, even Parzel between gasps of air. She turned then to look at Eden. "Thank you," she half smiled.

"Up, everyone up," Petros called to them, he had already climbed the bank and stood over them smiling, pleased at his success.

"You will not have any more of your stupid arguments. You will trust each other; you will be a team or I will kill you making you one," he stopped smiling at that point and they all had to wonder if he really would. "You have the remainder of the afternoon to yourself.

Train, study, rest. Tomorrow morning on the field at dawn," he turned and left them before they had even made it to the top of the bank.

Eden spent the afternoon in Migdal. She wanted to go back to that sword maker's shop. She wandered through the stalls on her way, taking a look at the various wares that the shopkeepers were selling. There was a shop for everything. She found a great armory, another that sold the leather vests that she had been given, a tailor who had some interesting styles of pants and dresses. Another soled shoes and boots, others were obviously farmers selling their produce. Everything seemed to be in season here. There were oranges, and corn, rice and vegetables – she couldn't imagine importing the stuff, so it must all actually grow here. She bought an apple, now that she had a small salary from serving, then made her way through the dusty streets into the animal area. The smell greatly increased here, as farmers were selling cattle and sheep – others had pets and birds. As she passed a stall with several sheep tied up, she couldn't help but remember what that shepherd had said to her about the sheep that always strays. She bent down and rubbed the nose of one, "I hope that's not what you were doing," she said to the animal, and received an angry bleat in return.

"Hey, don't bother the animals unless you gonna buy one," the angry merchant shooed her away.

"Sorry," she tried to apologize, but decided just to leave. Finishing her apple, she found the blacksmith stall. She stood across the street first to watch. She remembered what Nasah had said, and she wanted to look at the swords when the smith was either preoccupied or not there. She could see the man bustling around the fire inside, and she felt that this was probably a good opportunity, so she made her way across the street and tried to stand in the shadow as she looked at the swords.

Most of them were rather modest looking, average, any farmer might have one for protection, but then the glint of silver caught her eye and she saw the sword that drew her heart. Instinctively her hand went to her own side and the belt that hung beneath her jacket. She wasn't often allowed to wear it, never to class and that was basically all the time. But this afternoon she had strapped it on with a smile before heading out.

Now that she saw the sword again, she could see that there was no inscription on this one. But its style was remarkably similar to her knife. She slid her hand down the central ridge to the cross guard. Even its weakest part seemed strong.

The grip was a hand and a half, with two thirds covered in a tight black leather, and the bottom third and the pommel were silver that had been smoothed down so the butt was flat. Out of the corner of her eye she spotted someone else moving in the blacksmith's shop. She vaguely remembered the smith saying his apprentice had made the sword and wondered if this was the man. He was obviously very strong, she could tell just by the size of his silhouette. Eden slid back further towards the wall of the shop so as not to be seen. Just then the man moved into a beam of light and Eden could see his face and she stifled a gasp. There was Sela, moving around the smith like a professional, but it was the conversation going on inside that was interesting her more.

"What do you mean you aren't coming back?" the smith yelled at Sela.

"I mean, I'm done with you," Sela said quietly. "I've paid my debt and now I have found service for the King."

"Service for the King eh?" the man barked at him. "You'll leave when I'm done with you," he held his hammer threateningly.

"No Grippa," Sela shook his head, "I'm done. I've found my call, and it is much more than taking bribes and ripping off customers."

"Oh, so now you have a conscience?" Grippa the smith laughed "All those times you seemed pleased with the extra money – I didn't hear any complaints from you then."

"I didn't know better," Sela mumbled, "but now I do and I'm done, I am taking my stuff and you will not bother me again," he turned and continued collecting his things. He had a sack on his back that he kept filling with tools of the trade, and he also began picking up pieces that he must have made.

"Oh no, you are not going to steal from me too," Grippa came at him with the hammer now enraged by what Sela was doing. Eden gasped, and she knew that Sela had heard her as he paused a moment, but turned to face Grippa. The smith brought the great hammer down on his apprentice, but Sela caught it with one hand and with the other he raised Grippa up by his throat.

"You have oppressed me long enough," Sela snarled now into the face of the smith. "I may not be very bright, but I have finally figured you out. I will not be used by you any longer. We will see how you fare without someone to do your work for you. And yes, I will take all that I have sweat over, even the sword," he released the man's throat, but not the hammer. Grippa stood only for a moment holding the handle before he released it and fled to the back of the fire.

"You will never get anywhere," he shouted at Sela as he continued to pick up his things. "What would the King want with a man with only half a mind?" he hurled insult after insult. "It's a blessing your parents never learned what you really were before they died. I did you a favour and look what you do? It will never leave you, it will always follow you."

Sela's head was dropping lower and lower as the words seemed to almost be sitting on his back. Eden could stand no more of it and she moved out of the shadow and stepped up beside Sela. He raised his head startled and looked her in the eye.

"Don't believe a word of it," she whispered, "do you have everything?"

"I don't know," he mumbled.

"I think you have enough," she said, then cast a scowl at the blacksmith, and with one hand on Sela's arm, she reached up and took the sword down and handed it to him. "Let's go," and they left the shop.

They walked in silence for a while as people passed, oblivious of the internal battle that had just raged inside this strong man. Sellers called their wares, shoppers jostled with each other, and Sela and Eden walked arm in arm until they were able to turn down a side street and sit on some overturned crates.

"Thank you," he said quietly, looking at the sword resting on his knees.

"Any time," she smiled at him, realizing that for the first time she felt protective of her teammate. "Who was that guy?" she asked.

Sela took a deep breath. "My uncle."

"Oh," Eden nodded and just sat there, waiting for him to speak.

After several minutes he went on. "My parents were Chayil, that's where they met. Grippa is my mother's brother. They had me just a few years after they married but were caught in an uprising in a town south of here. Both of them died, but they managed to smuggle me out with my uncle. He says he did it to save me, but I think now it was an excuse not to have to fight. So, we came here and I grew up as his slave. I learned the trade and out matched him until he simply used me to do the work," he paused and a tear fell down his cheek. "Last year I saw a battalion of Chayil come in from battle with several wounded. I couldn't help but think of my parents, so I ran away one night because I was too scared to tell Grippa what I wanted to do, and I joined the recruits in the palace. I came back once this year to tell him where I was thinking maybe he had worried. But all he cared about was lost wages, and a job I never finished. So, I left again, but swore I'd go back to get my things someday. After that water thing today I decided that this was the team I was going to give my life for. Even though I'm not smart and don't have much to give, I have my life."

"Sela, that's terrible," Eden shook her head. "What a jerk that guy is, you were totally right for leaving," trying to think of what to say to comfort him.

"You know, I saw some of your work," she reached over and took the sword. "This is incredible, it's why I went back today, I just wanted to see it again," she turned it over in her hand and let it balance itself on her fingertips. "I have a feeling that this is what you never finished, the pair?" she pulled out her own belt knife and laid it in her open palm beside the sword and they did match perfectly.

"Where did you get that?" he asked quickly, taking the knife from her and examining it.

"It was given to me by the King the first day I arrived here," she explained, "but it was Nasah who told me what the inscription was and what it meant."

"We were commissioned to make this for the King. I finished the knife, then had done the majority of the work on the sword, minus the inscription when the King's servant came to see the work. Grippa decided to demand a thousand more than what was paid, the servant argued with him, so Grippa said we would not finish the sword. The servant took the knife and left. That was over six years ago now. The sword never was displayed before, I think Grippa thought they'd return for it, but they never did," he smiled at the knife, "this was my best work."

"I can tell."

"Thanks," Sela said again quietly, "if you hadn't come in I think I might have lost my courage to leave. I have nothing now."

"That's not true," Eden smacked his huge arm. "You have a new family, a team. That is if you still want us, or me," she turned her gaze away, realizing how she had behaved before.

"I don't care what they say about you, I think you're alright," Sela smiled a big lopsided grin.

"No," Eden shook her head, "They are probably right, but I think I see that now. I'm sorry for being a jerk – I'm going to work on it I promise," she looked down at her feet, "I've never really had a team either, or friends for that matter."

Sela smiled, "I'm not sure what this 'jerk' is you keep referring to, but you did act like a donkey," he laughed, "but I think we all have work to do," he took the sword back and handed Eden the knife.

"Hey, want to come see the sun set?" she asked him, smiling too.

"No, I think I'll head back to my room. I'm tired, and we have an early morning. But thanks Eden, for everything," he reached over and gave her an awkward kind of hug then stood and headed back into the busy street.

Eden sat for a few minutes longer. It was an interesting turn of events. Sela was really talented, and now she knew that they had similar backgrounds. She couldn't imagine having had to live with such a creep though. Ian and Heather were so good to her, and she never really appreciated them.

"Man, I have been a donkey, to a lot of people too," she admitted as she pushed herself up off the crates, brushing the dust from her pants. She slid the knife back into its little scabbard and made her way through the crowds.

The dust in the city was choking, as many made last minute purchases on their way home, and shop keepers were cleaning up. Eden decided to walk around the outside wall to her favourite spot before heading back into the barracks.

The air outside town was much fresher. The walk was a bit more cumbersome as she had to trek around little ravines and streams, but the view was idyllic. A golden light falling on the farmer's fields; a little cottage off in the distance had a small plume of smoke coming from its chimney, 'probably supper cooking' Eden thought. There were pastures with sheep and cattle. She wondered if one of these farms might be her shepherd's.

It was funny to her that through such a short conversation she could see and understand so much about herself. She really did want to meet him again, just to thank him even, and get his name.

By now she had reached the King's pastures, and she could see the horses ranging around as the sun was dropping. She waved to one of the Chayil she recognized, and he returned the wave, and pointed. He drew her attention to the great black horse that she had ridden on her first day. Ruach raised her head and trotted over to Eden. They had some strange bond now and Eden always saved a bit of sugar or something for the horse. Ruach snorted and shook her mane as she approached, then circling Eden she rubbed her head against Eden's shoulder almost knocking her over.

"Easy girl," she laughed, and she could see the Chayil laughing as well from his station. "You're making me look silly," she rubbed down her nose, "okay, okay, you know I always do. Stop being so pushy or next time it's nothing," and she pulled out a second apple and held it out to the horse. Ruach took it in one great bite from her hand then dropped her head as she chewed.

"Sure you don't mind?" she asked, putting a hand on Ruach's side. Then taking a bunch of mane in her hand, she swung her leg up and let the horse trot her over to the gate as she ate her apple happily. Eden had improved a lot on her riding skills just from her times with Ruach in the field. She felt fairly confident on the great war horse now, which probably had more to do with Ruach than herself. She was able to ride bareback around the fields and had had the grooms teach her to saddle and groom her.

"Hello Eden," The Chayil smiled. "That horse is something," he scratched his head. "I've never seen anything like it, she always comes when you walk into the field and then to let you ride bareback. You know she will barely let any of us ride her anymore."

"Really?" Eden said surprised, "I thought she'd never throw anyone?"

"Throw, no, but since you've ridden her, she won't hardly let anyone other than you close to getting a saddle on her. Seems to be waiting for you," he laughed and pet the horse's nose. "Guess you'd better join the cavalry eh?"

"I guess so," Eden smiled at the little pleasure the animal gave her. "But it's probably just because I bribe her. Try apples, it might work," she slid from the horse's back and gave her a pat. "Oh, I meant to ask, what does her name mean?"

"It's an old word that sort of means wind or spirit," the Chayil replied, also patting Ruach's neck cautiously.

"Appropriate," Eden nodded her thanks and headed off towards the barracks still thinking.

7

"For many are called,
but the few are Eklektos"

On her way back to her room Eden slipped into the kitchens to grab what might be left from supper. Parzel was just finishing her own meal and glanced up as Eden approached. She looked her in the eyes and raised her chin in acknowledgment. Eden returned the gesture and kept moving towards the food, and Parzel picked up her dish and headed out the door. "Hum." She muttered to herself.

"What was that lass?" the old cook asked her, looking up from what must have been some form of stew. Eden skewed her nose up at the look of it, but held her bowl out. "Oh, nothing, I just think maybe I'm starting to learn something finally," she tried to smile as the stew slopped into the rough clay bowl.

"They say it takes time here, lots to learn, not many do well you know." The cook threw her bit of wisdom in.

"Thanks," Eden swirled the stew around in her bowl, "what exactly is this?"

"Why it's potato stew, it'll put hair on you," the cook grinned.

Eden's eyebrows raised, "Great, just what I'd hoped for," she shook her head a bit and went to sit and eat as quickly as she could. The first bite was a bit of a shock, but it was warm and surely there must be something wholesome in it, so she swallowed the whole bowl down. Her mind was running over the day again, wishing that she had learned this lesson earlier in life, "could have made a difference on that fire test," she murmered to herself with a rueful smile.

As she finished her stew, Shephel came into the dining hall. He paused at the door looking around, and once his eyes zeroed in on Eden he made a beeline over to her.

"Hi Shephel," she pushed her bowl aside and gestured to the bench in front of her. He quickly threw himself onto it, his knees hitting the table and knocking the bowl and Eden's cup of water over. She scrambled to catch it before it rolled off the table.

"Sorry," he muttered, looking embarrassed.

"Don't worry," she replied, giving up on trying to contain the water that now dripped down onto the floor. "What's up?" she turned her attention to her teammate, starting to get used to that word.

"Well," he started kind of sheepishly. "umm, well, I'm just going to ask." Then he paused, and Eden raised her eyebrows, trying to urge him on.

"Ineedyourhelp," he said it so fast that all his words slurred together and Eden had to think a moment before she understood.

She nodded when she got it, "With what?"

"Well, I don't know if you realized," he started playing with Eden's wooden spoon, "but I'm not the most athletic person on our team."

Eden stifled a laugh but contained herself to look very seriously at Shephel.

"and you kind of are, at least in some things," finally he looked up at her, "so I wondered if you might help me?" he finished, his eyes desperate.

Eden nodded, "What do you want me to do exactly?"

"I'm not sure, but I need help with running, swimming, some co-ordination…" his voice trailed off and Eden's mind finished the list.

"Okay," she pushed her bench back and stood. "Let's go."

"You'll help me?" he asked surprised, jumping up and knocking his bench over.

"Yep, but we're starting right now," she walked resolutely out the door with Shephel trailing behind her.

"Where are we going?" he asked, as she led him towards the back of the kitchen.

"Well, the gates are shut, but if we're going to train, we need to get outside to the river," she said matter-of-factly, and slipped down into the culvert with the garbage.

"What are you doing?" Shephel stood on the edge, his head swinging back and forth nervously looking for who might be around.

"Come on," Eden's voice carried back to him as she'd already slipped under the wall.

Shephel stood a moment longer looking at the garbage, "I didn't really expect to start right now," he said.

"Do you want help or not?" Eden called back to him.

He heard a door open near them and in a panic he jumped down and scrambled to catch up to her. He was panting by the time he joined her in the garbage piles. "It stinks here," he closed his eyes and wrinkled his nose at the stench.

"Sure, keeps everyone away," she smiled and started to head out.

"How did you find this?" he asked, trying to follow her footsteps.

"The first time Moreh let me out, I went looking around and found it. Thought it might come in handy," she stopped and took a deep breath once they were past the trees. "There, that's better."

They stood with the garbage behind them and the still town ahead. "Okay, we have to be quiet. We're going down to the river," Eden led them carefully through the dark. They slipped from house to house, avoiding any pools of light cast from windows. They passed by the blacksmith and Eden felt a bit uncomfortable, but couldn't see any reason to, so they continued on.

Finally, the two reached the river. It looked rather threatening at night, the dark waters flowing swiftly east, and the trees encroaching the banks. Shephel was looking around nervously at the shadows from the moonlight as Eden inspected different areas of the bank.

"Okay, here's where we'll start," she pointed to a little path that led down to the water. It was made of various roots that had been uncovered and made a natural staircase up the bank.

"What am I supposed to do?" Shephel stood beside her, examining the pathway. "Am I swimming?"

"No, you're climbing," Eden smiled at him.

"What?" he asked, his brow furrowed.

"You'll start up here and go down, then run up and back down again," she explained, "and you'll keep going until I stop you," she smiled again.

He took a deep breath. "Okay," and down he went.

He stumbled a few times on the way down, but always caught himself. Once he reached the bottom he turned with a look of satisfaction at accomplishing that and then headed back up. He was out of breath at the top and paused for a moment.

"Go, there's no stopping," Eden spun him around and pushed him back down. He stumbled over his feet again and fell to his knees but got back up looking at Eden.

"You're not going to get stronger if you don't push yourself," she said with compassion.

They worked there for over an hour. Shephel running up and down and Eden switching between the harsh teacher and encourager, she was starting to feel sorry for him as he struggled up the bank again and was about to say something when suddenly he stopped. An expression of fear fell over his face and his hand pointed to something behind Eden.

"Look out!" he cried, and as he did, Eden spun around, dropping to her right shoulder and rolling away.

As she rolled, her eyes caught the shadow that Shephel was looking at. It loomed behind Eden in the trees and had started moving forward when she moved. By the time she was up on her knee, her belt knife was in her hand and released but a ray of light caught the intruder for a moment and there was something familiar there.

A shocked cry came from the shadow and the thud of the knife burying itself into something thick. Eden stood, thinking that she had hit her mark. Shephel had made it to the top and was now panting to her left, but the shadow started to move from where it had dropped to.

"What are you doing," a voice cried out and the shadow stood to its full height.

"Parzel?" Eden asked, now afraid she'd wounded her, she hurried over.

As her eyes adjusted to the shadows of the trees, Eden could see Parzel brushing herself off and looking at Eden's knife buried up to the hilt in the tree beside her. "Good thing I have better reflexes than you," she gripped the hilt and tried to pull it from the tree with no success.

"What are you doing sneaking up on us like that?" Eden exclaimed, throwing her hands up. She had been frightened and the natural response was anger flowing out of her.

"Well," Parzel turned to face them, "I saw you two sneaking off behind the kitchen and I wanted to know what kind of trouble you were going to get us in, so I followed you. Watched you slip under the wall, but then the cook came out with garbage and I had to hide back in the yard until they finished cleaning up from supper. Once they did I followed you."

"But how did you know where we came?" Shephel asked, finally having caught his breath.

"Well, at first I was able to track you into town from your footprints. But once you got to the blacksmith's there were others that covered yours, so I had to go with my assumption that you were doing some extra training and I figured, you were probably going to come out here. So I made my way to the river, and started to follow the bank until I could hear Shephel's gasping. I just waited a moment and was going to come talk to you when you both freaked out," she explained.

"But how did I miss you?" Eden asked, looking to her knife, "I know this was exactly where I was aiming."

"Like I said, you're not always the best you know," Parzel replied rather self-righteously. Then she sighed and dropped her eyes. "Actually, I don't know."

"What?" Eden asked confused.

"I don't know," she repeated, "I saw the knife coming right at me and the next second it was buried in the tree beside my arm," she shrugged, and pulled on the knife again, still to no avail.

"Strange." Shephel murmured, looking at the hilt.

"That is weird," Eden too was examining the knife, trying to figure out how to get it out of the tree. She couldn't bear to lose it like this. "Guess I'll have to get Sela to come back here in the morning and try and get it out," she shrugged, upset to leave it behind tonight.

"No," Shephel was intent on the knife, "Eden, you try and pull it out," he instructed.

"Why? If Parzel can't even move it I don't think I'll be able to do anything," she said, but let her hand grip the hilt.

"Just try," he was watching her hand anxiously.

"Okay, but…" her voice trailed off as the knife slid smoothly from the tree without any exertion at all. "That's so weird," she whispered in awe.

"I knew it," he cried, tripped himself and fell on his butt.

"How did you know that?" Parzel asked, taking the knife from Eden and turning it over in her hand.

"Well," he stood up brushing himself off, "I'd read, well actually Nasah read and told me, that this knife has special powers, but only for the one who it is chosen for, which would be Eden. So I just guessed that since you couldn't move it, maybe the true owner would be able to," he smiled at his own thought process, then his eyes grew, "and I bet you were aiming right at Parzel and the knife knew it wasn't an enemy."

"How can a knife know that?" Parzel asked skeptically.

"The knife didn't know, but I did," Eden said slowly. "When I let go of the knife you caught just a bit of moonlight and I didn't know who it was, but I thought it was someone I knew," she was thinking through the whole thing and speaking slowly, "so maybe my intent changed and that did something. The inscription says 'rightly dividing the truth' and Nasah had thought that meant that the knife would show enemies or something like that."

Parzel looked skeptical, but Shephel was getting excited.

"Let's test it," he exclaimed.

"What?" both girls asked surprised.

"How on earth can we test it unless I throw it at someone?" Eden rolled her eyes.

"Exactly," his eyes were full of fire now, "throw it at me."

"No," Eden shook her head.

"Yes, throw it," he stood against a tree just a few feet away.

"No, I'm not going to throw a knife at you," she shouted, getting angry and nervous.

"Wait," Parzel interrupted, "we need to prove you can actually hit a target to begin with."

"What?" Eden turned on her, "are you saying I missed you because I can't aim?" she was letting her anger boil up again.

"No," she rolled her eyes this time, "relax." and took a half-eaten apple out of her pocket and set it on a stump beside Shephel. "I know you can throw, we are just doing a real experiment," she stepped back. "Hit the apple."

"Fine," Eden was so angry now, whether at Parzel or herself she wasn't sure, that without any thought at all she hurled the knife at the apple and pierced it right through the core, pinning it to the stump.

"Perfect," Shephel cried, "now throw it at me."

"No," Eden cried again, pleading this time. "What if your theory isn't right? What if I hurt you?" she turned away again and stared off into the woods behind them.

"Okay, okay, just throw it at my foot then, even if you hit it, it won't do much damage, nothing that can't heal quickly enough," he finally conceded.

"You think you're giving me some great compromise?" Eden's voice was getting louder with the extra stress. "Oh, don't kill me, just wound me," she mocked his voice. "How would I explain that to the masters?"

"You won't have to, we'll make something up, but I really think it won't hit me as long as you know I'm not an enemy," he tried to talk calmer and slower.

"I think so too, just try it Eden," Parzel encouraged her, being more convinced by Shephel's confidence.

Eden stood there feeling like a little kid in the playground at school getting bullied into doing something wrong at recess. She looked back and forth from Parzel who was still coaxing her, to Shephel with his left foot extended for her to have an easy shot at it.

"Argh" she grunted, quickly she retrieved the knife from the apple and without pausing hurled it directly at Shephel's foot.

The next second all of them were holding their breath. Shephel's face was a mask of astonishment, and Parzel had her hand over her mouth.

Eden was dumbfounded. The knife had hurtled towards his foot until at the very last second when, rather than imbedding itself into his boot, it suddenly was impaled in the ground beside him.

"Did you, did you see that?" Shephel finally took a breath.

"No, it just was in a different spot," Eden said honestly, "I didn't see it move."

"I thought it was going right through his foot until I looked closely and saw it beside him," Parzel bent down and was looking at the knife. She reached to pick it up but just as before it wouldn't move. "I can't budge it again," she waved Eden over.

Eden stooped down and easily picked the knife up. "So strange," she murmured.

"I wonder who made it?" Parzel asked.

"Why?" Eden's eyes flew to her's to see if she knew Sela's secret.

"Maybe they could explain more about it, so we'd know the other things it does," she shrugged.

"Oh, good idea," Eden agreed quickly, catching herself added "maybe I can find out from Moreh or someone."

"Hey, it's like matin, we'd better head back before we get caught out," Shephel suggested, looking up at the moon.

"So you're saying you're tired?" Eden smiled.

"Yes I am," he agreed immediately.

"Yeah, let's head back," Parzel agreed. "At least we have determined that Eden actually likes us," she looked at Shephel, smirking.

"Sort of," Eden shrugged with a smile, and as quietly as they had come they slipped back into town and under the ditch to the kitchens, never noticing the dark shadow that followed them to the edge of the town's gate

8

> *"For you are a people holy to Melek, your King.*
> *Melek your King has chosen the Eklektos*
> *to be his treasured possession,*
> *out of all the peoples who exist."*

During the next several weeks Eden was anxious to get Sela alone to talk about the knife, but she could never get the opportunity. He always bolted from training, and then no one would see him till the next day. She didn't feel she could ask people about him, in case she gave his secret away, but she was beginning to get frustrated.

Meanwhile, their training had finally begun to include swords. Granted, they were still the practice swords, but they were now learning how to use them rather than just holding them. Eden had to admit that Petros was a good teacher. He was certainly the most skilled swordsman out of all the masters. It wasn't often that Eden had a chance to think about talking to Sela during class as they were working so hard now. Master Petros had them sparring with each other on a foot wide log that was suspended over the practice area. It meant a lot of falls, twisted ankles, bruised wrists and backs. More often than not, one of the masters would be sending students to the hospital wing for minor treatments. But they were improving. Eden knew she was getting better as she was able to hold her own now with Parzel who had been sword fighting her whole life.

Although Eden had burning questions for Sela, time was passing quickly, and for the most part much better now. She and Parzel were still taking Shephel out after dark to do some conditioning and training, and although it was doing nothing for his clumsy nature, it was improving his endurance and physical skills. Perhaps the most interesting part was that it was bringing the group together as a team.

Even Nasah noticed it. Yesterday while they were sparring on the log she had asked Eden, "What's up with you and Parzel?" followed by a swift down stroke.

Eden blocked it easily, but her concentration was broken and she gave a weak stroke in return. "What do you mean?"

"You – never – seem – to fight – anymore," Nasah punctuated each word with a strong blow to Eden's sword, driving her backwards.

"I don't know," Eden replied, catching her balance, and trying to return the blows. "We just sort of understand each other more I guess," she tried to spin and catch Nasah off guard, but resulted only in losing her balance and falling ungracefully to the dirt below. She grimaced as she looked up to Nasah smiling down on her and sighed, tucking the pala stone back into her shirt and pulling herself to her feet.

Today as she moved herself through her stances alone, she was trying to figure out exactly when things had begun to change. It might have been at the river, or maybe that first night with Shephel. What she did know, was that she respected Parzel now, and she thought that Parzel was becoming less snobby too, she didn't seem to be showing off anymore either. As she finished her last moulinet with her sword extended in front of her, she spotted Sela heading back to his room. Quickly Eden glanced around to see that everyone was busy, and she leaned her practice sword against the wall and stole away after him.

By the time Eden got to his room he was just leaving again.

"Sela," she cried, not too loudly to call attention to the fact that neither of them were where they should be.

He turned quickly for such a big guy and hushed her immediately.

"What are you doing?" he said in a quiet voice.

"I have to ask you a question," she demanded, coming right up beside him.

"Couldn't you ask me in class?" he asked as his eyes darted back and forth looking for something.

"You're never around long enough," she replied, following his eyes and seeing nothing. "What's wrong? You're being all secretive," she asked, puzzled and a little worried now.

"Nothing," he replied, looking directly at her and taking a deep breath, "sorry, what's your question?" he tried to give her his attention.

Eden decided to drop it and went on, "you know that knife I have, the one you made?"

"Yes, what about it?" he answered somewhat suspiciously, narrowing his eyes as if trying to discern why she had asked.

"Did you do something to it?" she asked vaguely.

"What? I haven't touched it - are you accusing me of stealing it or something?" he got offended, "because.."

"No you goof," she stopped him, "but it seems to sort of – well, I don't know have special powers," she screwed up her face as she said it, realizing it sounded ridiculous.

Sela just stood there for a moment with a blank look on his face. "Really?" he asked. "I'd read that about it, but I never did anything special, so I never believed it," he looked her in the eye again. "What did it do?"

"Well, I accidentally threw it at someone I thought was an intruder, but they were a friend and even though I was aiming right at them I missed completely."

He smiled, "Are you sure you just didn't miss?"

"No, You oaf," Eden shouted sharply, then caught herself. "We tested it, and I can't hit anyone that I don't think is an enemy."

"Really?" Sela was shocked. "I can't help you much. I mean, I made it following instructions exactly, but when I gave it to Moreh it was just a silver knife with engraving on it. I didn't even know what it said."

"Moreh?" Eden asked.

"Yes, she was the one who came and took it finally," Sela nodded, then something caught his eye. "I have to go – sorry I'm no more help. I'll talk to you later," he rushed away from her and around the barracks.

Eden stood there dumbfounded for a moment, she glanced all around and couldn't see anything that could have startled Sela. He was acting strange. But he did give her one important piece of information. Moreh had had her knife.

"I'm just going to have a talk with her," she said aloud. "But I'd better get back to class," she realized she'd been gone too long, and quickly ran back to the practice field.

They continued to work on their sparring, with Master Petros yelling at them constantly. Parzel was by far the best in their group, but the rest of them were not too far behind.

"Okay, come here," Master Petros waved them over to him. It was a third before vesper, and the other groups had already been released for supper. "I am mildly impressed with you," he gave them a backhanded compliment, and shook his head, "but whether I think you are ready or not, you are being sent on your first field mission."

The whole group's eyes widened in disbelief.

"But sir, you haven't even let us use proper swords yet," Nasah cried.

"Whatever you can do with a dull blade, you can do that much more with a real sword, it will not matter," he waved off her remark. "I am more concerned about your ability to work as a team," he sighed, "but my opinion is not considered apparently. So tomorrow before dawn you will meet here to receive your instructions."

"What kind of mission is this?" Parzel asked.

"It is still a training mission right?" Shephel asked.

"Yes, it is still training, but it is training out in the field and anything can happen in the field," Master Petros explained. "You will be given a contained mission, but it plays out with real people and places, those are things you cannot prepare for, and at times our enemy likes to target our trainees," he added ominously.

None of them knew how to respond, they just looked at their master. He finally smiled, realizing they needed some confidence. "You'll do fine. Go and choose your swords from the rack. Practice your moulinet tonight in your rooms, get the balance right for your sword, know it well, feel its grip," he paused, taking the measure of them. "Before dawn here," he turned and walked off into the deepening shadows.

"What the heck are we supposed to know about a mission!?" Nasah exclaimed.

"And where is Sela? He hasn't heard any of this," Parzel threw up her hands, "how are we to be a team if we're missing members already?"

"Calm down everyone. Just calm down," Shephel kept his head. "We wouldn't be doing this if someone didn't think we were ready. Let's just choose our swords, eat and rest tonight," he walked over to the rack and began picking up swords and testing them out.

"I think we need to go over our notes too," Nasah added, getting her composure back.

"Why?" Eden asked, as she followed Shephel to the swords.

"Well, remember, the King's words are life," she reminded them. "I think they might help us on whatever this mission is."

"King's words are life," Eden muttered, she remembered Moreh telling her that the first day. She had spent much time before learning those words, but lately she had left off a bit as she had focused on the sword and her own conditioning, but something was resonating in her that Nasah was right, they had to know those words or they would be doomed tomorrow. She determined to go over everything tonight.

Quickly choosing her sword, she waved goodbye to her team and hurried to the kitchen to grab something to eat while she studied in her room. However, her plans were quickly changed when she found Moreh standing at her door when she returned.

"Hello Moreh," Eden tried to smile, but the small woman's somber face worried her.

"Leave your food, but bring your sword and follow me," she set off at a brisk pace towards the tower. Eden threw her things and food in her room and clutching her new sword she jogged to catch up with her teacher.

Moreh did not say a word but led Eden in through the front gate of the tower. She had not been there since her first day in Kaleo, they walked up to the tapestry that had so caught Eden's attention that first day and stopped. Moreh looked at the tapestry for a moment, then at Eden. "Give me your sword."

Eden extended it to her. Moreh held it in her two palms, "Tomorrow is a very dangerous day for you," she began, "you must complete your field training, but there are others who know you are here and will seek to use this opportunity to try and get rid of you before you are fully trained. I did not want you to go out so early, but the King sees you and he chose the day and the mission."

Eden soaked in her words.

"So you go out tomorrow in peril with your new team. You must rely on your team, you cannot do this alone, although it is you alone that brings the peril to your team," Moreh paused, waiting for Eden's mind to grasp all that she was saying. "Use the gifts and talents you have, and you will succeed as a team."

Now she looked down at the sword in her hand. "This will not do," she laid the sword aside so that it leaned against the tapestry.

Moreh threw back her cloak and revealed a plain leather scabbard. Its chape was polished silver and the locket matched, but the leather was simply a thick black, with small braids crisscrossing its width.

Eden recognized the sword itself immediately from its hilt, which was a very familiar ivory and silver. She took it from Moreh's hands and pulled the sword from its sheath. It rang clearly as the steel passed over the locket and Eden stared at what was Sela's work. However, the sword she had admired before, now had similar engravings to her belt knife.

"What does it say?" Eden asked, as she let her fingers trace over the unknown letters.

"Even the darkness is not dark to you, and the night is as bright as the day, darkness and light are alike to you," Moreh's voice took on a deep and dramatic tone. "You will find the meaning of those words as you use the blade. Sela has been working hard on it for you, under my orders."

Moreh's words suddenly reminded her of her questions about the knife. "What did you do to the knife?" she asked abruptly. "I mean, it does strange things for me, and Sela didn't know anything about it."

"Yes, there have been blessings given to your blades. They have been chosen for you, long before you knew, and watched long before Sela knew what he was making," Moreh smiled at Eden, she had let her harsh professor look fall for a moment and said, "I am proud of you, you have been growing and improving. Do not forget the words of the King," she looked back at the tapestry and her hand lifted to touch the image of the lamb. "Don't forget," she whispered.

Eden slid the sword back into its scabbard and stood awkwardly behind Moreh. Feeling that she was supposed to leave her teacher alone, she slowly backed out of the room and through the main gate

9

"Of old you spoke in a vision to your chosen one
and said, 'I have granted help to the one
who is gibbor chayil,
I have exalted my Eklektos from the people.'"

It was a damp morning with a chill in it that found Eden, Parzel, Sela, Shephel and Nasah huddled together on the practice field. They tried to stay out of the wind as they awaited their instructions. None of them spoke. It didn't seem the right moment to be making small talk.

Eden's mind was racing through all she had tried to recall last night in her bed. She had let her mind drift through her studies, the King's words, her sword fighting, Moreh's words, all the time lying with her new sword on her chest. She pulled her jacket up closer to her neck as the chill had begun to seep in. Her hair was wet now, Sela and Shephel were wiping the mist from their faces. There wasn't much chance of the sun breaking through today. The clouds were thick above them and to their north it looked like full-fledged rainstorms weren't far off.

Petros and Moreh came around the tower and headed towards the cold group. Neither of their masters seemed bothered by the weather as they traveled with cloaks open, the wind apparently afraid to touch them. Moreh had a piece of parchment in her hand and Petros had some fabric thrown over his arm, which as he approached, appeared to be cloaks Eden thought.

"Good morning," Moreh met them looking nervous, "we trust you have rested and are ready for the journey that lies ahead of you," she did not wait for any of them to reply, before rolling out the

78

parchment. It was in fact a map of Kaleo. "You will hopefully already have this map entrusted to memory, as well as ones with more detail. You will recall here," she pointed,

"to the south west of us there is an old ruin of one of the King's guard posts. It was lost a long time ago and left in disrepair. However, recently we have had reports that slaves of Nachash have made their way to the ruins and are now using it as a stopover in their raids of the King's lands here in the North. Your mission is to clear out the guard post, once you do we will send a battalion of masons and carpenters to begin repairs on the ruins and rebuild it to the strength it once knew."

She folded the parchment up and slipped it inside her cloak. "You will be traveling for two days to reach the post; however, you must keep in mind that it is *slaves* of Nachash, not his soldiers that remain there," she emphasized the word. "These slaves were once free men and women of Kaleo or your world Eden, you must try first to free them – not attack them. Force is acceptable; however, it should be a last resort in this case. The King wishes for all who are slaves to be free, he does not want any to perish. You are charged to this task."

Parzel raised her head to meet Moreh's eyes. "Teacher, just one question. You said we will travel for two days, that journey will take us much longer than two days, unless..." her voice trailed off.

"Yes, unless..." Moreh smiled at her understanding, "Eden can you reveal your necklace?"

Awkwardly, Eden reached under her shirt and pulled out the stone. The brilliant blue stone shone on its chain. As Eden looked at it in her hand it seemed that the stone was filled with a liquid, the turquoise colour of a Caribbean ocean. In all the times of examining it, it had never looked so 'alive'.

"Here is a pala stone," Moreh waved her hand at the stone. "It will take you within two days hike of the guard post. Any closer and your position will become known," she paused and looked around at the group. "You know how to use this?" she asked, looking at their astonished faces.

"I do," Nasah replied, her mouth still gaping at the stone.

"Good, to you I entrust its uses then," Moreh smiled. "You will instruct your team."

"And your weapons? They are ready?" Petros now spoke up.

He nodded, pleased as they each pulled their jackets back to display sword hilts and belt knives. "Good, throw these cloaks over top of yourselves, they will keep the chill out and give some protection from prying eyes," he handed out the brown and green cloaks.

Eden was amazed that they did immediately give warmth, she quickly pulled the hood up over her wet hair and felt instant energy from its comfort.

"You will be in our eyes, but we cannot get to you quickly should you be in trouble. You must keep your wits about you and rely on one another," He took a deep breath as if calming himself. "Remember my disappointment if we lose any of you."

"Really Petros," Moreh chided, "the King's guard go with you," she raised her hand over them. "Now quickly, surround Eden, each place one hand on her shoulder or arm and hold on," Moreh instructed. "Ready Nasah?"

"Yes," she was staring at the stone around Eden's neck.

"Go ahead, we will see you all soon," Moreh's words were fading away quickly.

Eden wasn't sure what was happening but all the buildings, the practice field and even the rain was slipping away from them. They were the only solid objects as everything else slid past. She looked at Parzel who's eyes were wide with wonder too. Then she heard Nasah's voice,

"Let go of Eden and bend your knees."

Eden watched as Parzel, and Sela vanished before her eyes, then Shephel and finally Nasah and the world suddenly jerked to a stop, like an elevator, and despite having bent her knees, she found herself crumpled amongst a pile of leaves in the midst of a deep forest. Parzel was already standing beside her, and Sela was pulling himself up. All of a sudden Shephel appeared and collapsed into a heap just behind

Eden, and Nasah with more grace than any of them was just as suddenly standing beside Parzel.

"Wow," was all Eden could say as she picked herself up.

The weather was different here, cloudy she could tell, but the wind and chill had not moved this far south. She pushed her hood back and helped Shephel to his feet.

"That was incredible," Nasah pointed to the stone, "you should put that away," Eden quickly slid it underneath her shirt. "I'd noticed your necklace before but never realized what it was."

"How did you do that anyway?" Parzel asked her.

"Well, I'd read about it before, and it said you had to fix the spot you were traveling to in your mind then say these words, 'open to me the gates of righteousness; I shall enter through them, this is the gate of the King.' And here we are. As far as I can tell, there are certain markers across the kingdom that this will open to you. There's a map somewhere that shows them all, I've never seen it, but obviously one is here. We'll have to fix Migdal in our minds when we travel back."

"I'm very glad that you're smart," Sela smiled at her, still brushing leaves from his clothes.

"I think we all are," Parzel nodded.

"Okay, so we are two days hike from the guard post, I suppose we ought to be careful where we camp and stay off the main trails," Eden pulled her notebook out from the back of her pants and flipped to her pages of maps.

"Where did you get that?" Nasah asked, awed at the detail on the maps. "It looks like a textbook."

"When I first arrived Moreh gave me lessons for a week and spent days and hours on these maps, I'm a quick transposer so I just copied them out, I've used them lots around Shammah too," Eden shrugged and flipped to a page showing the area around them.

"I've never even seen a map like this and I've lived here all my life," Parzel exclaimed.

"Really?" Eden was puzzled, "I thought I was just getting the same stuff you guys got in class," her mind went back to those lessons, and she remembered Moreh insisting on the importance of geography.

"I guess they thought you'd need to know more," Shephel remarked. "Doesn't surprise me really, we have a different case here than any other trainee group."

Nasah looked at him, "What do you mean?" she asked confused.

Shephel looked at Eden who was starting to grasp where he was going with this.

"Do you want to tell them or should I?" he asked.

"Tell us what?" Parzel demanded and Eden honestly shrugged, not knowing what information Shephel was hinting at.

"I overheard you and Moreh last night, when she gave you that," he pointed to her sword hilt protruding from her cloak.

Eden was shocked at being overheard.

"Moreh said that we were in greater danger on this exercise because the enemy knows Eden is here and wants her dead," his sentence ended abruptly and caused all of them to swallow uncomfortably.

They all seemed to be taking in the danger of the situation they were in having Eden on their team and were shuffling their feet nervously for what felt like an eternity.

Eden wasn't sure what she was supposed to do. She was willing to sacrifice anything for this team now, but it really wasn't fair to them to put them in such danger just because of who she was. "You know what, I'd give anything for this team, and if it means stepping out, I will," she replied resolutely, though it was the last thing she wanted to do. "I'll go back if you guys don't want me on this team. It's not fair, I realize that you didn't ask to be here and be marked just because I'm on the team. I don't even know why the Nachash guy wants me dead, but I don't want any of you being in any sort of danger," she took a step back from the group and pulled the pala stone from her shirt.

"No," Parzel said quietly, "no, if he wants you dead then that's the very last thing in Kaleo I will ever let happen," her voice was unwavering and strong now. "I would die for this team too, and this team includes you Eden. Whether or not you're the chosen one, you are my teammate, and even my friend," she added that part a bit self-consciously, "so forget Nachash, he isn't breaking this team up."

"That's right," Sela agreed, "I made that sword for the eklektos, and I knew her name was Eden and she was my friend. I will not see it go to waste," he threw his arms around her, crushing her to his chest.

"Thanks guys," Eden smiled, after being freed from the hug. "Are you two okay with it as well?" she asked, looking at Nasah and Shephel.

"We wouldn't have it any other way," Nasah agreed, then turned her gaze to Sela. "But Sela, you made Eden's sword?" she raised an eyebrow at him, and his eyes went huge, realizing that he'd let his own secret slip in his excitement.

"Um, uh, well…" he stuttered.

"Yes he did," Eden gripped his arm. "Sela was a blacksmith before he came to Migdal, and he was commissioned to make the knife I have and the sword for me. I think they are the finest workmanship I have ever seen too," she smiled at him.

"Not that that says much since you've been working with swords for what, two months maybe?" Parzel scoffed at her good-naturedly and leaned over Eden to pull her sword from its scabbard, "but I *have* been around swords my whole life and had an uncle who made them and …" she examined the sword in her hand, and let her fingers trace the words slowly, "I believe this is one of the finest swords I have ever seen," she agreed, and handed the hilt back to Eden.

"Well, now that we have had these warm and fuzzy moments, perhaps we should get moving?" Shephel asked.

"Right," they all agreed, suddenly feeling silly.

"Okay," Eden looked back at the notebook in her hand. "Right here, there is a trail just up that ridge that runs almost parallel with the main one we're standing on, yet it seems to always have the high ground," she traced it with her finger, "we should be able to take it right to, oh about five kilometres outside of the guard post. Then we'll have to go cross-country to get in sight," her eyes followed the trees up the hill on their right hand side.

"Good, let's get off this road before someone else arrives," Parzel led the group up the hillside, and there at the top was an overgrown path that did indeed follow along the main trail.

They set off at a good pace, the path was clearly unused and they had to cut through some branches and maneuver around trees, but they were always able to keep a close watch on the road. Once or twice they heard voices and even a horse so they quickly took cover in the trees and watched as what appeared to be regular townsfolk made their way down the pathway.

After one such group passed Eden asked, "So if these people are slaves and are raiding the King's land, why do they look so normal?"

"That's the biggest problem," Nasah answered her, as she slipped underneath a fallen tree trunk in the path. "They come off as regular citizens, look and act the part, then all of a sudden there will be a raid from Nachash's soldiers and these people will vanish. The King's guard think that they will move into areas, get known, find out all the comings and goings of the towns, when the King's guards are around and stuff, then pass all that information on to Nachash, who in turn, eventually sends his soldiers to do the raid and then these slaves just move on with them."

"That's why, if you notice, most people have a terrible suspicion of any newcomers. It's made moving very difficult for loyal citizens and has affected a lot of commerce and trade within Kaleo," Shephel finished the explanation.

"Is that why I was given such strange looks when I first was moving around town?" Eden asked, following the path that Nasah was now striking for them.

"No, you were stared at because you came dashing through the city on a huge warhorse with three of the King's gibbor chayil," Parzel laughed letting a branch swing back into Eden.

"Oh, people noticed that?" she joked, ducking out of the way.

Night had fallen by now, and they were making their way along more carefully. They had progressed well during the day and were at least two thirds of the way to the guard post. But their chosen path was difficult to navigate in the dark and they didn't dare use any torches here.

"I think we should settle down and make camp," Parzel finally suggested, breathing heavily as they had just crested a steep hillside. "Eden, do you think we've come at least halfway?"

"Oh easily," she replied, pulling the notebook out again. "In fact, I think we're here,"she pointed to their approximate location and the group all nodded with satisfaction at their progress.

"Good," Parzel nodded, dropping her pack to the ground.

"So we should set a guard?" Nasah asked, trying not to give orders to her team, but make a wise suggestion.

"Yeah," Eden agreed, looking around her. "What do you think if we each take a third for a shift and then we'll be able to move out very early tomorrow?" she looked pointedly at Shephel to make sure he was going to make it with so little sleep.

"I'm fine if that's what you're asking," he remarked, "I haven't run all those hills with you for nothing."

"Good," she smiled in return then looked at Parzel, "want to divide up the watch?"

"Sure, I'll take the first shift, then wake Eden, then Shephel, Nasah and Sela?" she asked it as a question to make sure they all agreed.

"Sounds good," Sela nodded and the others seemed in agreement so they quickly found comfortable spots, or as comfortable as tree roots and rocks can afford, and huddled under their cloaks. They didn't want to risk a fire, to cook or for warmth so had to rely on the cloaks that Petros had given them before they left. Parzel found a spot where she could see the main roadway as well as her team and pulled her sword out and let it rest across her knees. Eden's eyelids struggled to watch Parzel for a few minutes, but despite the cold, and uncomfortable position she could not ward off sleep any longer.

The others slept quickly too, having been tired from their hike. It felt like only a few minutes to Eden when Parzel shook her awake. She startled and Eden almost cried out, but Parzel put a hand over her mouth and signaled for her to be silent and follow her.

She pulled her own sword out and crept to the spot Parzel had been in. She pointed to the path below them and there Eden could see in the darkness a small caravan of people stealing along in the direction of the guard post.

When there was a break in the group Parzel leaned towards Eden and spoke right in her ear. "It's been like this for the past half of my shift. Groups of them slipping along. Occasionally I see some coming back, it's as if they are reporting in or something. Be careful," she slipped quietly to where Eden had laid and was almost immediately asleep.

Eden sat with her own sword out and watched the strange parade of people. Nearing the end of her shift the flow had stopped, but her eyes continued to scan the path and she could hear the faint sounds of travel off in the distance in front of them. When she woke Shephel she quietly explained what had happened and instructed him to keep a close eye out, and thankfully fell back into an exhausted rest.

It was about a third before dawn that Sela woke each of them. Eden stretched and pulled a rock out from under her side and tried to work the kinks out of her back.

"Did anyone else pass by?" Parzel asked, biting into a piece of dried beef from her pack and looking at the others.

"Lots for the first half of my shift, then they seemed to stop," Eden replied.

"I didn't see anyone," Shephel answered, he too eating a bit of breakfast.

"I started to see them coming back," Nasah informed them, "just a few though."

"I saw a few too at first, but not as many as you guys have said went on," Sela replied, "and no one for the past half third."

Parzel and Eden looked at each other, "I think that we had best expect more people at the guard post than the masters knew," Parzel mused.

"I think you're right," Eden nodded, having thought the same thing. "Did any of you see any soldiers?" but they all shook their heads. "Well that's good I guess, they must just be these slaves, but either they are meeting someone else there, or they've been told to keep an eye out. We are going to have to be careful," she finished her own beef jerky and stood adjusting her sword. "Come on we'd better go."

They moved quickly and as the dawn came, their way got easier but they had to move more stealthily, keeping well back from the edge of the ridge. It was just after sext that they had to stop as the trail they were on now branched away to the north.

"Here's where we have to go off road," Eden examined her map. "We should come to the guard post in the next five kilometres over this small ridge."

"At least we'll come down on it right?" Nasah asked.

"Yeah, that's to our advantage. I wonder how big it is anyway?" Parzel wondered aloud.

"Not big, maybe three thousand square feet, just enough for a small troop of chayil, the rest lived down in the town at the base of the hill, but it's been burned down long ago," Sela answered.

Everyone turned to look at him.

"How do you know that?" Shephel asked confused at Sela's sudden astuteness.

He swallowed hard for a moment, looked away from them and answered, "I believe this is where my parents were killed," he said quietly.

No one knew how to respond to that and stood waiting for Sela to say something else.

He waited awhile, trying to get his composure. "At least there can't be more than ten people in the place, there's no way an army could be waiting for us in it, as long as there is no one around it," he stopped and swallowed hard, "I spent some time in the library after I found out where they had died studying the place and the battle, it made me feel I was closer to them or something, silly I know," he wiped his eyes with the back of his hand.

"Good - I guess - that you know that," Parzel tried to move the conversation on seeing Sela's pain. "So, we need to take real caution approaching the post, let's flank out on my point, give each other say ten or fifteen paces between. One whistle for danger, two to come together on my spot," she gave orders, but none of the rest argued, leaving her to lead.

They spread out, each with their sword at the ready and moving cautiously through the trees. They saw nothing out of the ordinary, but Parzel was several paces ahead of their line and raised her sword for them to stop. Everyone crouched low and froze, their eyes focused on her. A moment later she let out two low whistles, and they all carefully approached her spot.

From her vantage point she could see the guard post below them. Sela was right, there could not be more than ten people inside that place, but there were at least that number around the outside.

"Hum, that presents a problem," Nasah surmised, "there's got to be at least that number inside too, making it twenty that we five are facing."

"And these ones seem armed," Shephel pointed out, "Sela are you alright?" he put his hand out to Sela who was weeping silently while looking at the post.

Sela took a stuttered breath, trying to stop the tears. "I've just…" he sniffed again, "I've never seen it, but it happened here. They were right here."

The sight of this big strong man weeping was heart breaking.

"We are going to claim it back for them, Sela," Eden said, "for you." She too put her hand on his shoulder, and then the others followed suit.

"This is for you Sela," Nasah spoke their hearts.

"Thanks," he smiled while tears still fell. "I'm fine," he brushed his face with the back of his hand leaving a dirty streak there.

"Okay, so we need to figure out how to clear them out, and without fighting, and with offering them freedom from the King," Parzel listed their requirements out.

"Small order," Eden raised her eyebrows with sarcasm. "Any suggestions?"

No one spoke. There didn't seem any way to offer freedom without fighting these people and with odds of four to one, things didn't look so good.

"Wait," Eden suddenly exclaimed, "I do have an idea." She looked at Parzel with excitement. "Do you remember the words of the King that say, '*the cords of the wicked have encircled me, but I have not forgotten Your law. At matin I shall rise to give thanks to you.*' ?" Eden was ready to burst with excitement.

"Vaguely, I could never have quoted it," Shephel admitted.

"So - you're saying," Nasah was working it out in her head, "that if we offer them freedom at matin they will remember the law and the King?"

"I think so, Moreh kept drilling into my head the idea that the King's words were everything in battle, they would keep us alive. I think this might be it," Eden was so confident now, it was spilling over into the others.

"Okay, so then we just have to wait till matin and then one of us offers freedom to any who will return to the King?" Parzel suggested.

"Yes, but I think it would be wise if the rest of us split up and surround them, and if the offer goes wrong, or if any don't accept it then we will have to fight and trust that we can each take – what four people?" Shephel counted.

"Yeah, four is right," Nasah agreed, "that's a good plan brother… and what if we bluff that there are more of us here than we are?" she was examining details in her mind.

"How would we do that?" Parzel asked, waiting as Nasah was obviously still thinking.

After several moments she continued, "Well, what if we each make a torch, and when Eden, I'm assuming it'll be Eden, gives this offer, she can call out to the 'captains of the guard' to light their torches, which would suggest the idea that for the four torches that will be seen, there would be a whole troop behind it, instead of just four people."

"Risky, gives your positions away though," Eden offered, worrying about their safety. She assumed that if any know she's the chosen one and see her there, that most of the battle will revolve around taking her, but if they give away their positions -.

"But we have to trust in the King's words like you said Eden," Parzel was smiling, confident, "I like the plan, it's all about timing, you have to make the offer right at matin and call to us just before that and we hope from there."

The others seemed completely in support of this plan so Eden had no other choice but to agree. They spent the remaining hours of daylight setting up their posts, making torches and then finally Eden was to slip down to her hiding place where she would appear from at matin.

Dark had set in, and it must have been close to a third past compline at night, but the moon was full and gave a great light so that they were able to see all of the enemy as they continued to mill around the outside of the post. Only a few seemed to actually be guarding anything or watching the woods, the rest seemed uninterested really and bored.

"I guess this is it," Eden looked into the eyes of her team. "Be careful all of you."

"We go with the King's guard," Parzel placed her sword into the ground and put her hand over the pommel. The others all reached in and put their hands over top of hers.

"The King's guard," They agreed in one voice, then quietly each headed off to their place.

Eden slipped down the hillside carefully, watching the two men on her side that actually seemed to be paying attention. Had they all been on guard it would have made things much more difficult, but as it was she got into her position rather easily.

There she remained, cramped beneath the overhanging branch of an evergreen. She could see people's feet as they walked by and she planned her quick dash for the center of the open space in front of the post. She realized that she'd have to speak quickly and be on her guard for an immediate attack as well. As she crouched, she let her mind again run over the King's words as she had studied them. She prayed she had this one right about matin, could be a short lifetime in Kaleo if she was wrong, she thought.

Looking at the sky she determined it must be almost matin, I have to get my own sentinel, she thought and readied her sword. She waited a moment longer for the feet in front of her hiding spot to move away, then she took a deep breath, prayed her team was ready and dashed out into the open, her sword in front of her.

She obviously startled all of the people that were there as they turned to look at her with fear on their faces. She took their surprise as the opportunity to call out, "Slaves of Nachash. See the torches of the captains of the Kings guard around you," she used her sword to gesture to the woods, but though she heard her teammates call out in a war cry all she could see around her was a deepening darkness.

What was going on? Her mind immediately flew back to the dressing room in the King's tower as this darkness seemed to press out every light around her. It covered the moon and seemed to give strength to the slaves that now had recovered from their surprise and seeing nothing but the darkness of matin, were moving towards her.

10

Eden's mind was racing. The darkness was pressing in on her and she was unable to move, she knew that she would not even be able to defend herself when these people reached her. Her arm felt like lead holding her sword and she started to tremble.

Her eyes flew from one person to another until she focused on one man that had been standing guard earlier. His gaze was fixed on her, his eyes shone with a strange sickly yellow colour, and his pupils were black holes that didn't dilate. He had one arm raised towards the sky and a sinister smirk on his face as he approached her. Claustrophobia gripped Eden as fear crushed her from every side like a physical vice and she struggled to breathe. But then, just as powerful as the darkness felt, the inscription that Moreh had read to her on her sword blazed in front of her eyes, blocking out the evil that approached.

> *Even the darkness is not dark to you,*
> *and the night is as bright as the day,*
> *darkness and light are alike to you.*

With all her strength she forced her sword to point directly at the man and cried out in a shaking voice, "Darkness and Light cannot dwell together."

Instantly an explosion of light ripped from her sword. The darkness was gone and the torches of her team blazed as if each held ten.

Everyone froze.

Eden blinked.

The man that had been approaching her with his arm raised was lying immobile on the ground. Eden's sword continued to blaze with unnatural light and the slaves cowered back from it.

Gaining confidence again, she took a deep breath and called out. "Slaves of Nachash, the cords of the wicked have encircled you, but you have not forgotten the King's law. At matin you shall rise to give thanks to the King. You have a choice right now, you may lay down your arms and you will be free."

It was like a veil had been lifted and these slaves that seemed so bored and uninterested in what they had been ordered to do suddenly came to life. They looked at Eden, her sword, at each other and then one by one they threw down their weapons.

One or two ran for the hills, only to be met with Eden's team. From her spot in the clearing, she could hear fights going on, but it was not long before Sela appeared, dragging an unconscious man along with him, then Shephel and Nasah and finally Parzel with a blade dripping blood. Each came to stand beside Eden, swords still at the ready, but there was no one left to fight. All of the slaves had sat down to await their fate at the hands of what they thought were the captains of the King's guard.

They stood that way for quite a while.

"Is it safe to put down our swords?" Nasah finally asked out of the side of her mouth, keeping the people in her line of sight.

"I don't know," Eden replied, keeping her eyes on the people too. "Are you guys okay?" she asked, she could tell that Parzel had a cut on her arm, and Sela's fist was bloodied too.

"We're fine, just a few ran up the hills, but we had them all. What was that darkness?" Sela asked.

"I don't know, but it happened to me once before when I was in the tower with the King, and the words I spoke were what Moreh said to save me that time, so I thought maybe it would work with my sword," Eden explained. "I think that guy there was the one doing it," she motioned to the body that still hadn't moved in front of her.

"Do you think the chyail will be here soon?" Shephel asked.

"I hope so, my arm is killing keeping my sword out," Parzel answered and the others laughed, which drew the people's attention to them again and they tried to look serious.

Finally, they heard movement on the path, and there emerged a troop of the King's chayil coming towards them. Petros was at the head, and quickly gave instructions to his men then headed over to their location.

"Well done all of you," he said.

He went over and touched the man in front of Eden with his foot. "We did not expect this," he muttered.

"Who is he?" Eden asked, finally lowering her sword.

"What, is a better question," Petros replied. "Look at his eyes," he pointed to the man's face, his eyes frozen open, still yellow but unseeing. "That is the mark of an Ebed of Nachash. Like the Gibbor Chayil, the Ebed serve Nachash directly and receive power from him. I don't doubt that it was he who was calling down that unnatural darkness on this place. We did not have any knowledge that any Ebed would be here, thank the King you had the presence of mind to use your sword Eden," he sighed. "We will have to see how he got to this place unnoticed by our intelligence. But enough of that, you have succeeded in your mission and with flying colours," he congratulated them. Then noticed Parzel's shirt that was now soaked through with blood from her left arm. "Are any others hurt?" he asked, looking them all over and noticing Sela's hand. "So not without resistance?" he sniffed, "Well, it would seem you learned something in class then as you are still here. Your adversaries?"

"He would not turn, I had no choice once he attacked me," Parzel explained, "he's up to the south west."

"Mine's right here, but I think he'll have a headache when he wakes up," Sela pointed to another man lying just a few steps away.

Petros smiled, "I am proud of you," He looked at Eden, "You still have the stone?" when she nodded he continued, "then fix Migdal in your minds, hold on to Eden and go back. Go and see Master Rophe in the hospital and make sure all is well with you. We will finish here," he turned and walked away.

"Nasah?" Eden looked at her as she held the stone, too tired to try it herself.

"Open to me the gates of righteousness; I shall enter through them, this is the gate of the King," Nasah's voice was clear and bright and they all found themselves in the practice field of the palace moments later.

"Nasah and Shephel, are you two hurt at all?" Eden asked as everyone but Nasah pulled themselves up off the grass again.

"No."

"Worst I got was a burn on my thumb lighting my torch," Shephel laughed.

"Good, then you two go back and sleep, it must still be early, I'll take Parzel and Sela to Master Rophe," she instructed.

"I'm fine, no need to bother him," Sela waved her off, "I've had much worse working the forge. I'm going to bed too," he paused, "unless you need help with Parzel?" he asked.

Eden looked at Parzel, who had her hood pulled up but was standing. "I think it's okay, thanks though."

Sela nodded, took Nasah and Shephel by the arm and the three headed off to the barracks.

"Okay, come on Parzel, let's get that arm fixed up," she turned to her, and could see that the wound was worse than she had let on. Under her hood Parzel's face was pale and her left arm hung there lifeless, blood dripping from her fingertips. "You're not good are you?" Eden started to realize the gravity of the wound, she glanced towards where the others had left but they were already around the corner and gone.

"I don't feel real good, kind of cold," Parzel was sounding distant and her eyes were not focusing on Eden.

"Come on, we have to get you help," Eden put her arm around Parzel's waist who draped her arm over her shoulders. Supporting most of her weight, Eden tried her best to hurry them to the hospital wing. It couldn't have been more than the second watch, the doors were shut and no lights were lit.

Parzel was getting heavier on Eden as she was losing more blood. Eden began to bang on the doors, "Master Rophe," she cried out, "we need help. Please open up, Master Rophe," her voice gave away her own fear for Parzel and finally she heard the doors unlock from inside and a gentle looking man in his night clothes holding a torch stood there looking at them.

"Oh dear, you were the team out on mission I suppose?" he asked lifting Parzel's chin from where it was resting on Eden's shoulder, he pushed back her hood and opened her eye lids to look at her. "Okay, bring her in, we'd better attend to this quickly," he waved her to follow him, as he lit more lights and pointed to a room on their right. "In there, I'll be in in a moment, have her lie down," he instructed. "She'll be fine," he added as an afterthought.

"Come on Parzel, you're going to be fine," Eden kept talking, she flopped Parzel's body down on the open bed, lifting her legs up so that she was lying down, she put a pillow behind her head and pushed her hair out of her face. Parzel had stopped talking and was all but unresponsive at this point. Eden's brow knit in worry, begging Master Rophe to hurry in her mind.

Finally, he reappeared in the room. "Oh dear, don't worry, don't you know the King's words are life?" he lifted the book in his hand to her. "She'll be just fine, you leave and wait outside. I'll get you when she's better," he waved her out. "Go on, she'll be fine."

Eden moved slowly to the door and let it swing shut behind her. She could hear the Master reading or speaking to Parzel, and finally took a seat in the hall.

She must have fallen asleep because it was Moreh who shook her awake and the sun was up and shining outside. She rubbed her eyes trying to remember what had happened, where she was and why

Moreh was waking her when she was so tired. Suddenly it all came flashing back to her. "Is she okay?" she jumped up from her chair, only to have Moreh guide her back down and sit beside her.

"Yes, Parzel is fine," she nodded, "she's sleeping so let's not disturb her, although I am glad to see your concern," she smirked. "I want to talk about what happened out there," she looked Eden in the eye. "Tell me everything."

Eden took a deep breath and began to recount the whole thing, including all the people on the trail at night, the Ebed and the blazing sword.

All the time Moreh was nodding and encouraging her to continue the story. When she finished Moreh sat back in her chair for a moment.

"Interesting."

"What does it all mean?" Eden asked.

"I don't know, I will have to discuss it with the King. But one thing is sure, your presence was known and prepared for. Thankfully, you are smarter than they know and more prepared than they expected, but that will not happen again. I doubt they will underestimate you next time."

"It wasn't just me, it was the team," Eden was quick to add.

"Oh, I know that, but the attack was directed at you. But they had given you a clue that first day, that was what did them in here, you remembered. All in all, I am very proud of each of you. You faced a threat worse than any trainee should ever see and you battled well and won," she glanced at the door to the room that Parzel was in. "I think she is awake now, you should go and see her. I'll be back to debrief all of you in a few minutes, then you have the day off today to rest and recover," she stood and walked down the hallway.

Eden quietly went into Parzel's room. She was sitting up in bed, a bandage on her left arm, but her hair was washed and combed, her colour had returned and a light was back in her eyes making the grey twinkle like silver.

"Hi," Eden called from the door.

"Eden, come in," she responded, her face lighting up.

"How are you doing?" Eden asked, examining the bandage on her arm.

"Oh, I'm fine, just a little scratch now, Master Rophe has the healing touch to be sure. He says I can leave today after I eat," she smiled, then added, "thanks for getting me here last night. I remember most of it, up till the hospital anyway, you basically carried me here."

"Well, I would have had Sela carry you the whole way if I'd known you were hurt so bad," Eden explained.

"Guess that's my stubborn side," Parzel grimaced, "I didn't want to let anyone know it was that bad. Sorry," she looked away.

"Whew, well at least I'm not the only one with issues," Eden pretended to wipe her forehead and laughed. Just then Nasah and Shephel walked through the door followed by Sela, still rubbing his eyes from sleep.

"Hey," they smiled, seeing Parzel up and laughing. "We just heard you were in here," Nasah explained. "We didn't know you were this hurt or we would have all come last night."

"Don't worry, I don't think I even realized how bad it was," Parzel smiled at all of them. "Master Rophe fixed me up without any trouble and Eden got me here fast enough so it's all good," she smiled again, clearly thrilled that all of her team was here with her.

"Hey, who let you all in?" Master Rophe came in through the door. "There should be no more than one visitor at a time. Get out all of you before..." he was interrupted by Moreh coming into the room as well.

"How many times..." he began again, but she raised a hand to him.

"Master Rophe, I asked them all to meet here, I need to debrief them from their mission, and seeing as you have not released one of their team we are forced to meet here," she stated matter-of-factly.

"Well, I – that is, well..." he blustered a bit, then finally smiled and seemed to give up. "Just don't touch anything," he threw up his hands and left shaking his head.

"Good to see you all here and awake," Moreh began, looking at Sela as he continued to rub his eyes, but stopped as soon as he caught her gaze and put his hands behind his back. "I just want to go over a few things with you," she took a seat on the end of Parzel's bed and gestured that they should all sit.

Each found a spot and got settled before Moreh continued.

"You did very well yesterday. Particularly that you remembered the words of the King. They are your salvation in battle, not your own skill. Thankfully, when it came to physical fights you were not outmatched, but I dare say it is lucky that it was Parzel that faced that man, he was in fact a regular soldier in Nachash's army and not a slave, he would have been well trained and must have been leaving to bring a report. If any of the rest of you had met him I would say he would have bested you. Parzel, your swordsmanship is exceptional, but even you were not unscathed," Moreh looked at her arm, "you must not give false hope to others that you are not injured, you could have died from the loss of blood if you had been out a few minutes longer," her eyebrows furrowed in disappointment.

"I'm sorry, I just…well, I was wrong," Parzel admitted.

"Good, as long as you realize that," Moreh pushed her glasses back up her nose. "Now for you Sela," she turned her attention to where he was still struggling not to yawn. "What was your difficulty?"

"Well, it was that I was pretty sure that was where my parents were killed," he said slowly.

"And that was a problem why?" Moreh continued to question without a hint of sympathy in her voice.

"Well, it was sort of emotional and all. I mean, I joined the army because they were both in it and gave their lives for it. I guess it made me sort of angry to be there," he shrugged as he answered, unsure if he was saying what she wanted him to or not.

"Our pasts will haunt us at times, but we cannot give in to our emotions. Yes, that was the very spot your parents were killed, they died giving their lives for others and are honoured for it, but if you cave to your emotions you make their gift worthless in you," she was trying to discipline without being too harsh Eden thought. "You are still here because you possess talents to serve the King in this way, do not let your past pull you down," she seemed to know more about his past than she was really saying, and Sela was nodding quickly as if he understood.

"Now Eden," Moreh turned her gaze again, "You did well, you have studied well and acquired much knowledge. I am most concerned about the information about you that is obviously getting out. Nachash certainly had information that a team was coming to the guard post, and that you were also there. I can see no other reason he would have had an Ebed there otherwise, it would have been overkill to be sure. Somehow information is getting out of Migdal," she was talking more to herself now and staring out the door into the hallway, having forgotten the rest of the group.

Nasah cleared her throat and Moreh jumped a bit, "Where was I?" she stumbled over her words, "oh yes, so I will be discussing what you have told me with the King, in the meantime your team will be training within the confines of these walls," she said the last very pointedly. "So I mean no evening excursions outside the walls into Town or elsewhere."

Shephel's eyes widened and he tried to avoid eye contact.

"We must keep your movements unknown as much as we can until we discover the source of our leak," she continued. "However, I must say, that I am proud that this team has really come together. You have grown to like each other I'd even say, and your choice to remain strong together in the face of unasked for danger is a testimony to your hearts," she gave them a thin smile, or at least Eden thought it was supposed to be a smile. "I believe that Parzel will be released from here shortly and I would suggest that you all meet tomorrow on the practice field to work on your sword skills. Sela, your fists will only help you so far, you all need greater skill with your blade. Parzel can instruct tomorrow then you return to regular training," she stood, "but today, rest," she swept out of the room, her scarf the last thing to leave as usual.

"I wonder how they know where you are going?" Nasah mused, "I mean we didn't even find out until that morning."

"I don't know but staying in these walls isn't going to find the answer. We need to do more," Eden stated, hating to be cooped up in the castle.

"You heard Moreh, we need to practice, and she obviously knows that we've been getting out, I don't want to get in any more trouble," Shephel's voice cracked with his worry.

"Well, at least all we have to do have is rest today," Parzel smiled. The others nodded, Sela yawned and everyone took their leave.

11

"And if the King had not cut short the days,
no one would survive.
But for the sake of the Eklektos,
whom he chose, he shortened the days."

The afternoon dragged on. The team was out on the practice field for most of it going over drills and steps with Parzel. Eden had to admit, she really did know what she was doing with a sword. Occasionally other groups would come by and ask questions about their training exercise. Apparently news had traveled about Parzel and the battle already, giving more fire to the need to stop any leaks of information. Moreh and other masters would often shoo students away and send them back to their own studies or other tasks, trying to contain the information as best they could.

'It doesn't seem to work though,' Eden thought to herself as Master Petros was just finishing sending another group of recruits off to the kitchens to clean since 'they were so bored'.

"Ah," he muttered as he turned back to the team. "You will not talk to these groups, no information do you hear me?" he shook his finger at them.

"Yes sir," they replied, some smiling at their notoriety and others trying to look serious at the dilemma their masters were facing.

"Youth," he spat and stalked away to the Tower.

"This is crazy," Nasah smiled, "suddenly everyone wants to talk to us," fixing her blonde hair as another group of students approached.

"Yeah, and have you noticed that a bunch of recruits have been watching our practice from the walls?" Shephel waved his hand towards a cluster of students who suddenly tried to look like they were inspecting the walls above them. "It's like we're famous now," he too ran a hand through his short hair, wondering how he looked.

"Don't enjoy it too much," Eden warned, "It means the masters are going to be keeping a closer eye on us and it's going to make it that much harder to get out of these walls," she spun and clashed swords with Sela.

"What do you mean harder?" Nasah questioned, "Moreh said we can't go out," she turned her attention from the students to look at Eden in disbelief.

"You don't honestly think we're going to stay here and let them try and find the leak do you?" Eden asked, twisting her sword until she had Sela turned around with his back exposed, she slapped it with the flat of her practice sword.

"Ow," he cried out.

"Sela, you have to counter her actions, not just roll with them," Parzel corrected him. "Try again."

"But if she knows we've been getting out, then she's obviously watching us. We'll get in loads of trouble if we disobey orders," Nasah continued.

"But it wasn't really a direct order, she just hinted that she knew, we'll just have to be more careful about how we leave. I can't imagine they know about the kitchen route, or they'd have stopped it up by now. I mean that could very well be how the information is getting out to begin with," Eden argued, again clashing swords with Sela who was concentrating so hard on thinking of defensive moves to her attacking ones he wasn't listening.

"Parzel, talk some sense into her," Shephel pleaded, agreeing with his sister that they needed to stay put.

"Well," she paused, watching them all practice in unison for a second. "If there's a good lead then maybe we should follow it. But I don't think it's worth going out for Shephel's training, we can do that here, but like I said," she added quickly, seeing Eden's look of incredulity, "if we get some sort of a lead, then I think we'd be the best people to follow up on it."

Sela took the moment that Eden had paused to look at Parzel for his opportunity to strike back at her, catching her off guard she struggled to regain her composure in the face of the strength of his attack and quickly found herself on her backside with Sela's sword at her throat.

"Good Sela," Parzel exclaimed, "you need to be more focused Eden, little things draw you off and look what happens."

"Well, Sela," Eden took his big hand to stand back up, "if you get the advantage for a second you'll be able to beat your adversary into submission, your strokes are so strong," she smiled at his strength and shook her head at her own mistake.

"So you want a lead do you?" she muttered as she switched opponents and now faced Nasah. "Well, we're just going to have to find one."

That night after everyone had headed off to bed, Eden started to get dressed. Rather than her pyjamas, she slipped on her belt and knife, pulled on her coat and tied her boots. She waited awhile longer, until she figured everyone had to be inside, with the exception of the guards on duty, and then slipped out of her room. Her intent was not to discover her 'lead' tonight, but if she was going to be able to get any information discretely in town she had to have some kind of disguise. She had thought about it all day, trying to think if there was anything inside the palace that she could use, but everything there would at the very least draw attention to the fact that she lived or worked here and would most likely be loyal to the King. She had to find something that would cause people not to even notice her.

She waited carefully behind the kitchen until she saw the guard on duty walk down to the next parapet, and then she slid under the garbage gate (her name for their secret exit). Thankfully the guards were mostly concerned with keeping people out and not keeping them in, so her excursion was uneventful. She only hoped that there was no one watching. She did not go in her usual direction and was careful to avoid the blacksmith's shop. She did head towards the worst part of town she could think of. As she got closer to the area she was looking for, there were more people out and about, many of them drunk and stumbling. Some were arguing and fighting, others seemed to be having a great time. As she neared what appeared to be a busy pub that evening, she quickly slipped down the alley beside it. She took a breath to calm her nerves and was rewarded with the stench of garbage. She wished she could have brought her sword, but that was the problem, it made her much too noticeable. Even now she had collected quite a few looks in her clean and obviously well made clothing. She had nothing distinguishing on but was still relieved that most of these people would remember little in the morning, and hopefully only a rich kid looking for some fun.

Her real goal lay in the stench beside her. There were boxes of just about anything tossed here. She had heard some of the other guards talking about the mess this district was and that all the pubs and establishments down here became dumping zones for everyone's garbage. She just hoped she could find what she was looking for.

Taking a deep breath, she began pulling boxes from the pile and digging through them. Most of it was just that, trash. But slowly a small pile of items rose beside her. After about an hour of searching, she finally wiped her hands on her pants and examined her spoils. With a nod, she scooped them up in her arms and headed to the entrance of the alley. This became a bit more difficult now, as the hour was late enough that most people were either passed out on the street or home. There were few out walking and those who were looked unsavory enough that she didn't want to face them without her sword. So, it was a long trip back to the castle's garbage dump. She stopped often and waited for long periods of time for people to pass. Twice she pretended to be passed out, and once just outright ran to escape prying eyes. But finally she managed to slip back into her room.

With a relieved sigh she dropped onto the bed, letting her collection fall to the ground. She took several deep breaths trying to get her heart rate to slow, then took a closer look at what she had picked up. She had a pair of worn gloves that were missing most of the fingers, there was a worn knit cap that she was going to have to wash before she could imagine putting on her head. She found several ratty scarves that would work well to cover her face. But her best find, and what she had been looking for particularly was a long black overcoat. It reached right to the floor when she put it on, and was worn and dirty enough to pass as a beggars find. But it had deep pockets, and would cover her sword easily, and a large hood that would also help to hide her face. Finally, she lifted up several pieces of old ripped cloth. Her intent was to wrap her scabbard in the cloth when she went out, so at least if it was spotted, its true radiance would be disguised.

"A profitable night," she smiled. Looking at the sky that was already starting to lighten, she quickly threw her disguise under her bed and tried to sleep for a couple hours before she had to train.

* * * * * * * *

"Eden," Moreh called her name sharply. Eden's head snapped up and she looked around wide eyed, until she saw the displeased look of her master glaring at her. "You can stay afterwards and run some more stairs as it would appear you are so rested this afternoon," Moreh scowled at her, then resumed her discussion on the fourth entry of the King's words in their classroom.

Eden struggled to keep her eyes open, and at the end of the class, she sighed as she packed her books and headed to the tower stairs to complete her punishment for Moreh.

"Eden," a voice called behind her. 'Wait up," Parzel was running to catch up with her, black hair swinging in its ponytail.

"What's up?" Eden yawned as they continued on together.

"I was just wondering if you're okay?" raising an eyebrow at her friend.

"Sure, I'm fine, why do you ask?" Eden was evasive and looked ahead towards the tower, not wanting to give herself away.

"Well, you've been awfully tired for the last two weeks, and you are always going to bed before the rest of us," Parzel was still eyeing her, "I just thought you'd be more interested in finding out what's going on around here, but you haven't mentioned it once, and you're falling asleep in class now," she finished hurriedly, seeing Moreh coming up behind them.

"I'm fine, just studying late, I figured I need to stay ahead for whatever might happen right?" Eden knew that Parzel wasn't buying it, but Moreh's firm admonition that she hurry to the stairs saved her. "Don't worry okay?" Eden looked her friend in the eye now, "I'll be fine, I'd better go."

Parzel stopped, letting Eden go on. She watched until she went inside the doors, then walked back towards her room shaking her head. Eden couldn't be bothered with what she suspected, she was exhausted and now had to run stairs before she could start out on her evening foray. "This better pay off some time soon," she said to herself with a sigh and started up the first set of stairs.

As Eden came down the final flight of stairs she saw Moreh waiting for her.

"You're done, now come here," she called her over.

Eden wiped the sweat from her forehead, pushed the stray hair back from her face and took deep gulps of air, as she came to stand in front of Moreh.

Her master looked her up and down with a suspicious frown on her face. "I don't know what to think of you right now," Moreh began. "You are one of my best pupils, but now you are falling asleep in class," she stated the facts as a question, looking to Eden to crack.

Instead, she just shrugged. "I've been studying a lot more," she gave it as an excuse.

"Humm," Moreh sifted her words in her mind. "I think there is more here than you are letting anyone know," she narrowed her gaze on Eden. "Be aware, you need to be rested to be at your best if you are to face this unseen enemy. Rest is key, no warrior can go on indefinitely, no matter how great. The King rests, and so must you," she put her hand on Eden's back and turned her to the barracks. "Your supper is in your room, eat and sleep tonight," with a gentle push she watched Eden practically stumble back to her room.

Once there Eden eyed the steaming bowl of stew and fresh bread lying on her plate. A cup of warm herbal tea was also sitting there and a fire lit. She sighed, "Oh, all I want to do is enjoy this and sleep." But with resolution, she knew she couldn't. 'If nothing comes of tonight I'll tell the others and maybe we can make another plan,' she thought as she let the stew warm her insides. She ate ravenously, it was amazing how hungry you can get exercising, she thought, then she dug out her disguise.

It had been two weeks of slipping out of the castle at dark and then dressing in her disguise and sitting outside the blacksmith's shop. She'd been up most of the night for these two weeks and for nothing. Not so much as a new mouse had gone into the shop and Grippa never left at night. She was sure that he was the source of this leak, some way or another, but nothing seemed to be happening there. She began wrapping the cloth strips around her scabbard to disguise it, then stuffed the rest of her clothes into her bag. "At least I smell like a beggar after all that running," she laughed to herself, and quietly slipped out her door.

She was always amazed at how easy it was to get out of Migdal without being seen. Once she graduated and was a full-fledged Chayil she would have to let them know, but not now. She slid through the shadows, waited for the guards to pass then ducked out through the garbage. Here in the dump she quickly pulled on her disguise. The ripped gloves covered her hands, she wrapped the scarves around her neck and face, rubbed some extra dirt on her face, and pulled the cap on, then swung the overcoat on to cover the rest of her. She pulled the hood up before taking a slouched gait and walking out of the dump.

Most of the lights were already out on the street, but the blacksmith's was still blazing. This was nothing new, he usually stayed up later than most, working the bellows. Eden found the doorway to a shop across the street that had become her home and curled up. She put an old tin cup in front of her with a few coins in it to make the act complete, and with head slumped on her folded arms, she watched. It was predictably boring, and as the sentinel neared laud, she was feeling she should pack it in when she heard footsteps coming down the road. A tall man in a boot length dark jacket stopped in front of the blacksmith's shop. He put his back to the door and glanced up and down the street, his eyes resting on Eden for a moment. Her breath caught as she saw the yellow flash of his eyes as they swept over her. Her mind flashed images of the Ebed approaching her with his hand raised so many weeks before. She tried not to move, and appear passed out. Finally he turned and rapped on the door.

"About time," the blacksmith grumbled.

"Shut up Grippa," the man snarled, "what of that man there?" he asked pointing at Eden. Her heart skipped a beat and she thought of what her first move would be if they approached.

"Oh, an old bum, he begs here everyday, usually passes out from the drink by matin and doesn't leave till morning. No worries there," he sniffed and led the stranger into the shop.

Eden breathed a sigh of relief. Granted she was pretty confident in her skills now, and she would have had the element of surprise, but that stranger was at least 6'2" tall, and obviously an Ebed, he would have made a daunting opponent, but one she had bested before. She tried to focus her attention on the conversation inside the shop, she slid across the street and slouched under the shop's window in the side alley to try and listen. Unfortunately, work was still going on in the shop and it was not a quiet place so the conversation was mostly muffled, but she caught a few pieces.

The stranger was obviously upset at Grippa for something. It sounded like he was supposed to give him something, but Grippa didn't have it. "I tell you, they just took it, threatened me and took it." This seemed to be Grippa's excuse but the stranger was having none of it and growled some reply.

Grippa must have moved closer to the window because Eden could hear him better. "I can't fight him, he's too big for me, even if he is dumb, and with her I wasn't taking chances, you can deal with that, I'm just for information," Grippa shouted.

"Keep your voice down," the man was closer now too, "you are for information, and you are failing miserably, perhaps we will need to dispatch you."

Eden could hear boots moving towards the window and she dropped even lower. "That might solve many of my problems. Perhaps we can't trust you any more now that you have a nephew in the service of the King? A change in loyalties?" the man was now looking out the window and had gripped the window with both hands. Eden held her breath as she looked at his white knuckles straining on the sill above her.

He turned away again and they seemed to have retreated further back into the smith. Eden took the moment to slip back across the street to her doorway and resumed her position. What she should have done was gone back now and brought news to her team. She considered it, but just then the door opened to the smith and the stranger emerged. He stood in the light for a moment, this time not looking twice at Eden, and put his gloves on. He glanced behind him, then turned, leaving the door open and walked back in the direction he had come from.

Eden paused for a moment. She looked to the open door, and then to the retreating cloak as the man turned a corner. Finally, a real lead to the information leak and without another thought, she leapt up and ran to follow the man.

12

"And Melek said to Nachash, 'I rebuke you, O Nachash!
I, Melek, who has chosen Migdal, rebuke you!
Is not this Eklektos a brand plucked
from the fire?'"

As Eden trailed behind the man on the dark streets, her pride kicked in. She couldn't wait to get back to the barracks and tell the others what she'd found, though she wasn't sure what exactly that was, but if they wanted a lead she certainly had one now.

The man in front of her paused for a moment, and Eden threw herself against a wall. Even though she was disguised he had spent enough time looking at her in the doorway that he would recognize her now. She breathed deeply, trying to slow her own heartbeat, until the man took up his pace again. They were in a district of the city that Eden had never been in. Here there were still a few people up and about, and she passed several, like herself slouching in doors, and sleeping in rags. She tried to put them out of her mind as she saw the man's open jacket trail behind him into a darkened house. A light went on in an upstairs room. Eden mulled over the possibilities from the street. She could go back and get her team, but she would have little to tell them.

"I need to know more," she decided nodding to herself. Besides, she was pretty confident in her skills since her success at the guard post. Surely just getting more information would be less dangerous than that. She let her hand rest on her sword hilt and slipped into the alley between the houses. She kept an eye on the light upstairs as she looked for an open window or door where she might be able to overhear more conversations. There was nothing within reach on this side of the house, so she determined to get into the backyard. There was a rough wooden fence where she was able to pull enough boards apart to allow her to slip between them. As she was halfway through, the scabbard of her sword caught on the ground and she couldn't pull it free.

Eden tugged several times but to no avail. "Argh," she grunted in frustration and quickly undid the buckle on the belt. She had just released it when her world went black.

A rough woolen hood had been thrown over her head and a hand was pressing painfully hard against her mouth to keep in the scream that was struggling to escape her throat. Eden's heart was racing. She realized the instant that the hood had gone on that her sword was lost to her. The arms that encompassed her had prevented her from being able to even grasp the hilt of the weapon as the belt had fallen from her waist. She had been dragged forcefully into the very yard she was trying to get inside of, and her weapon was lying on the other side of the fence.

"Stop struggling or I'll end it permanently," a raspy voice whispered in her ear. It was not the same voice that she had heard in the blacksmith's shop she was sure, but she did not stop struggling. She thought if she could free one hand she might be able to get her belt knife out. But her captor was obviously tiring of having such a handful to deal with.

"I told you – to – stop," and what must have been the pommel of a sword smashed into the back of Eden's head and she dropped with a thud to the ground.

The sound of a cart rattling past in the distance was what brought Eden slowly back to herself. She tried for several minutes to open her eyes, and when she was finally able to accomplish it, she was rewarded with a splitting headache as light pierced her dark world. She winced, closing her eyes in pain. Slowly she tried again. She was lying in what appeared to be a damp and dirty pit of some sort. She tried her limbs and found that with the exception of a lot of bruises, she seemed unhurt. She gingerly sat up and rubbed the back of her head. When she pulled her hand back her fingers were covered with a sticky substance that she could only guess was her blood. She was a bit lightheaded.

She glanced around her surroundings more clearly and was in fact in a damp pit. "Probably an old well," she mused as she felt the slick walls of what was her prison. She glanced up and again winced with the pain in the back of her head, but she could see that the top of the well was covered by some sort of wooden barricade, and only one ray of light was coming down. She tried to stand and instantly collapsed back in a heap as her right ankle screamed in pain. She pulled off her boot to see that it had swelled dramatically and was a lovely shade of purple. She could move it, but it refused to hold any weight. She sighed, and leaned back against the wall to try and get an idea of how high the top was. Disappointed she realized that there were at least thirty feet between her and the barrier.

"Good thing this ground was soft," she dug at the wet dirt with her good foot, "or else I'd be having broken bones not sprains from that fall." She tried to grasp onto the stones that made up the walls of the well, but they were so moss covered and wet that there was nothing for her to hold, even if she'd had the strength to climb without an injured ankle.

"I'm so stupid, why didn't I just go back and tell the others?" she muttered to herself miserably, tossing a bit of mud at the opposite wall. "Always have to do it my way," she shook her head. Then she had a brilliant idea, the pala stone was still around her neck. Quickly she pulled it from her shirt and repeated the words that Nasah had said, concentrating on Migdal.

Nothing.

She tried again, exchanged a couple words, and still nothing.

"Why isn't this working?" she muttered. She kept trying for several minutes and then finally gave up, sagging against the wall.

After beating herself up for awhile, Eden realized she needed to do something. "Okay, at least I need to figure out what's going on." She looked longingly up at that one beam of light, that had now moved to the other side of the well. "So, the guy that grabbed me wasn't the one I was following, which means he must have been a sentry of some sort," she tried to wrack her brain to remember any details of the night before, but came up with nothing.

"I didn't see anyone, but he must have had a sword," she rubbed the back of her head again. "I wonder…" she began, suddenly remembering herself, and reached for her pant leg. There her fingers grasped the hilt of her knife. "Guess I wasn't searched," she shrugged, turning the knife over in her hand. "Maybe there's hope that he didn't notice my sword either," she thought. That had been what she was most upset about, that she might have lost what was supposedly part of her prophecy.

"I did see those eyes though," she shuddered at the sense of evil the memory brought.

Suddenly the barrier above her slid out of the way and a shadowed man's head leaned over to look at her. Eden had to shield her eyes from the glare of the setting sun.

"See, I told you, she has to be one of the King's guard," another man spoke, and leaned over and looked down as well. "She was dressed like a beggar, but those boots are a dead giveaway."

Eden closed her eyes and sighed, she hadn't even thought of her boots, of course everyone knew the boots of a Chayil, especially if they'd noticed the King's insignia on the side of them.

"Feels pretty stupid to be on the King's side now doesn't it?" one of the men yelled down and laughed. "You're going to rot down there, and there ain't none of your little friends as come looking for you." he laughed again.

The anger at their disrespect of the King was boiling inside of Eden and she clenched and unclenched her fists figghtin her way into a standing position despite the pain.

"Oh, looks like you got her riled," the other laughed, slapping his partner on the back, "you can't be very bright to come to this place with no weapons or support. What are they teaching in the castle these days?" he laughed again.

"What would you know of it?" she shouted back, her temper boiling over and her face flushed with embarrassment.

The man above stopped laughing and glared at her, "Oh I know enough from my time, worthless fighting for someone else to have all the power, you – you get nothing but a dirty hole to die in," his voice dripped with disdain.

"The prophecies say, 'behold your enemies will perish; all who do iniquity will be scattered.' That's all you have to look forward to serving Nachash," she shouted up at him, one hand supporting herself on the wall.

"Nothing's changed, throw out those stupid prophecies, the king's words," he mocked, "I ain't seen none of them fulfilled, only see Nachash doing me right," he laughed again.

"Come on," the other pulled the man's arm and Eden couldn't see them any longer, "we need to move if she found this place. Go tell him she's taken care of."

The other leaned over one more time. "Enjoy your final resting place, it'll take awhile I suppose for you to die, but thankfully there's no one around here to smell you when you do," he chuckled to himself, then the wooden barrier was slid back in place and Eden could hear no more.

"Argh," she grunted and slapped the wall beside her in anger. There was absolutely nothing she could do. Obviously they were unconcerned about her drawing attention from yelling, so there must not be anyone around this area. Though she did think she'd heard a cart when she was waking up. "I suppose it's good they don't know who I am, or they would have been doing something else with me I'm sure," she slumped back down to the ground.

She watched the thin beam of light fade as the sun set. Eden's only hope was that her teammates might be missing her by now. "But you didn't tell them anything, so how are they going to know where you are?" she slammed her hand into the dirt. She spent hours going over everything she had done wrong. Why she was a terrible Chayil, why she had let her team down, Moreh down, the King down.

It was hours later that in her frustration she yelled at the top of her lungs, "Who redeems my soul from the pit." It was the one passage that kept running over and over in her mind from her studies. "Oh, if only that applies to me," she let her head drop onto her knees.

"Eden?" a faint voice was calling from somewhere above her. Eden's head lifted slightly from her knees as she couldn't really believe she was hearing her name.

"Eden?" it came again.

"Hey," she pulled herself to her feet. "I'm down here, under the wood. Hey, can you hear me?" she yelled with all her might.

"I hear her," the voice called to others, "she's over here."

The wood was ripped off and since it was still dark, all Eden could see were a few stars in the sky. Then a torch was held down and Parzel's face squinted to see the depths of the well. Her eyes lit up when she saw Eden waving up at her.

"Thank the King," she exclaimed, "are you okay?"

"Now that you're here," Eden grinned, "redeems my soul from the pit," she whispered under her breath, shaking her head.

"Hang on, Shephel's got a rope."

Within minutes they had her sitting up on the edge of the well and Parzel, Nasah, Shephel and Sela were all hugging her in great relief. Nasah held the torch now and Shephel was examining the cut on the back of her head.

"It's pretty nasty, good thing you've got such a hard head or this could have been fatal." His fingers were probing around causing Eden to wince. "We'll have to get you to Master Rophe, it'll need his work on that gash, it's still bleeding, and your ankle must be sprained, but generally you're alright," he stood back and smiled.

"Is it safe here?" Eden asked, eyeing the house behind them.

"I think so." Sela said, "I went through that house already, there's not much there, people left in a hurry it'd seem, but no one's been around."

"And you might want to hang on to this next time," Parzel handed Eden her sword, still wrapped in the dirty cloths.

"I was so worried they'd taken it," she said with relief and pulled the blade from the scabbard revealing its true worth. "But maybe it was a blessing it got left aside, or they would have figured out who I was."

"Yeah, so you have a lot of explaining to do," Nasah stood with one hand on her hip as she held the torch aloft, a disappointed look on her face.

"Well, you guys need to explain too, how did you ever find me?" she asked, "and what time is it anyway?" Eden tried to get the attention off herself.

"Should be hitting Laud in a few moments, day after you'd gone missing," Parzel replied, "we had to wait till it was late enough to get out without being seen."

"You mean, no one knows I'm missing?" Eden was surprised. She'd figured Moreh would know for sure, and even though she was safe, she had expected her wrath.

"We made some excuse for you about being sick from running those stairs," Nasah rolled her eyes, "but I don't think we should have, you deserve to have Moreh rip you open for this, you could have died all alone without any of us here," she was almost in tears as she spoke.

"Yeah well…"

"No, just wait," Nasah held up her hand, her brown eyes flashing now. "we made a deal, we were part of a team, and we knew there were greater risks because you were something special. Well, if you think you're special , you sure act like an idiot," she was gaining momentum, "we are willing to die for you if it will serve the King, but we can't do that if you go off by yourself all the time. You are no better than us you know. You need us," she paused as if expecting some excuse from Eden.

"I know," Eden said quietly instead. "I'm sorry," her head was bowed and she couldn't make eye contact with any of them.

Nasah wasn't expecting that answer. Nor were any of the others by their faces. "Well, good – then - I guess," Nasah tried to have a dignified ending.

"I was selfish, not that I meant to be, but I was. I thought I could do this on my own to prove my point to you guys. At home they told me I had a hero complex, maybe it's just my pride," Eden mumbled, "but I was wrong," she looked up at each of them this time, "trust me, I have gone over all the stupid things I've done for the last twenty-four hours here, and I've come up with a lot," her shoulders slumped even lower. "Will you forgive me?"

They all stood, in the dark back yard with only one torch illuminating their faces.

"Come on," Eden implored them, "someone say something. I realize I'm not very good at apologizing, or asking for help or - a lot of things but..."

Each of them smiled at her. Parzel put her arm on her shoulder. "Never, do anything like this again," and gave her another hug, and they all laughed in relief.

"Okay," Shephel said, "start talking. We're standing in the worst part of the city and we need to get out of here, but we also need to know what went on," he sat himself down on a piece of wood, his sword over his knees.

"Yeah, let's hear it Eden," Sela took a similar stance on the other side of her.

"Okay", Eden began with a deep breath. At least she had them on the edge of their seats the whole time, but she cringed every time that Nasah reminded her of when she should have either come got them, or done something different. She couldn't really fault her, she'd thought the same things herself while sitting in that well, but to hear someone else reaffirm them was hard.

"...until you guys showed up." Eden finished ashamed. "You guys haven't told me, how in Kaleo you found me?" she glanced back and forth between them.

"Well, I have to say it is a bit of a miracle," Parzel began. "When you didn't show for training this morning we knew something was wrong, but Nasah came up with the sickness thing, and I think Moreh must have been worried about something else because she never questioned it. The most difficult part was getting through the day."

"Yeah," Sela interrupted, "we just wanted to come find out what was going on, but today must have been the worst day of training we've had in months. They didn't even let us have lunch," he rolled his eyes in disgust, and Eden stifled a laugh.

"Right," Parzel continued, "so we had to wait till after we had supper to go to your room, so all of us went down and broke in…" she paused.

"Yeah, sorry about that, but we can fix your lock later," Shephel apologized, "we thought this was important."

"I'm okay with it, really," Eden reassured him.

"So, we got in your room and obviously you weren't there, but Sela found some old dirty cloths laying on the floor, your coat was there, but no sword or knife, so we figured you'd gone outside the walls looking for that lead."

"And then we all seemed to understand why you were so tired all the time, it was because you were up all night," Nasah interrupted.

"So, we figured we'd better find you, but unless we wanted to tell Moreh, we couldn't go till it was dark.'

"I wanted to tell Moreh right away, but these guys thought it might jeopardize a clue or something stupid like that," Nasah again threw her two cents in.

"And see, it worked out," Shephel gestured to Eden.

"Barely," Nasah muttered.

"Anyway," Parzel tried to continue, "we waited till it was late and then all met in the dump. It was really easy still to get out, but then we didn't know what to do, we had no idea as to where you were or anything, the only thing we found was your duffle bag in the garbage dump."

"So we figured you were disguised, but still didn't know where to start," Shephel interjected.

"Right. So we just started walking. We were a bit obvious, four of us, obviously recruits, walking together but thankfully most of the people we saw were either drunk, or so busy trying to avoid us that it wasn't a problem," she shrugged and continued. "but we had no luck, no sign of you and no idea where to really look until we ran across a young shepherd that was heading back to his inn. He asked what we were doing, and we were just surprised that he wasn't drunk, and I really don't know why we did, but we just told him we were looking for you," she paused as if trying to figure something out.

"Yeah, it was kind of stupid really," Nasah agreed, "why did we just tell him like that?"

The others were of no greater help, so Parzel went on. "Anyway, it was good we did, because he said he'd seen someone looking like you following some other guy. He told us exactly where you were going, so we took his directions and got to the alley here. When we were outside the fence, Sela went through the front and Shephel saw your sword all wrapped up out here, plus the boards ripped apart on the fence, and then we heard you yell 'redeem my soul from the pit.' Some of the King's words right?"

When Eden nodded she went on, "And so we found you in here."

"Wow," was all Eden could say. Her mind was stuck on the shepherd. She knew it had to be the one she met earlier, but how could he have seen her? She was all disguised, there's no way he'd have known it was her.

"Eden, what do you think?" Nasah was asking her.

"Sorry, what did you say?" Eden shook her head, and gave her her full attention, realizing she had asked her a question.

"Do you think we should go and look in on Grippa?" Nasah repeated herself.

"Maybe," Eden nodded, "leaving that door open seemed a bit odd to me."

"Wait, I have a question." Nasah stopped them. "Why didn't you use the pala stone to get back to the castle?" she pointed to the necklace protruding from Eden's shirt.

"I tried, it wouldn't work, what are the words again?" she asked. Nasah repeated them.

"That's exactly what I said, but nothing – I don't get it," Eden shrugged.

"We'll have to ask Moreh about that, I've never read of it not working before," Nasah scratched her head.

"Okay, now that we've satisfied your curiosity, let's get going if we're going to the smith it's on the way back anyway," Parzel agreed. "Keep your swords up and Eden, you stay in the middle, you're not in any condition to fight."

They made their way through the streets with ease, Eden was partially expecting an attack and partially expecting the shepherd. But nothing occurred, they hardly even saw anyone out. She leaned on Shephel as they walked, trying to hide the pain in her ankle. They finally arrived at the blacksmith's shop to find the door was still open, and lights still burning, if a bit lower than normal.

Sela decided to enter first, and he kept his sword at the ready. Parzel followed behind, with instructions for Nasah and Shephel to guard Eden until they called it all clear.

The three outside stood anxiously for a while, with Eden leaning on Nasah. There was no noise inside, until Parzel finally called them in.

"You'd better come see this."

The three quickly came inside to find Sela down on his knees beside the still body of his uncle Grippa.

"What happened to him?" Eden asked. The man's face was contorted in terror, but other than that, there wasn't a mark on him. With the exception of the fact he was dead, it didn't look like anything was wrong with him.

"That's weird," Nasah muttered. "Are you okay Sela?"

"Yes," the big man answered. "I mean, I shouldn't feel anything for him, he was horrible to me and obviously a traitor, but still – he was so – lost," he stood, still looking down at Grippa. "Is there a sheet or something around here I can put over him?" he asked.

In a moment Shephel handed him a large cloth that he pulled off a work bench. Sela draped it gently over the blacksmith.

"I don't think there's any way out of this," Parzel looked at Eden. "We've got to tell Moreh."

"Really?" Eden whined, already knowing the answer. "I know," she agreed, after Parzel raised her eyebrows. "I just know I'm in big trouble is all," she muttered, "well, let's not wait any longer."

The team shut the door behind them and slipped back inside Midgal to find Moreh.

13

*"Who shall bring a charge against
the King's Eklektos?
It is the King who justifies."*

Eden was sitting on a rough table in the medical building listening to Moreh rail on her. Her head was slumped onto her chest, and with each word her teacher spoke, she heard the same ones echoing in her mind while she sat at the bottom of that well. Master Rophe had fixed her ankle, and the cut on the back of her head was stitched and bandaged. He told her he wouldn't take all the pain of it away so that she'd remember what happened more vividly. Like she was apt to forget this night ever.

It seemed that Moreh was wrapping up when Master Petros came stalking through the door. "I tell you Moreh, she should be thrown out for this," he waved a hand to stop her from speaking. "I don't care what the prophecies say, there must be a mistake. Do you have any idea what could have happened tonight? What did happen to that blacksmith? You have no idea what you're getting into!" He was inches away from her now, and Eden just wanted to hide under the blankets and wake up in some other place. She wished she had the pala stone on her, but Moreh had taken it when she came to see her.

"Master Petros, that is enough," Moreh pulled him away from Eden by his cloak. "Do you possibly think that criticizing and yelling at her will cause anything to change? Or that she has not thought the same things in her own mind?"

Eden's eyes widened, shocked at Moreh's sudden change of heart but she didn't dare look at either of them.

"Well, I still think we should throw her out, but I do care what the King says," Master Petros grumbled. "You are to report to his throne room immediately."

Eden almost swallowed her tongue. "What?" she stammered, "Me?"

"Yes you," he shouted again. "You're the one in trouble aren't you?" he moved back to the doorway. "Hurry up, the King doesn't have all day to wait for disobedient children," and with those words he was gone in a swish of his cloak.

"Moreh, I can't see the King. It was bad enough having to face you, but Him?" Eden was gripping the edge of her teacher's cloak with eyes full of fear.

"Now child, you cannot avoid a call from the King," Moreh's voice had an edge of warmth to it, but her face still looked disappointed. "It won't be as bad as you think, remember he is a just King." She took Eden's hand and pried it from her cloak. "Go on, Master Petros is right, you shouldn't keep Him waiting when He's called you." She gently pushed Eden to the door.

"Wait," she turned back to Moreh. "Why didn't the pala stone work for me? I tried to use it in the pit, to get out but it didn't work."

Moreh nodded gravely. "That's the trick isn't it?" she paused. "The gifts of the King are not toys for our amusement, they aren't given to us to exploit and use for our own motives. He gives them purposefully and they will only truly work when we are working in line with the King's will. When we step outside that, we misuse his gifts and although we can sometimes fake the results, ultimately his gifts will fail us, even if we are the only ones who know that. Your's is a very public gift, a rare one, and with that comes great responsibility because the use of it will always point to the king, so it will be very public failures if you try to use it for any other reason, like last night. It is not just power for power's sake, and there are always consequences for our actions."

Eden listened carefully and nodded. She fingered where her necklace normally hung around her neck, then turned without another word and headed to answer the King's call.

Eden's legs felt like lead as she walked ever so slowly across the field to the tower. Life had slowed down, and she noticed a little song bird perched on top of the great lion statue, the dew that was wetting her boots, the sun peaking up from behind the clouds in the East. It felt like her final moments on earth. She didn't have a clue what the King would do. What do they do with recruits that disobey and cause problems, let alone get someone killed? Probably kick them out like Petros said. Would the King kick her out? Just the thought of the disappointment she would have caused Him was ripping her heart out. All she could remember were His eyes from that first day. She had rarely seen Him since, and then only from afar when he had been going in or out of the tower. "Oh, you messed this one up real good," she muttered to herself.

She now stood in front of the great doors. It seemed so long ago that Moreh had first led her through them. She took a deep breath and pushed them open. She was immediately confronted with that tapestry of the lamb in battle. It certainly meant nothing to her, looking at the way she had performed in her battle. Her head dropped a bit lower, and she dragged her feet towards the stairs. She certainly had not faced opposition as the lamb did. She sighed as she passed the picture and began her ascent.

With each flight her heart pounded more and more. This time she knew it wasn't from the climb, but from the fear of a King who would expect more from his eklektos. As she reached the fifth floor, she could see that the doors to the great hall were open and there were generals and rulers gathered around the table anxiously discussing something. In the midst of them, Eden noticed the King was standing and talking with several of the men. She paused, unsure of what to do. She certainly did not want to interrupt the King in a meeting, yet he had called her here. She'd never considered that he might not be in his throne room.

She stood for several minutes watching the heated discussion until suddenly one of the generals noticed her.

"You there?" he pointed at her. "What are you doing interrupting the King's session?" anger ran over his brow, as the rest of the men turned to face her.

"I'm sorry, it's just, I mean…" she stammered to answer them.

"Eden," The King called, waving her into the room. "I have called her here, she is not interrupting," he addressed the others. Eden slowly walked into the room. Her footsteps echoing on the stone floor as she approached the King; the men in the room sizing her up.

"I'm afraid I'll be unavailable for a few minutes, I need to take care of something. Please carry on without me," the King dismissed the men and put his arm on Eden's shoulder as she had finally reached him and he guided her out the back of the room, into a smaller sitting room. Eden heard the discussion start up behind them again, as if she'd never been there as the King closed the door.

The King waved her towards a chair by the fire. Eden took it sheepishly, she was having a difficult time making eye contact with him.

"So, I hear you had quite an adventure last night," he sat in the chair opposite her, letting his chin drop into his hands as he watched her.

Eden kept her head down and answered. "I am so sorry Sire. I just never think of others, I was only interested in getting this great lead to who's leaking information. I thought I was better than I am, I mean they call me the eklektos, so I figured I can do whatever, so I wasn't thinking, then I got that man killed, though he was obviously a traitor, but still and then I got in trouble and just was barely saved by some great teammates of mine and…" The King raised his hand and she stopped finally taking a breath.

He sat back and just looked at her until she lifted her head and cautiously looked him in the eye. His face broke into a gentle smile.

"Oh Eden," he chuckled quietly. "You have so much to learn," he paused again, just looking at her.

He settled himself further into his chair. "Yes, you are eklektos, but that doesn't mean you are any more important than anyone else."

Eden frowned. She felt she'd just been insulted, but looking at his face she was sure that wasn't true, yet, what had he just said?

He laughed louder this time. "Yes, you're eklektos, but your only importance is that Nachash thinks you're important. He has made you what you are. You have no special abilities, you have talents and gifts and intelligence, but really no more than other exceptional students we have here," he could see that she was completely confused. "I think I will leave that with you to consider," he smiled reassuringly. "But now, let us deal with last night," and he made his face somber, Eden steeling herself for his judgment.

He stood, putting his hands behind his back and pacing the room. "Let us start with your first error, you disobeyed a direct order from your master to stay inside Migdal. Suggesting you felt you had a better handle on the situation than your master."

Eden felt she should explain but then thought better of it and kept her mouth closed. This seemed to make the King smile again, but he continued. "Your second mistake was in thinking that you could undertake such a plan on your own, suggesting your egotistical opinion of your own skills in relation to your team."

With that comment Eden could not even look at his back as he paced. Her heart breaking again. "Thirdly, you completely underestimated the situation, and your enemy. He far outmatched you in skill and knowledge, had you had to face him you would no longer be with us. It is a miracle that they never discovered who you were or took your sword," he began to stir the fire. "Fourth, once you uncovered this situation, you again felt you were more than strong enough to handle it on your own and failed to get support. Then you entered an unknown area unarmed and without any visual on your quarry, which resulted in your capture and injury. How'd I do?" he turned from where he was squatted by the fire to look at Eden.

Her head could not get much lower, but she felt that maybe she could fall on the floor. In answer to his question, she remained silent and just nodded.

He smiled and stood. "Well, you have at least learned to admit your faults," he stepped closer to her and put his hand on her right shoulder. "I forgive you."

Eden wasn't sure what to do. Those were the last words she expected to hear. She was waiting for a punishment, or instruction, or expulsion, but she hadn't thought she needed forgiveness.

"I forgive your selfish behaviour. I forgive your pride, and I forgive the actions that resulted because of these things," he was still gripping her shoulder and somehow in it she felt release, but she didn't understand why. She raised her head, looking him in the face she began to weep.

He remained just as he was, watching her cry and continued. "This is not to suggest there are no consequences to your actions. Obviously a man died, however, the man was a traitor and you have exposed our leak. Grippa serviced many of our Chayil, even our Gibbor Chayil and I'm sure information was inadvertently divulged to him. In fact, do you remember the mirror in your room that first day you arrived here? Well, we found pieces of its glass in Grippa's shop, it matched the piece I took that day. I'm not sure how, but it would appear that he was involved in whatever power Nachash was using to get to you. However, we do need to correct your behaviour, so…" he paused making sure she was fully focused on his next words, "your punishment will be that outside of your training hours you will attend me."

Eden wiped the tears from her eyes as they widened in wonder. "You must be dressed properly in your dress uniform each time, and you may not leave these grounds unless ordered to do so by your masters or myself." He reached out his hand and opened it to reveal the pala stone. The stone lit up and glowed a brilliant blue for a moment, then faded back to its opaque colour. "Now I will know if you leave these grounds. I expect you will obey this order now," he handed her the necklace.

He stepped away from her and started towards the doors to the great hall. "Do you have any questions?" he turned with his hand on the door handle to look at her. Eden stood and shook her head. "Good, you will report for your training this morning, and I will see you in my throne room when you are finished. You can leave through the back stairs that way," he gestured towards a door on the far wall, and began to pull open the other letting in the sounds of his men arguing. "Oh, and Eden, ask yourself what has won the battles for you and you will be closer to understanding why you are eklektos." He turned and left the room.

14

"You are my witnesses declares Melek,
and my servant whom I have chosen,
my Eklektos, that you may know that I am he."

The next several weeks were excruciating for Eden. She'd spend her days in training, then would quickly wash up and change so that she could appear in her dress uniform, a smartly cut black jacket overtop a fitted white linen shirt buttoned up to her collar; very different from the flowing shirts they wore for battle and training. The pants were similar to her usual ones, three quarter length that were tight on her calves, and perfectly polished black boots that laced just below her knees. Her sword and belt knife completed her ensemble. Dressed for ceremony she would spend the rest of the day in front of the King – to stand there. That was what drove her crazy, she looked the perfect part of a Chayil, but she did absolutely nothing. He would acknowledge her when she arrived, but nothing more. He would go on about his business. His generals would meet with him, people from the town, occasionally dignitaries from other regions; and all the while Eden just had to stand there beside his throne or by his side on the fifth floor meeting room. If he left the room he would sometimes have her follow behind him, other times he'd leave her standing in the throne room alone.

"This quite possibly is the worst punishment ever," she muttered to herself as she watched the King walk out of the room with a governor, again leaving her alone. She had simply stood there until he returned the first few times this occurred, but she soon realized she could hear him coming so she would wander around the throne room. Not that that was much more interesting.

"Argh, what is he trying to teach me in this?" she grumbled, as she walked over to the window that looked out on the pastures. From this vantage point she could see the grooms exercising the horses. Ruach was fighting with whichever groom was trying to walk her on the lead. "Silly," she laughed to herself, "Oh, I wish I could be down there and ride her." She gripped the edge of the window with all her strength trying to keep the tears from her eyes.

"I just don't get it," she said to herself through gritted teeth. "Why can't he just use me?" Just then she heard footsteps outside the door, and she rushed to get back to her position by the throne. As she straightened her jacket the King walked in, intently reading a piece of parchment. The governor who had left with him had been replaced by Moreh.

Eden gasped, as she noticed a tear fall from the King's face onto the paper. The noise caused the King to look up and remember her. He looked over at Moreh, "We must do something for these people." He gestured towards the table and gave the parchment to her, then addressed Eden. "You may leave early today, but you are not permitted outside the walls, with the exception of the horse pastures," he turned and headed over to where Moreh stood.

Eden was thrilled to leave early, but part of her wished she could overhear this conversation. She had never seen the King this way before. But she took her leave and bowed her way out of the room. She had heard many privileged conversations before. In fact, she'd been instructed by one general that some of what she heard could result in her death if she spoke of it. He was quite irate with the King that a recruit should listen in on these discussions, but the King had waved him off. Eden was hurrying down the stairs, she'd heard plans for raids on the enemy, she'd heard of rescues, she'd heard of complaints about the King's rule, she'd heard of discipline of some Chayil and even captains, there was no conversation (except this one) that she had been excluded from.

At the bottom of the stairs she rushed to get outside, partly wondering if the King might change his mind, and partly wanting to get to the pasture before they took the horses in again. She rushed across the grounds, and could now hear the whinny of the horses. Some of the groomsmen waved at her as she approached them.

"Hey Eden, we haven't seen you in ages," one called to her. "But you're looking important in that uniform."

"Yeah, heard you were in a lot of trouble," the other said prying for information.

"You're right, I've got punishment every day after training, which means no time for the horses, but I was let go early today," she explained as briefly as possible, her eyes had quickly caught sight of Ruach fighting with her groom in the midst of the training ring. "She's not very happy is she?" she asked watching the horse buck and toss the groom around the ring.

"No, I think she misses you," A Chayil of the calvary came up behind her. "In fact, she's not letting any of us ride her any longer," he smiled at her. "I'm not sure what to do," he shrugged.

"Do you mind if I go out to her?" Eden asked, her eyes still focused on Ruach.

"Not at all, she needs real exercise," he waved towards the groom with Ruach. "In fact, why don't you ride her around the pasture if she'll have you," he gently pushed Eden into the ring and watched as she whistled. Immediately Ruach's ears perked up and she spotted Eden. She gave a great snort and galloped up to her side. The horse nuzzled her head right into Eden, almost knocking her over.

The groom who had been holding the lead, tossed his hands in the air in exasperation and stalked off.

"What's up with you girl?" Eden rubbed the horse's nose. "You know you need to run, why don't you let them work with you?" she whispered, and the horse responded with a shake of her mane. "Telling me no are you?" Eden laughed, rubbing her neck. "Well, I guess you're just as stubborn and alone as me," she gripped a handful of mane and swung herself up onto Ruach's back. "I need some refreshment, will you run?" she had leaned forward to whisper in the horse's ear and it was a good thing, because as quick as a lightning bolt Ruach was flying out of the ring.

The horses that were grazing quickly got out of the way as the horse and rider galloped at breakneck speeds around the pasture. Eden just let Ruach have her head, they didn't have too far they could run, but the wind and the lack of walls made her feel like she had been freed from the castle at long last. The sun was beginning to set and Eden could see the fires and lamps being lit inside, but she couldn't bear to go in yet.

After awhile she slowed Ruach to a walk, and they wandered over to the edge of the pasture. Here some trees had grown over the fence and Eden slipped off Ruach's back and let her graze. She hopped up on the wooden fence and began playing with a branch from the tree Ruach was nibbling on. She took several deep breaths, trying to enjoy the moment, knowing it would end all too soon.

"Hello there," a man's voice called suddenly, startling Eden that she fell right off the fence. When she stood up again she saw her young shepherd friend walking up the hillside to her. "Sorry, I didn't mean to scare you like that," he looked embarrassed. "I thought you'd seen me coming up here."

"No, I didn't," Eden laughed, brushing herself off. "I was in my own world there," she leaned on the fence to talk to him. "What are you doing out here?" she asked.

"Oh, I have a flock just down in the valley, but I saw you riding and thought I'd come and say hello," he smiled.

Eden glanced down the hillside and could just see a white speck that must have been a sheep. She nodded.

"I heard you got into some trouble up here," he raised an eyebrow with a sympathetic look on his face.

"Yeah, and I suppose I should thank you for directing my friends to me. I don't know how you saw me," she remembered his role in her rescue now.

"Oh, just a coincidence, but a good one," his smile grew bigger. "What have they got you doing for your punishment?"

"I have to 'attend the King'," Eden said with mock seriousness.

"What does that mean?" he asked, looking puzzled.

"Well, it means every day after training I have to put on my dress uniform and stand beside the King," she shrugged.

"Just stand there?" he leaned on the fence, interested.

"Yeah," she shook her head and reached over to pet Ruach's nose. "It's the strangest thing. I literally just stand there while he does whatever he has to do."

"Huh," he too reached up and pet Ruach's nose. The horse wasn't sure if she liked it or not, but after sniffing him once, she rubbed her head against his arm.

"That's actually a pretty interesting thing," he laughed at the horse, and pushed her head away.

Eden was surprised Ruach behaved that way, but more so the interest he showed in her attendance of the King. "What do you think is interesting about it?" she asked him.

"Well, you're getting to see how the King behaves. You see his anger, his strategies, his thought process even. You'd know when he gets upset and when he's happy," he paused to think. "In fact, I think it'd make you that much better of a Chayil."

"Why do you say that?" Eden frowned, not understanding.

"Well, you'll learn what he loves and what matters to him, then you can serve him that much better. If you know how to please him, you'll be his best subject. If you learn to love him, you'll be his best Chayil, because you will think like he thinks, do what he would do and you'll never turn aside," he had stepped back from the fence and was glancing down the hillside. "I should go but try and pay close attention while you're in his presence and see what you can learn." He waved to both Eden and Ruach and headed off down the hill.

Eden watched him until he was out of sight, still pondering what he had said. She had been learning a lot about how the King did business, and thinking back she could probably tell you what was important to the King after hearing him talk so often. But she hadn't been focusing on that because she was so frustrated with not doing anything. She knew she had lots of skills and abilities, and all she was allowed to do was stand still in his presence. But to pay attention. It was worth some thought.

Just then Ruach almost knocked her over with her head. "Okay, you must be hungry, I suppose I should eat too., she took ahold of her mane and swung up on her back again. "Let's go," and off they went at a brisk trot towards the stables.

This morning, Eden decided, was going to be different. She dressed quickly, since she didn't have to train today she was going directly to the King for the entire day. It was actually the first time she'd spend the whole day with him and wasn't completely sure what to expect, especially after having been excused the day before. "He can't just sit in his throne room all day can he?" she mumbled as she tied her dark hair back, observing her appearance in her small mirror. Satisfied, she slipped her sword on and hurried out of her room.

The fields were quiet as she walked. It was an unusual day, no one would give them an answer as to why they didn't have to train — but all the instructors were away somewhere. There were even different guards at the posts on the walls Eden noticed. She nodded to the two that were standing outside the main door as she pulled it open. The morning was quiet inside too. There were no servants bustling around, in fact, Eden didn't pass anyone as she made her way up the stairs into the King's room. She opened the door quietly, but the King was already pouring over some maps or something on his table.

"Good morning Eden," he waved as she entered.

"Good morning your Majesty," she smiled. "Do you have anything for me to do?" she raised an eyebrow hopefully. She was determined that today would be different, she was not going to be sullen or upset or complain or anything about it. Her talk with the shepherd was still running over and over in her mind.

The King paused for a moment and stood up, and Eden's hope rose with him. "No, I don't think so," he said, leaning back over the table and her face fell. She took her place beside his throne, shoulders stooped. She was still considering that question he had asked her, 'what has won the battles for her'... At least she had lots of time to think.

The watches dragged by as they did every day, but she tried to remain hopeful. She spent her time observing the King. He was very methodical in all he did. He spent the first third by himself pouring over what she had figured out were in fact maps. He studied each one carefully, often writing notes in a journal beside him. Then two of his generals, who Eden had seen often here, came in and they discussed some locations of Nachash's troops, what activity had been seen in the last twenty-four hours. Who was best suited for what mission. She tried to pay attention to all the King did and said. Most often he listened and rarely gave any advice. He let his generals make the decisions. If they were completely off he would step in, but usually he would simply say something along the lines of "have you considered this aspect or that?" and then they would come to whatever conclusion and eventually he'd nod and they'd move on.

Next a local merchant was escorted into the room. The King politely dismissed his generals, and they very courteously gave a deep bow to the merchant who looked mildly shocked that such high ranking officials even noticed him. He immediately fell to his knee and bowed his head to the King. But the King put a hand on his shoulder and raised him up, greeting him with a solid handshake, then leading him over to Eden he instructed her to get their "guest" a chair, while he took his seat on the throne. She hurried to do so, and then stood and listened as this merchant explained a story of injustice by another man in his business and how it has resulted in his own loss of a substantial amount of money. He wasn't seeking retribution but wanted to ask grace to pay his taxes next month rather than this.

Eden watched as the King pondered the situation, he asked some questions then leaned over to Eden and said, "Go and get my ledger from the anteroom, and ask the Sergeant at Arms to come here." Then his attention went right back to the merchant, and he asked some questions about his family while Eden left the room.

She quickly found the ledger and brought a quill and ink with it, then stuck her head out in the hall. She knew the Sergeant, he wasn't new today. "Sir?" she spoke just above a whisper. He glanced down at her. "The King would like you to attend him, when the merchant leaves," she knew he hadn't given that specific an instruction, but after seeing his attention to the merchant, she felt that he wouldn't want the intrusion until after so as not to disrupt the man. The Sergeant nodded and resumed his stance and Eden slipped back into the room. She handed the ledger to the King who quickly wrote a note in it about the man's taxes, then even in mid-conversation, he handed the ledger to the man to sign.

The merchant was startled. "Forgiven?" he asked, the quill hanging from his fingertips.

"Yes, until the fall, you shouldn't have to think about taxes for the time being," he smiled.

"Thank you, your Majesty, thank you," the man stood and bowed again before quickly signing the ledger.

"Go take care of your family, enjoy today without any worries." The King stood as well and shook the merchant's hand before he left.

As soon as the man was out the door, the Sergeant at Arms slid in behind him. "Your Majesty?" he asked, head slightly bowed.

"Take this name and find this merchant for me. He has defrauded a friend and is going to make restitution in an anonymous donation. He will need to come to the treasury to pay, he may not be willing but you will convince him it is that or the dungeon," he held out a slip of paper to the Sergeant who took it from his hand.

"I'll take a few other Chayil with me just in case," he bowed, spun on his boot heel and left.

The King turned to Eden and smiled. "You knew I would not want him here with the merchant." It was more of a statement than a question. "Well noted," he went back to his table of maps.

The joy that Eden felt at being recognized by the king faded as the afternoon wore on and nothing more significant happened. She watched the King read, talk with a few advisors, eat lunch, rather mundane events. She was trying desperately to stay positive and learn all she could from him.

Suddenly the doors burst open at the end of the room and Moreh, Petros and another master rushed in. They barely bowed their heads in acknowledgement of the King, and all three looked weary and worn from traveling. Each was dressed for battle with thick wool cloaks draped over their shoulders as they stalked up to the King.

"What's wrong?" he stood immediately, leaving his reading aside.

"Nachash is what's wrong," Petros exclaimed, pushing his hair from his face and displaying a deep gash from his ear to his chin. "He has attacked the southern villages again like the report yesterday said, but this time with a huge amount of force."

"We've been able to hold them off in most places since we did get advanced notice and we were prepared, but we are spread very thin my Lord," Moreh continued, "so thin, that I think we need reinforcements," she cringed as she told him this.

"What reinforcements do you suggest?" the King asked, "since we have already taken away almost all of our own guards here, should Nachash take the opportunity, we might have a great difficulty in keeping our own capital from him," he was obviously aware of the situation. "I don't think I can give you anymore," he shrugged.

"We knew that my Lord, and what we propose should in no way hinder the guards here. We really only need help with a small mission," Moreh nodded to the King. "You see, an entire family was taken captive in the southern village of Nagdesh earlier this month. We believe they are loyal to you sire and have served you faithfully but were unwittingly taken captive by Nachash's troops. Now that we have some stability in the area, we have a plan to get them out, and would only need a few Chayil in order to accomplish it, we just can't spare what we have, so I'm proposing we send one of our recruit units," she finished, gazing boldly into the King's eyes.

He stood for a minute pondering her idea. Eden was terribly excited, she couldn't think of any other recruits better suited for this sort of assignment than her team, especially with her right here, they'd send her. She tried to look uninterested but was sure she was failing miserably.

"Okay," the King nodded in agreement. "Send a team." He turned to look at Eden. "Your team is good at this sort of task correct Eden?" he asked with a raised eyebrow.

She returned his gaze sheepishly, remembering them pulling her out of the pit not so long ago. "Yes, your Majesty they are."

"Good," he smiled, and turned back to Moreh. "Get them from their rest today, give them the information and send them out," he turned back to his chair to sit. "Send word when they return as to the outcome."

"As you wish Sire." Moreh and the other masters dipped their heads and started to the door. Eden, assuming this meant she was to follow and go with her team took a step or two away from the King.

"Eden?" he responded quickly.

"Yes Sire?" she paused, praying that her worst fear was not going to be realized.

"Where are you going?" he asked, as if he had no idea at all.

"Well," she swallowed hard and tried to look him in the eye without crumbling. "I just thought it's my team going, that I'd be going with them?"

"Actually," he smiled slightly and picked up his book, "it's my team going and I don't need you to accompany them. I want you here. Moreh?" he called her back just before she turned out of the door. "Take the pala stone and give it to Nasah to use," he instructed. Eden reluctantly pulled the necklace over her head and handed it to Moreh. Trying to plead with her eyes, to step in on her behalf. But her master simply nodded and strode from the room. She turned to the king, but he was already absorbed in his reading again.

By this time Moreh and the other masters were gone. Eden could hear their footsteps down the stone staircase. She glanced at the King who was paying no attention to her at all. She looked longingly at the door to the hallway and fought back the tears. She took a deep breath and went back to her position and waited.

'He said he didn't need me' she thought as she stood there. 'but what possible good could she do here? She could help them, surely she could do something? He'd said she was the eklektos and had special gifts, why was he leaving her standing here not doing anything at all? The tears were brimming in her eyes. All she wanted was to be used, to be helpful, to please the King. How could standing in a room all day accomplish anything when she could be winning battles and leading her team? She was more than frustrated and struggled to not break down right here. She tried her best not to sniff or anything so he wouldn't see, but all she really wanted to do was hide in her room and sob. He didn't need her. Can anything be more painful to hear? Then why did he bring her to this crazy country in the first place? What if her team did really well without her? Would they start to think they didn't need her either? I mean, she's messed up enough times to make them want to be free of her, if they didn't see her as a necessary component of the team they might just be happy she's gone.

Eden's mind was all over the place and her spirit got darker and lower with each passing minute. She imagined the exploits of her team and them telling her about it later. How was that going to feel? She'd probably start crying then which would totally take away from their success and make her look like an idiot.

She was startled out of her depression by the King's voice. "Pardon me, Sire?" she asked, not daring to look at him.

"You may go now." He repeated himself.

'Go?' she thought 'Not a third more than when Moreh leaves with the team, I don't do anything and he says go. What is that about.' But she just slowly nodded her head and began to head to the door.

"Eden," his voice came from behind her and she stopped, not turning though. "I know you're upset, but you must know that I don't need you. Until you realize that, you will never make a suitable Chayil," he paused. "You did well today."

Eden sort of sniffed at that comment, then turned, her head still lowered and did a little bow to him – and hurried from his presence. She ran down the stairs faster than she ever had before. The tears were flowing quickly and she was glad that no one was around that could see her like this. She burst out the front doors, startling the guards there and ran straight to the pasture. She could barely see for the tears, and her shoulders were heaving as she sobbed.

Ruach was on the far end of the field, but as soon as she heard Eden's whistle she hurried to her. The horse brushed her shoulder with her head, as if sensing something was wrong, and Eden buried her head into the horse's side and sobbed. Ruach just stood there like a statue and let her cry. Eventually, Eden lifted her hand and grabbed a handful of mane pulling herself up onto the warhorse's back. Ruach trotted about a bit, until she realized that she was not being directed, then she headed back to the far side of the pasture and continued grazing. Eden sat there and stared unseeing at the trees surrounding the pasture. She felt a bit paralyzed. She didn't know what to do. She'd never been flat out told she wasn't needed. Her ego didn't deal with that well, she always wanted to be needed, it was how she fit in, how she felt some sort of purpose, or love. What was left now? A horse who wanted her? She was so confused. She didn't honestly know what to feel even.

"And what's with telling me I did well today?" she almost spat the words out, startling Ruach so that she threw her head back to tell Eden of her disapproval. "I didn't do anything today, how do you do nothing well? And what the heck did he mean that I'm chosen but not special, and what really won the battles? I just need some answers," she threw up her hands to the clouds and slumped forward against Ruach's neck. The horse stood for a minute with her head up, then decided to keep eating and stooped again, sending Eden tumbling over her onto the ground.

The fall startled Eden enough to stop crying. Once she caught her breath, she lay there for a few minutes with Ruach grazing near her. She watched the darkening clouds as the sun set and tried not to think of anything at all. Finally, the horse nudged her again and she sat up. It was then she could see the grooms gathering the horses into the stables. She sighed deeply, "alright you poor source of comfort, let's be nice to the grooms today and head back." She climbed back up, dug her heels in and with a whinny, Ruach jerked herself to a slow trot. She had decided to obey, but in her own timing apparently.

When they got close, Eden slid from her back and hoped the young groom coming would be able to corral her. She didn't want anyone to see the mess that she was so she hurried the other way and quickly slipped across the training field and back to her room. She could tell her teammates were still away, and really, a mission like the one Moreh described could take days to complete. "I suppose I might not be training tomorrow either?" she muttered to herself. She opened her door and slipped inside, collapsing on the bed. She hadn't eaten but figured all she really wanted to do was sleep and stop thinking so she pulled her pillow over her head and prayed she could fall asleep.

The morning was a long time coming, but as the sun rose Eden finally got out of bed. She hadn't slept much, if at all, and looked as bad as she felt. Her eyes were still swollen from crying. She felt stuck, as bad as if she still sat in the pit she'd been rescued from. She moved slowly to dress and eat breakfast. Her team was noticeably absent from the meal. "What do you expect? Them to have some super important mission and be back for breakfast?" she angerly stirred her oatmeal around the bowl. She figured everyone in the room knew she'd been left behind. They were probably all talking about her right now, being alone and forgotten. She finally couldn't take being there anymore and pushed her food aside and left, sure that every eye was staring at her back.

She fought back the tears even as she crossed the training yard. A few of her classmates were out working on skills together. Some raised a hand in a wave that Eden tried to return without looking too pathetic. Having no direction, she just assumed she'd have to be with the King today and trudged up the stairs in the tower. As she pushed open the door to the throne room it was still dark. She lit several lamps and then the fire and wandered over to the window to watch the sun rise higher in the sky lighting up the fields around Shammah. For a few moments she was caught up with the beauty of the world and forgot her own misery. Deep down she recognized that she did not have the attitude in attending the King today that she had yesterday, but at the moment, she preferred to wallow in her own self-pity.

A few moments later the King pushed open the door from his study and entered. She dropped her head in a bow.

"Good morning Eden," he said, with concern in his voice. "It's good to see you here early."

Again, Eden nodded, then quickly took her place by his throne.

The king sat there beside her for a while not saying a word, just staring at the fire that she had started. Finally he almost mumbled, "I'm concerned for your team." Eden raised her head a bit, but didn't know what to say. "It was not an easy situation I sent them in to and keeping you here will change their dynamics. I am hoping they will fare well," his voice was low, and he continued to watch the fire.

Eden took a deep breath, "I know they will do well your majesty. If I may say so, I think they are the best," she wanted to be able to say, 'they don't need me.' but wasn't able to get those words out.

Malek waited a few more minutes before glancing at Eden, then rose to examine his maps again. He spent much of the day pouring over the maps, on occasion he would ask Eden's opinion on a strategy or tactic and she was happy to give it. Eventually several local merchants and farmers arrived with various requests and difficulties for the king to oversee, and they were lost in economics and land disputes for a while.

The day wore on, and Eden honestly hadn't noticed how much time passed until the last farmer left and the king turned to her and asked, "would you care to eat with me tonight?"

Eden was startled at the question and not sure how to answer. His piercing eyes seemed to be questioning her heart right then and she had to look away. "I – I would be honoured, your majesty, to eat with you," she stumbled over her words.

"Good, I have enjoyed your company today, ask the guard to have two dinners sent up, then join me in the study," he picked up a map and headed to the opposite door.

Eden watched him leave and was stuck to the spot. She was so taken aback by being invited to eat with the king she didn't know what to do, or think for that matter. Finally, she shook herself out of her daze and ran to the door to send for their dinners. The guard raised an eyebrow when she asked for two, but he nodded nonetheless.

"Okay, just relax. Everyone eats, no big deal if I happen to have dinner with the King," she straightened her jacket. "What in the world. I'm having dinner with the king," she whispered out loud, running her hands through her hair. Exhaling strongly, she took a few deep breaths and walked into the king's study.

He was already seated and gestured for her to take the seat opposite him. "So, tell me Eden, how have you found your training so far?" he sipped from a steaming mug as he talked.

"Well, it's been good I guess," she stammered. "Hard, for sure, harder than anything I've ever done before, but good," she looked down at her own hands nervously.

"And the transition from your home?" he questioned again. "Has it been difficult?"

"No actually," she smiled and dared to look up. "I never fit in at home, I feel much more at peace and home here than ever before. I guess that's probably odd isn't it?" she thought about what she was saying.

"No, it's good to hear and I actually would have thought that would have been the case," he smiled back at her.

Just then the door opened and a kitchen worker brought in their dinners. He too was a bit startled to see Eden sitting with the king and not standing beside him. She was sure there was going to be some great talk in the servants' quarters tonight.

After he left they both began to eat. Eden tried to do all she could remember from her etiquette book but she'd definitely skimmed those sections. She'd never eaten with royalty, not even someone remotely famous before and she desperately didn't want to offend.

Part way through their meal she cleared her throat, "Um, Your majesty?" she began.

"Yes, Eden," He swallowed a piece of chicken and followed it with a large gulp of wine.

"May I ask you a question?" she tried to be patient.

"Of course, you have my permission to ask anything that you want, any time you want," he broke off a piece of bread and buttered it as she began.

"Well, I'm just wondering why you knew I'd feel more at home here than in my world?"

"Ah, you ask a question that I have been preparing to answer for a very long time," he bit into the bread and pushed his chair back a bit from the table. Eden was intrigued now and stopped playing with her own food and sat back to look at the king, forgetting all her nerves and worries over etiquette. "Well, you see Eden," he paused to swallow, "this is your home."

15

"For you are Eklektos.
Melek has chosen you to be his, out of all the peoples."

Eden sat dumbfounded, she tilted her head to the side, frowned and said, "What?" her food most definitely forgotten.

"I said," the King repeated, "this is your home, you were born here." He smiled somewhat awkwardly as if trying to figure out how Eden would take this kind of news.

"I was born here?" she repeated the words again. All her memories were of her home with Ian and Heather and the kids. She remembered her parents vaguely, saw the news clippings, knew what happened to them. How was any of this possible? She put a hand to her head ."How is that possible? I remember my childhood, my parents had friends, jobs what do you mean?" she shook her head again, confused.

"I realize this is a bit of a shock, but what you know about your past is slightly skewed. We had to make some adjustments in order for you to have a chance in your new home," he looked at her with sympathy. "I'm not sure how to explain this - or go on."

"Please try," she gripped the table with both hands to steady herself. "I'm really confused now. Were my parents really my parents?" all kinds of conspiracy theories were running around her head.

"Yes, of course," he assured her, "but Roy and Hope were not their names. Here they were known as Roi and Miqweh, the shepherd and our hope," he smiled at the recollection of them.

Eden was just sitting there, gripping the table and staring blankly at the king. Everything that she had ever known was a lie to her? She wasn't sure what to do. Be angry, happy, throw a temper tantrum – what do adopted kids do when they find out they were adopted?

"I suppose I should tell you the whole story," when she didn't answer he continued. "Your parents served in my Gibbor Chayil just as you are training for. However, they had a different sort of task ahead of them. They spent much of their time traveling to your world and bringing people back here. They were seeking the prophesied eklektos. They were friends with Ian and Heather, and they did have jobs, so to speak, in your world. They recruited many to our kingdom, but one day they found they were pregnant with you. They were taken off active duty and served me here in more of a ceremonial office while you grew," he smiled again, staring into the fire. "They were a remarkable couple, loved each other greatly, and loved me as much. I have not found the like in the kingdom. But as they were here they spent much time studying and it was then that they discovered the truth of the eklektos. You were born shortly afterwards and they poured their souls into raising you. However, their secret knowledge of the eklektos was betrayed by an informant within the guards. Nachash knew they had found the answer, and he concluded it had to do with you."

The king paused to look at Eden before going on. "Nachash set about to kill you. Unfortunately, we did not know anything had been leaked, and did not know until too late that he was seeking you. Your parents had taken you with them on a trip to your world. They were without my protection and alone, and that is when the serpent chose to strike. He sent assassins to your home, his intent was to kill you, but obviously your parents stood in the way. I do not know the full details of it, but from what we could gather, your mother died protecting you. Your father it would appear killed the assassin, but your home was set ablaze and he had to get you out. He died as you thought from the fire, but was able to save you first," he stopped and waited.

Eden wasn't sure what to think. Part of her life was a lie, part was truth. It explained why she felt home here and why she'd never fully fit in before. She was proud to hear her parents were honoured

Chayil, but it made the ache in her heart to know them even greater. "So, I was just left there?" she asked, looking into the king's eyes.

His heart reflected in the tears that rolled down his cheek. He sighed and knelt in front of her. "We thought it safest if Nachash assumed you'd died too and didn't return here until you were old enough to understand and train," he took her hands. "I am sorry that it's so difficult, and I wish I could return your parents to you. But I know that they would be so proud of you now. They longed for the prophecies to be fulfilled," he said quietly.

Eden wiped a tear from her eye. "So, now he knows I'm here, and he still wants to kill me?"

"Yes, the eklektos will help lead to his downfall, so the prophecies say," The king nodded, taking his seat again. "You see the danger you face, he will do whatever he can to prevent that from coming true which he believes requires him to destroy you."

Eden was still dumbfounded. She pushed her food around with the two tined utensil that served as a fork. "Is there anything of my parents still here?" she asked hopefully.

"I don't know," The king answered, "I suppose that their possessions would have been collected here. I will ask Moreh to look into it, she served with them for many years and saw you grow up."

"May I be excused your majesty?" Eden asked suddenly, standing with her head bowed. "I need some time alone," she explained. The room had begun to close in on her.

"Of course," he nodded understanding. "Please, take tomorrow as well for yourself. If Moreh returns I will send her to find you, she can perhaps tell you more about your parents."

Eden bowed quickly and hurriedly headed for the door. She needed to be outside, to breathe fresh air, to think clearly. She all but ran down the stairs of the tower and out to the pastures. She spent the next several hours pacing back and forth along the fence line of the pastures while Ruach watched. Her head would follow Eden's progress for a while like a tennis match, then she'd drop to graze some more before some exclamation from her rider would cause her to look up again for a time.

Eden was trying to put everything together that the King had told her today, as well as deal with her feelings from the day before. "Can't I get a break?" she asked aloud to the sky. "Just a few minutes, maybe even a whole day, where I can understand what is going on?" Ruach snorted behind her. Eden turned to the horse and rubbed her nose. "Is that a no?" she pushed her face against the animal's and took a deep breath. "Okay, I can handle this, the King said Moreh will be able to tell me more, all I need to do is - just do my job. Stop focusing on the things I can't do, focus on what I can do," she stood upright and seized Ruach's mane, startling the horse. She swung up onto her back and kicked her into an instant canter towards the gates. She determined in that second to do what she could, and what she could do was study and practice. If she wasn't needed on her team, she would make herself needed, make herself invaluable for her skills. The rest of this stuff about her family, it'd figure itself out.

She spent the rest of the night, as long as it was light out, going over and over sword drills and exercises. Once it was too dark to continue, she went to her room and started studying the King's words, she was determined to have them all memorized. She fell asleep that way, sitting up at her desk, book in hand.

The physical exhaustion from practicing so long the night before, and probably the emotional trauma she had gone through, caused her to sleep late into the day. Somehow she'd managed to get herself onto her bed at least, but she woke to the afternoon sun, her lamp still burning low and she was fully dressed. What exactly had awoken her she wasn't sure at first until the noise came again. Someone was knocking on her door.

Immediately she thought she was late to serve the king, but as quickly as she thought it she remembered him giving her the day to herself. "Maybe someone is worried I haven't been at meals.," she thought as she stood, trying to straighten her disheveled appearance and opened the door.

Moreh stood there with an expression of relief and empathy on her face. She was still dressed in her traveling clothes which made Eden think that she had retuned and come straight to see her.

"The King told me he had a conversation with you," she began almost apologetically.

Eden nodded, but for once thought her questions could wait. "Yes, but you obviously haven't rested or anything since returning, you can do that first, my questions can wait."

Moreh smiled and pushed past Eden to take a seat at her desk. "I think you look more in need of rest and refreshment," gesturing to Eden's appearance, "and you smell like an overworked horse."

Eden glanced down at herself and nodded again. "I was a bit caught off guard yesterday, and well, I can go bathe first if you'd prefer?"

A rare laugh came from Moreh, "oh child sit down and we will talk, we can both smell better afterwards," her eyes danced as Eden had never seen them. "I have longed to tell you of your parents, let me have my wish."

Eden took a seat on the bed.

Moreh took her wool cloak off and began. "First, your team is back, they were both successful and teachable, it wasn't a perfect mission, but they are safe and will grow," she paused, "you can see them after we are done and you are clean. They too are refreshing themselves." She pulled a box out from her vest. It was small and not very ornate but obviously hand crafted. She handed it to Eden. "This was your mother's, I kept it for her when she would go to your world, hence I've had it since their deaths," she nodded at Eden's unspoken request to open the box.

Eden eased the lid back to expose two rings. Both appeared to be white gold, one was smaller and obviously a woman's ring, it had a sapphire set in the middle surrounded by starbursts. The man's ring had a similar sapphire, but it was surrounded by lions, similar to the king's emblemas.

"They were their wedding rings, they had others in your world I believe, but I am sure she would want you to have them," Moreh smiled. "We were great friends, we served together, trained together, got into much trouble together. You remind me of them both. You have your mother's love of animals, and way with them according to the grooms here, and your father's stubbornness and knack for trouble. She kept him safe most of the time. They served the King faithfully, I have never seen two people so committed to their calling," she paused again, "and they loved you. Were willing to do anything so that you would be raised well. They never explained what they had discovered to me about the eklektos, but the way they talked it was obvious that they knew it was you and so were determined you would have everything they could give you, the best teachers, the best of everything. We had no idea what to expect from Nachash," her eyes welled up. "I'm sorry, I haven't thought on this for so long," she turned to wipe her face, "they were my closest friends and I have replayed what I know of their deaths hundreds of times, wishing I could have been there, wishing I'd seen something to prevent it," she turned back to Eden. "They didn't have much here, other than home furnishings and that box. But once you are done training and are able to have your own apartment I can get their things from storage in the tower," she rose and moved to the door. Eden wasn't sure what to say or ask. Her teacher turned again as she opened the door, "They would be proud of you," she nodded and was gone.

Eden breathed deeply. She chose to let Moreh's final words be what she dwelt on, and hurried to bathe and find her teammates.

"Parzel," Eden banged on her friend's door. Funny, she thought in that moment, that now she considered her a friend. "Par-" she was cut off by the door pulling inward and Eden surprised herself by throwing her arms around Parzel and hugging her.

"Hey," Parzel replied awkwardly, not sure how to respond to the unexpected emotion, but finally she simply hugged her back.

"They let you out of the tower?" the deep voice behind her caused her to jump, but again, Eden's response at seeing Sela was to embrace him too. Nasah and Shephel both came up to the group smiling at Eden's enthusiasm.

"Stop looking like a bunch of kids who haven't seen each other in a year," Parzel swept them inside her tiny room, "we need to at least look like Chayil." Once the door closed she smiled again and sat down beside Eden on her bed.

"So really? They let you out of the tower?" Sela asked again.

"I don't really know, they did today anyway," Eden shrugged, not sure what the King intended now. "But that's beside the point, I want to hear about this mission. I did get to tell the King he should send you guys as you are the best."

"Well, I'm not sure we deserve those accolades," Nasah replied.

"What? Why?" Eden looked around at her friends, they really were her friends now she realized. "Moreh said you were successful," she decided to leave off the other comment for their sake. "Tell me everything."

Parzel sighed, "Well, they came and told us that it was a rescue mission, that there was a family that had been captured by Nachash's troops and we were to go in and get them out. They had the pala stone and gave it to Nasah," at this point Nasah pulled it out of her shirt.

"Here, I was told to give it back to you now," handing it to Eden who slipped it over her head.

"So, the plan was we would use the stone to get to the edge of town, then we had been given a detailed map of which house the family was in. There were supposed to be two guards out front, but other than that and a routine patrol wandering the town it was supposed to be simple," Parzel continued.

"But it wasn't so simple," Sela interrupted. "We got there fine, stole up to the house easily enough, but there were no guards outside so we were a bit confused. So Shephel goes around back and sneaks a peek in the window," he shrugged at Shephel who took up the story.

"So, there's the whole family, sitting around the fire, they had fruit and bread out, seemed to be having a great time. It was so strange, they seemed completely content there, no fear, nothing. So we talked about it for a minute and decided it must be an act they are putting on for Nachash, so we carefully picked the back door lock and got inside."

"Shephel and Sela step into the living room first and immediately the wife starts screaming for guards," Nasah explained picking up the narrative. "So we were trying to shush them but she just kept yelling, the two kids hid by their dad who just wasn't moving or saying anything and finally Parzel pulled her sword and put it to the woman's throat and told her if she didn't stop screaming she was going to silence her herself."

Eden's head spun to look at Parzel. "I didn't know what else to do? She was obviously losing it and any longer and that patrol would hear her if they hadn't already," Parzel shrugged, "I felt terrible, I realize they were supposed to be loyal but they didn't seem it."

"So then began this long argument between the husband and wife," Nasah went on, "about how they had to leave, that the King had come to rescue them, but she was saying that Nachash treated them better, they had everything they wanted they were safe, he could just continue to work for Nachash and it was crazy to go back. But the husband was saying she was deluded and had forgotten all that they had in their home, their freedom and that this was all a trick and not real freedom. They went on and on, and I was looking down the street and saw the patrol start coming down towards us. I couldn't tell if they had heard anything but we couldn't take chances so I said we had to leave now, but the woman refused."

"So I said, fine, we'll leave without her," Parzel interjected.

"And that did not go over well, the husband refused to leave her, said we had to convince her and bring her, she'd remember the truth once we came back," Nasah sighed, "and we had been told that we *had* to bring him back, apparently he has some important skills the King needs so we were not allowed to fail."

"We all just stood there as the guards got closer not knowing what to do," Shephel said, "until Sela here, walks over to the wife, hits her on the back of her head with the butt of his sword and she drops like a rock unconscious."

Eden spun to look at Sela now who just smiled and shrugged. "Someone had to do something, so I picked her up and said 'Let's go'"

Eden laughed out loud at that comment. "Then what happened?"

"Well, the guard was at the threshold now, we still weren't sure if they knew we were there or it was a routine check, but they knocked on the door at this point, so as Sela carried the wife out the back and Nasah took the kids, Shephel and I waited as the husband opened the door. We were prepared to fight, there were only three of them, but they simply asked if everything was okay and when he said 'yes' they left. Apparently the wife had converted so much that they assumed the family wasn't much of a threat any more. Then out the back we went, got out of town and used the stone to get us back here."

"Wow, that's crazy?" Eden rubbed her head. "What happened to the wife?"

"We don't know exactly, they whisked her off to the medical ward and the family followed, the husband kept saying she'll remember, but I don't know, she was pretty adamant about not wanting to be here, it was so strange, I don't know what to do with it you know? I can't imagine thinking life out there could be better with Nachash, but they seemed so content," Parzel shook her head.

"Well, I am glad you are all back safely, I really hope I can be more involved in training soon and not always in the tower," Eden smiled at them all.

"Yeah, so what have you been doing?" Sela asked.

Eden paused, her mind running through all the complexities of the last few days and not sure what to share. The fact she simply stands beside the king all day, that she had dinner with him, that her parents were killed trying to protect her... "Not much really, it's truly punishment to not be allowed to do anything, but being in the King's presence is pretty great, I am learning how he thinks and acts which will make me better at understanding how to use his words I think."

That answer seemed to satisfy everyone enough, and they decided to go up to the kitchens to see what they could scavenge together.

16

"For we know chayil loved by the king,
that he has appointed you Eklektos,
because the truth came to you not only in word,
but also in power, from Sophia with full conviction."

The next day and everyone following, found the team of friends in training. The king released Eden from her duties of serving him and she spent the rest of her time working, training and studying. The days slipped into months and the months slid through seasons until the team was looking at the approach of their final exams. Eden kept referring to it as hell week, as they would have back home, but no one here seemed to get the allusion.

"How can you guys be so calm?" Shephel stared at his friends as they ate their supper. "Eating? Who can eat at a time like this? Exams start tomorrow," his voice rising in pitch.

"Shhh," Parzel hushed him. "You're freaking out and freaking everyone else out," she cautiously looked around the dining hall at the strange looks and whispered conversations as people nodded towards their table.

"What are you freaking out about Shephel?" Eden asked, as she stuffed a pile of potatoes in her mouth. "You're fine, you're a great Chayil!" she mumbled through her food.

"What? I'm the weakest link on this team," he dropped his head into his hands.

"Nasah, is he always like this with tests?" Sela asked.

"Yep, since he was little," she didn't even look up from her plate of food. "I mean, I'm nervous too though. Sometimes living it out on the field is easier than preforming in front of people."

"That's a good point," Parzel nodded. "I do get more flustered with people watching. I mean we don't even know who we have to fight or what we have to do exactly," she stirred her soup absently.

"Come on, stop it guys," Eden swallowed. "You know you're the best team here, and if you don't then wake up. The King sent you guys out to rescue people when he was short on troops, that's got to count for something." She looked Shephel in the eye, almost daring him to have a negative comment to that.

Nasah nodded, "True, but are we going to be judged as a team or as individuals. I'm not so strong without you guys picking up my weaknesses you know?"

"Why don't they give us some idea of what to expect? How is this stress beneficial?" Shephel avoided eye contact with Eden.

"I think that they probably want to see how we deal with stress you know?" Sela said slowly. "Being on a mission is pretty stressful, can't know what to expect there either, don't want us to cave then."

The rest of the table grew silent looking at Sela. "What?" he asked as he shoved a huge scoop of vegetables into his mouth.

"He's totally right," Parzel said what everyone was thinking. "We have to calm down."

Shephel took a deep breath. "Okay, I got this," he pushed his chair back. "I'm going to run laps around the pastures and then study some more. I'll see you guys on the field early," and he left.

Nasah and Sela followed him out leaving just Parzel and Eden finishing their drinks. "Are you really not stressed about tomorrow?" Parzel asked Eden, she too was amazed that they were actually friends now.

"Of course I'm stressed out, freaking out actually," Eden almost spat her qahua, the closest equivalent to coffee in Kaleo, on the table. "I just figured they didn't need to see that too, Shephel was losing it enough for all of us," she shrugged.

Parzel considered her friend for a minute. "Well, you've got the best shot of all of us, you're the most talented, but I also now think you're a pretty stellar leader to these guys - to us."

Eden took another sip, looking Parzel in the eyes. "You were such a jerk, I mean a donkey before, you know, trying to be all together so everyone would think you're a star - but really - now that you stopped the donkey part, you really are all together and everyone knows you are a star. I wouldn't want anyone else beside me on any mission I went on. Even if it was just to go shopping," she smiled a somewhat awkward grin, knowing she was not really good at sharing her emotions.

Parzel smiled in return. "Okay, you just made that weird," and laughed, "Let's go a few rounds in the ring with the practice swords then find the other guys and watch the sunset." She pushed back her chair, grabbed both their plates and headed to the door.

Eden paused a moment, watching her back, then laughed, grabbed her things and followed.

The next morning found all the recruits huddled around the outdoor training ring trying to keep the damp out. Some were stretching, others were doing exercises trying to stay warm, others were quizzing each other on various fighting techniques.

Finally, when the anticipation felt palpable, Master Petros and Moreh walked out of the tower and approached the group. They surveyed the fifty or so students in front of them, some looking better than others and then nodded to each other.

"Alright recruits," Petros bellowed. "Here is how your week will begin," he stepped up onto the dueling table for a better view, or to make the students feel even more inferior, who knew which? "You will compete in individual challenges; you will spend time with different masters as they quiz you on pertinent topics and finally you will have a team competition at the end of the week which will test how you put all these individual skills into practice and work together."

"Grades will be posted at the end of each day, but the final decision, as to whether or not you can continue on in the service of the King, will be decided with a pass/fail grade on the final day. Keep that in mind as you look at your grades, a student with exceptional marks individually may still fail if they cannot work well as a team, and vice versa," Moreh explained. "Good luck, listen for your name to be called and feel free to continue studying while you wait, just be in the ring so you can hear your name."

With that, both masters turned away and headed to different areas around the training ground. Eventually names began to be called out and students started to scatter to different rooms. Some went to Master Rophe to answer questions about injuries and healing, others competed against other students in sword fighting, wrestling, archery and even hand to hand combat. Others had to fight against masters. There was every possible type of exam going on and no one really had any time to talk until supper that evening.

When Eden walked into the dining hall she was struck with how quiet it was. Everyone looked exhausted and beaten down. She got her food and moved to sit by her team, most of whom were already done eating, or seemed to not have much of an appetite and were just playing with their food. "Hey guys," she whispered, not wanting to disturb others.

"Hey," Nasah replied for all of them.

"Soooo, how'd it go?" she asked as she started to eat.

"Well, got knocked off the dueling platform um, eight times by Petros so that went well," Shephel snorted.

"And I couldn't remember half of the parrying moves when I was fighting against Bauer, I beat him but pretty sure it was just by shear force, I got no marks for skill. The master was shaking his head the whole time," Sela mumbled.

"Yeah, I'm pretty sure I got most of the healing questions wrong."

"And I forgot the simplest of maps, to our own stupid city," Nasah raised her voice, then quieted down when heads started to turn.

"I know, I felt the same way," Eden agreed, deciding dinner didn't taste so good and choosing qahua instead. "I did okay in the fighting stuff, but then they started asking me questions and I just froze up.”

“Did anyone go look at the marks?” Shephel asked.

“I did,” Nasah said. “It wasn’t pretty but all of us are above average still, not sure how, and certainly not the top of the lists, but they aren’t kicking us out yet.”

Sela sighed, “That’s a relief, I guess I should go look just to know,” he pushed back from the table. “Then I’m going to bed, I’m so tired.”

Again, they all made their way out of the dining hall and back to their dorms. Eden slipped inside her room and collapsed in the chair. She was tired and frustrated with herself, but for the first time in her life she wasn’t really freaking out. She knew she belonged here now, she knew she was learning and even if she didn’t pass she was willing to do this whole year again and again until she got it right. “It’s so different knowing you are where you are supposed to be,” she said aloud.

Pulling off her sweat stained clothes she tumbled into bed and feel asleep almost instantly.

The friends struggled through the week of exams fairly well. As much as Nasah tried to be humble, her marks were well above the rest of them, with the exception of the sword fighting where both Eden and Parzel were near the top of the class. Sela was the only concern, his marks had dropped below average in several areas. But the week really hinged on the final assignment. Each of the recruits had been tested individually and now they were being put into a simulation that would test their teamwork. Their masters had informed them that even if you did exceptionally well in the individual skills, you could be failed if you did not work well as a team.

At breakfast Eden tried to rally them. “Look at the advantages we have,” she said, stuffing a piece of toast in her mouth. “We have been on a bunch of missions together already and worked really well.

You were even sent off on one that was filling in for real Chayil! This is just a training exercise, it can't be even close to what we've gone through," she looked at each of her teammates one by one. "Besides, I don't even care, if we don't all pass I don't want to move on anyway, you're the only team I want to serve with," she looked away and sipped her qahua. She was actually getting used to the strong bitter drink.

Sela took a deep breath. "Well ,if anyone isn't making it, it's me."

"This is stupid," Parzel spat, standing abruptly. "We are great, we work well together and we will not lose this," she glanced at the other tables of recruits that had hushed when she raised her voice. She sat back down then and said a bit quieter. "This is like war games right? We compete against another team, we take their position, we win. Eden's right, it's not even close to the stuff we have faced so get off your butts, lift your chin and lets go take on this test."

All of them stared at her for a moment, then Shephel pushed his chair back, grabbed his tray and they all followed him out into the practice field.

For this exam, the masters had them arranged out on a piece of property that faced the back side of the city. It was filled with hills and valleys, forest and a small swamp area. It wasn't huge, about two kilometres square. Eden's team was given the North side of the field. they had to construct a makeshift blind that could hide their team staff. Between them, they had to protect their base, and find the other team's staff. Once they had captured the staff, they had a special capsule they would crush and a green smoke would rise to signal the victory. If you were caught, or 'killed' you were removed from the game with no chance of returning, and a risk to be expelled from the program.

Parzel quickly took charge, instructing Nasah and Shephel to create the blind to hide the staff, and then setting up two positions for the two of them to watch the staff and be able to move quickly to intercept anyone who made it that far. "Alright, Sela, myself and Eden are going to advance across the field," she roughly sketched the area in the dirt from memory. "I'd say if they were smart they'd put the staff in that bog area, they know we have the high ground, so they have to draw us out into the open, their best move is to let us go to them and pick us off one at a time," she looked at Nasah, "so you guys will have to be prepared for that, and if we are all gone you have to move up." Nasah nodded understanding.

"Alright," Eden looked at the dirt map. "I say we cut around the sides first then, and see if we can take any of them in their hiding spots before we risk anything," she used a stick to show her idea.

"Good plan," Parzel agreed. Just then a booming cannon shot signaled the start. "Let's go team," and the three of them drew their game swords and moved out.

The game swords were interesting on their own. They had special blades that would not cut, but left streaks of blue paint when an attacker was hit. If you received more than five marks in non-life threatening locations you would become disabled, meaning you had a time delay before you could re-enter the game. But if you received one wound in a life-threatening spot, red paint would splash and you were immediately eliminated. They had been instructed that they could take prisoners by putting a sword to the throat, the prisoner always had the option of fighting. Being a prisoner brought less negative marks than dying did. How the sword knew the difference, Eden had no idea, but she liked the mystery of this new world of hers.

The three of them crept along for a while until they had managed to get themselves to the edge of the swamp land.

Parzel tapped Eden on the shoulder. She put a finger to her lips and pointed over Eden's shoulder so she could follow her line of sight to where a small recruit was well hidden under a large shrubbery, but her sword had reflected just enough of the sun to reveal her spot.

Eden saw her and nodded. Parzel pointed to herself and then across the field. She motioned for Eden and Sela to go around the closer side to continue to look for other recruits.

Eden and Sela both nodded and watched her slip off to the right. They slowly started to progress themselves, but Eden paused to watch Parzel creep up behind the other team's player and draw her sword silently across her neck. The other recruit looked shocked but threw down her sword. The only problem with taking prisoners, was that it meant that Parzel was now going to be out of the game for a few minutes as she took the enemy to the designated spot. That left Eden and Sela exposed Eden thought to herself. She tried to quiet her breathing in order to listen in hopes that the movement on the other side of the field would have stirred some of the other players into action.

It didn't take long, and two other recruits started to move from their locations just ahead of Eden and Sela. And it was a blessing they did move. "Didn't even see them," Eden mumbled to herself. Sela tapped her shoulder and pointed to them too and she nodded to him. There didn't look to be any way of sneaking up on them as they were moving right for their position, but at this point a fight would take them out faster anyway.

Eden held her hand up to Sela, and counted down on her fingers from five, when her fist closed the two of them sprang from their spots and as quietly as they could, attacked the two others. It was a short fight, both Eden and Sela's surprise worked to their advantage and soon each had delivered life threatening blows marked with red paint across their opponents. The two shook hands with them and sat down, removed from the game. They hadn't gone uninjured though, Sela had two blue marks across his sword arm and Eden had one across her left leg. They took a deep breath and slipped into some cover.

Sela was anxious to move, Eden could tell, but she just could not get a read on any of the other 'enemy' recruits. They had taken care of three, so there were two left. She debated over and over in her head whether those two would have moved forward towards their base, but like Parzel said, that just wouldn't be a good strategic move. They shouldn't leave three behind and two move up to begin with, but the two left should have moved to replace fallen team members and nothing was happening. She hadn't seen Parzel return and they'd been waiting for at least a quarter of a watch now.

Suddenly she spotted the briefest of movements. It wasn't even the recruit that moved, but a bird had settled on what appeared to be a tree branch, and then suddenly taken off again, startled. That was when Eden spotted their staff. It was in the middle of some marsh grass about thirty feet from their position. It was completely in the open so anyone making a move would be spotted and attacked and there appeared to be a recruit lying low in that marsh grass. But where was the other one?

Eden slowly reached over her shoulder and got Sela's attention. She pointed to the spot and whispered. "Staff, one down."

Sela nodded. "Where's the last one?" he whispered back and Eden shrugged. They both paused again. Eden was trying to work out a scenario that didn't involve being captured, but she just couldn't find one. She supposed that the two of them could try and out match the other team, but with both of them with injuries and the last recruit's location unknown it just wasn't good odds.

"I have an idea," Sela whispered. "I'm going to make a move on the staff," he held up a hand to stop as Eden opened her mouth to object. "I am sure I can take the one and it should move the last one out into the open at least for you, if not cause them to come at me."

"But Sela," Eden argued. "You can't take that risk. You've got the lowest scores and I don't want to lose you," she shook her head.

"I am not as important as this team," he said quietly, putting a hand on her shoulder. "You can't go because you're the best bet we have of beating the last remaining opponent and if we lose, we are all toast. If you make it, then I have a good shot of surviving too," he drew his sword. "Now shush," and he was gone.

Eden watched him slip much too quietly for a man his size, through the underbrush and then step out into the open. She could tell the recruit by the staff saw him, but she still didn't see any movement. She figured that this recruit had to be a good fighter if this was indeed their strategy, and she prayed Sela could pull it off. As he got about five paces from the staff, the recruit hiding sprang to his feet, sword drawn and attacked. He was a good fighter, Eden had seen him in his exams

beat Master Petros. She watched nervously as Sela fought valiantly, he
was gaining the upper hand as his opponent was tiring from the mere
strength of Sela's blows. As the other recruit stumbled and Sela moved
for the killing strike the final recruit on their team charged to his
teammate's defense. Sela didn't see him at first as he struck at his
target, and Eden, wanting to protect him shouted out. That caused Sela
to turn and just barely deflect a strike from the advancing recruit. Now
he had two men to deal with, as Eden struggled to get there to help.
She knew this was not a good plan, but she couldn't watch as Sela
sacrificed himself. She could tell Sela saw her coming, and she could
tell his decision in that moment too. His second attacker was still
focused on finding a deciding blow for Sela that he had not noticed
where Eden was coming from. With his back turned as it was and his
focus on Sela he was wide open for Eden to take him out and they
would win. So to assure that, Sela turned back to the recruit on the
ground and dealt him the final blow, exposing his side to the other who
quickly left the splash of red paint across Sela's whole right side. A
second later that recruit too had the death paint running from his neck
to his hip and his shoulders slumped, realizing they had just lost.

Eden, looked worriedly at Sela, who was grinning at her, then
grabbed the staff and crushed the capsule. A plume of green smoke
rose high and she could very distantly hear some shouts, which she
assumed were Nasah and Shephel.

They trudged out of the woods while chatting with the other
team who congratulated them. They exchanged strategies and discussed
what happened as they met up with Nasah and Shephel, and then just
as they got to the city wall where the Masters were waiting, Parzel and
her prisoner finally came trotting up. Eden explained what happened
and how Sela had sacrificed himself for the win.

"Sela, oh I wish I could have gotten there," she shook her head,
obviously worried for him as well.

"What happened to you?" Eden asked, "We expected you back
way faster."

"Well, I was walking her," she motioned to the other recruit who had come up with her, "when she stepped down a slope and fell. Or at least, I thought she fell, it was her plan, so when I rushed down she struck right away and got my sword, we went at it hand to hand, she's a good fighter. We had a good go of it, and both hit each other pretty often," she illustrated the splashes of paint all over herself and the other girl, "and then with one last struggle for my sword we both took a fifth hit and disabled ourselves. We were still waiting for the time lag on that when we saw the green smoke," she shrugged. "I'm sorry, it's my fault you had to do that," she said to Sela.

"I wouldn't have had it any other way," he smiled. "You should have seen it, it was perfect, I caught Eden's eye, turned on the guy on the ground knowing exactly what was coming and he took his chance and opened himself right up to Eden. Beautiful."

"But not if you're kicked out," Nasah said.

"Hey, what a way to go," he smiled.

Eden wasn't sure if he was being so confident because he really was, or because he was really worried. Just then one of the Masters spoke up.

"Alright recruits," he paused. "Your exams are finished, please go, clean yourselves up and you will be standing before the King tonight to hear of your results," he turned slightly and seemed to glance at Sela. "Good luck."

A few hours later Eden stood beside her team in their dress uniforms, nervously awaiting the King in his throne room. Several other teams had come and gone. Most had passed, there were one or two people who came out looking miserable and obviously had to repeat the training, but that was rare. Eden swallowed, as she anxiously looked at Sela. She was one hundred percent positive the rest of the team would move on, but she doubted that with his marks, and then 'dying' during their simulation he would do the same. She pulled nervously at her collar as she thought about it.

Finally, the king entered along with Moreh and Petros. He smiled at each of them.

"My loyal servants," he began. "You have had an interesting year no?" his eyes were laughing. "I see from your Masters that you have overcome quite the challenges. Training together, helping each other, even protecting each other. It is all quite admirable, and they are qualities that I would want in my Chayil. Now, I am sure that you realize what areas you need to improve upon, you are certainly not perfect, and if you want to be a part of the Gibbor Chayil you are going to have to improve those areas that perhaps you think you can skip over in light of your other talents," his eyes were penetrating as he looked at Eden.

He began to pace a bit. "Now your final practical exam was interesting," he continued to walk back and forth and seemed to choose his words carefully. "You definitely were very good as a team in strategy, you figured out your enemy's moves and countered them extremely well. You knew your strengths and weaknesses and played to them. Unfortunately, you lost a team member in your victory and had another disabled and alone. Yet, you did succeed, so I am granting you Eden, Parzel, Nasah and Shephel the rank of private, first class and after serving a year probational duty you may begin studies, should you choose, to join the Gibbor Chayil."

The entire team looked like they'd had execution orders given knowing he had not said Sela's name.

"Sela, you are a dear man and loyal servant and I do not doubt that with some more training, you too may join the ranks. However, with your loss of life in the final round of exams, combined with several of your test scores, your Masters and I do not think it wise you move forward."

Sela's head dropped to his chest. He nodded in agreement and started to turn to leave.

"Your majesty," Eden spoke up, surprising herself. "I stood in your presence for quite a while and at first I didn't really learn anything. But when I started to pay attention, I saw you surrounded yourself with the people you trusted the most. Not only loyal servants, but ones willing to lay down their lives for you, to give every ounce of their talents and abilities for your service. They weren't just your best warriors, they were your friends. I bet there are even men and women in your service that are better warriors than Masters Moreh and Petros," she grimaced a bit when she saw their facial expressions. "...but they are different than these two who you would trust with your kingdom, I am quite sure."

Eden paused to catch her breath, but as the King didn't speak she hurried on, "so, your Majesty, I respectfully decline your appointment and would prefer to continue to study with Sela. He might not be the smartest man out there yet, but I have watched him stand up to adversity beyond anything any of us have experienced. I have seen the talents he has with a hammer and his ability in battle and I have seen first-hand that he would lay down his life in order for any plan of yours to succeed. He did so when he did not have to today in our battle, he put the mission first and himself second. It was calculated and strategic and that is the kind of man I want on my team and to serve by my side, as I serve you."

There was an eerie silence that followed. Eden was quite sure no one knew what to do. Sela was staring at her, Master Moreh and Petros looked from Eden, to the King then to each other. King Melek simply stood and looked Eden in the eye. She didn't let her gaze drop and tried to straighten her shoulders.

"Is that what you think?" the King asked.

"I too, respectfully decline," Nasah suddenly squeaked out the same words.

"Me too your Majesty," Shephel nodded.

"They can't do much without my help, so I guess that includes me," Parzel gave Sela a big smile.

"This is quite a problem I see," The King looked both shocked and pleased at their responses. "Moreh, have we ever had someone refuse their appointment?"

"No, your majesty," she looked at Eden and shook her head, "this would be a first."

"Sela, what do you make of this? Do you deserve this sort of display of loyalty?"

Sela stepped towards the King. "No sir, I do not. And I would appreciate it if you denied their requests sir. I know I'm not very smart, but I do try my best and I will die for you your Majesty and for my team any day. But I will study harder and more and I will get better sir. I deserve to start over."

King Melek walked back towards his throne and sat down on it. He put his chin in his hand and seemed to be sizing up the five of them. He then made a motion for Petros and Moreh to come to him. In a swirl of cloaks, they knelt down beside him and began to whisper together for what seemed like ages, but Eden figured was probably just a few minutes. Finally, they stood up on either side of the king.

"Alright, I have decided," the King spoke in a booming voice that very obviously meant that no one should try and argue with his decision. "I deny your request Eden, and the rest of you. You will take your appointments and you will be serving on the front lines of my army for the next nine months." he paused to let his words sink in. "I will accept nothing but your best and expect even more than usual from you as you will be training a fellow private who must re-take his medical, geography and sword fighting exams at the end of those months."

Shephel's mouth dropped, and Nasah was obviously relieved. Eden and Parzel beamed as they glanced at each other, but Sela seemed confused.

King Melek laughed, "Sela, I hear-by appoint you as Private first class, but that's you who has to rewrite your exams," he explained, his voice slipping into his fatherly tone. Sela suddenly understood, and huge tear rolled over his cheek.

"Cursed be the day I try to separate a team who is so loyal to me and to each other. I thought that Moreh's idea of putting the five of you together at first might have been a bad one, but she has proven to be trustworthy as usual." he nodded to her. "And Eden, you are correct, I do have some Gibbor Chayil better than Petros and Moreh, at least on paper, but I would never trade these two for anyone," he smiled, "except maybe the five of you."

They all just stood there with stupid grins on their faces until Moreh shooed them out of the room, explaining that they would get their assignments on Monday morning and to go and celebrate.

17

"Listen my beloved chayil,
has not the king chosen the Eklektos
from the poor in the worlds, to be rich in truth
and heir of the kingdom which he has promised
to those who love him?"

The team planned to meet in the dining tent to get some food and then to head out to the practice area to celebrate together, but Eden excused herself. She wanted to get outside and ride for a bit to clear her head. She still couldn't believe that the King had gone for her ultimatum. She wasn't sure what she thought was going to happen but what he decided certainly wasn't it. Her heart was racing as she walked out into the pastures and whistled for Ruach who was grazing on the far side of the field.

The horse trotted to her peacefully, nuzzling her hand looking for a treat.

"Here you big suck, of course I brought you a treat," she whispered into her ear as she slipped her an apple. As Ruach crunched on it, Eden swung herself up onto her back. With a swift kick the horse was off, running like the wind. Eden clung to her neck and let the horse lead. They soon stopped at the far fence and Eden heard her name called from below.

She glanced over and down the hillside and saw her friend the shepherd waving and climbing up to her, his flock scattered over the grass below.

"Hi," she returned his greeting.

"Haven't seen you in a bit, how are things going serving the King?" he asked, leaning up against the fence, turned slightly so he could still see his flock.

"Good actually," she smiled. "I took your advice and it worked better than I could have hoped for," she laughed.

"Really?" he smiled, "That's great."

Eden squinted her eyes up and looked suspiciously at him. "What do you know?" she asked. Just the way he had smiled seemed to belie that he knew more than he was letting on.

"Oh, nothing really, I just overheard that you and your team were being appointed as Chayil!"

"Really?" she glanced down the hill. "Your sheep tell you that?" she laughed.

"No," he smiled, "I have my sources. I have lived here a long time you know."

"I suppose so," Eden was so overwhelmed with the whole day that she let it go. "Well, I guess I should thank you. Your advice really did change my attitude and ultimately my training to actually observe and learn from the King."

"I'm glad I could help," he smiled again, his face looking sincerely thrilled for her. "So where do you go from here?"

"I don't know yet," she replied, rubbing Ruach's neck as the horse was getting restless. "We get our assignments on Monday, I'm meeting my team in a few minutes to celebrate together. All I know is that the five of us get to serve together somewhere."

"That's great," he nodded. "It's hard to find people who will challenge and encourage you in your duty and life and that you can trust, much less enjoy. Got to hold on to those ones," he smiled again, then turned back to his sheep. "I should be going, moving the flock to new fields, I hope I'll see you again Eden. I enjoy talking with you," he started to move back down the hillside.

"Me too. Thanks again for everything." She watched him go thinking that he was probably as helpful in her training as any of her masters, maybe even more so. She hoped she'd see him wherever they placed her and her team.

"Well Ruach," she leaned forward, "wherever we go I'm asking for you to come with me, one more request can't hurt right?" the horse snorted and shook her mane and began trotting back towards the stables. "Alright, I get it, I've got some partying to do and you want to eat," she kicked her sides and again they raced across the field.

Monday morning came quickly. They had enjoyed a few days off, spent some time in town buying some supplies and things they thought would be helpful wherever they got sent. They tossed ideas around as to what their assignment might be, tried to get inside information from some of the servants who might have overheard things, but it was in utter astonishment that they stood now with Moreh's pronouncement ringing in their ears.

"Where are we going?" Eden asked again.

"That's hundreds of miles from here," Nasah said. "Is there anything out there even?"

"Of course there's something out there," Moreh responded, "the guard post you'll be serving at," she looked exasperated with them. "You all had a lot of nerve giving the King an ultimatum and the fact that he agreed still shocks me. You should not press your luck by complaining about your placements. You will serve as a front-line guard on the edge of the kingdom. You must protect the line so that all of those who live behind it never know of the troubles out there. It is a difficult and dangerous task, but one that provides ample time and space for extra training that needs to happen for Sela," she raised her eyebrows at him. "I expect an excellent score when you are re-examined."

Sela nodded, mouth still slightly open at the news.

"On a positive note, you are each assigned a horse, since your trip is a long one to your post and you will not be using any special transport. We want you to learn the kingdom firsthand as you travel, to know what you are protecting.”

Eden was thrilled with this knowledge at least and as she opened her mouth to ask about Ruach, Moreh looked at her and raised her hand. “I know what you want and yes, you may take Ruach, apparently she won’t let anyone else ride her anymore anyway,” she rolled her eyes, but seemed pleased all the same. “The rest of you can go to the stables and ask the grooms which horses are available and get set up with saddles and tack and such and get to know your horse a bit before you leave on Wednesday morning,” she looked at her notes again to seemingly make sure she had given them all the information they needed. “Oh yes, your commanding officer will be Allon, he has been serving on the outer limits for twenty years, knows what he’s talking about in terms of the wilds out there, but he is a bit distant, been a long time since he’s been back in civilization, or even to see the King. Remember that.”

Eden had no idea what that meant but at this point she didn’t care. Her mind was running over the things she wanted to get from Town, if she wasn’t going to be in civilization for a year she wanted to have some comforts with her.

“Eden,” Moreh’s voice startled her back to the moment. “Did you hear that?” she asked, her tone exasperated.

“Um, not exactly,” she mumbled, looking at her friends for help and finding none.

“Wednesday, by Laud, in the stables. Be ready to go, and you had better work on your attention. Allon will not stand for your sort of behaviour like I have,” and she turned and walked away.

“What the heck,” Parzel exclaimed. “We’re going to be in the middle of nowhere for a year.”

“And I heard those out-lying area guards are a bit crazy,” Shephel said nervously. “Too long without normal people around.”

“They are going to eat me alive,” Sela complained.

“What are you guys complaining about?” Eden exclaimed. “We get to serve together, the best team out there. If any of those old farts give us any problems we will just show them what made us the best set of recruits the King has ever seen," she was practically jumping up and down. "Now come on, we have to supply ourselves with everything we're going to want for a year. Let's hit the town and then get you all to the stables," she started to head back to her room to grab her money. She felt like a kid going to Disneyland. She laughed, 'Imagine trying to explain Disneyland to these guys?' She had no idea what she was getting into but was itching for the adventure. She had seen the area on the maps, but that was as much as she knew, so she had no preconceived notions, which could be good or bad, but for the moment she was thrilled and especially that she was taking Ruach with her. She sighed contentedly, grabbed her money purse from her room and ran to meet her friends.

It was still dark as Eden's team assembled at the stables on Wednesday. She slung her saddle bags onto Ruach who snorted, seeming to wonder at the extra weight. Her sword slid easily into the scabbard on the left-hand side of the saddle and she put her newly purchased hunting bow into the one on the right. She fastened her bed roll and blankets to the back and tightened her traveling cloak around her neck. The wind was strong across the pastures and clouds seemed forbidding. As she pulled her cloak tight, she felt the chain around her neck that now held both the pala stone and her father's wedding ring. She spun her mother's ring on her right hand almost unconsciously, smiling at the thought of them with her.

Sela bumped into Eden disturbing her thoughts. "Doesn't look like it's going to be a dry ride does it?" he nodded to the sky as he slipped his own saddle bags onto his horse.

Eden glanced around at her team as they packed up. Parzel seemed confident with the chestnut mare she had chosen, Nasah's palomino also seemed content with her rider, but Shephel was hesitant as he tried to get his bags and then himself onto his horse that the black gelding clearly knew he was the one in charge. "I'm going to die,"

Shephel moaned as he clung to the pommel on the saddle after finally being helped on by one of the grooms.

Sela laughed. "Sit up straight and try to pretend you can ride and maybe you can trick him," mounting his own grey stallion that was as oversized as he was.

"Are you all ready?" Moreh entered the stables behind them. She moved between the horses and shook her head as she passed Shephel. "Someone had better keep a tether to his horse or you might be short a team member," she swept her scarf back from her eyes as the wind whipped it around. She turned to face them all as they maneuvered their horses towards her. She looked the approving parent, sizing them up and sad to see them go. "Well, I confess I have a soft spot for this team. Please make me proud," she paused, "and don't die." she turned to face the doors. "Now go. And remember the King's words."

Eden and Parzel looked at each other and seemed to agree, "Ha" cried Parzel and Eden kicked Ruach into motion and all five galloped past Moreh and out of the gates. It wasn't until they were several miles down the road that they slowed to a walk.

"Talk about uplifting speeches?" Parzel laughed.

"Don't die," Eden mimicked. "Yep, that's a quality one," she joked.

Sela's hearty laugh echoed and warmed all of them, even Shephel, who had shockingly managed to stay upright on his horse, broke into a smile.

The sun never came out that day, and the clouds continued to close in. The wind was harsh and after several hours all of them were hunched over their horses' necks trying to get some relief.

"Why can't we just use the pala stone and travel to the outer limits?" Shephel murmured under his breath.

"Shephel, quit complaining," Nasah snapped at him. "You know we can't travel with the horses that way and we need all our supplies, besides Moreh said we had to learn the land."

Parzel grunted, "She also made some other comment about needing to grow on the journey."

Eden nodded, "And if you'd paid attention to the King's words you'd know that he values the journey - always. He almost always makes his Chayil travel without any powers. He directs our steps, so apparently we have something to learn. But.." she looked up at the clouds, dreading when they were going to open up on them. "but it would be a lot easier," she whispered to herself.

They trudged on for the rest of the day and mercifully the clouds did not unleash their wells, but as dusk was starting to fall they decided they needed to set up camp.

"We are still well within the realm, I think we can make camp pretty close to the road," Parzel pointed to a small clearing just a stone's throw from the trail.

"And we'd better hurry," Nasah pointed to the sky, "we are going to get soaked soon."

Each of them quickly set about making camp. Sela put up a tarp to shelter them from the coming rain, Eden tied up the horses and quickly started making a fire. The others took out some food and started roasting meat as soon as the wood caught, but it wasn't long until the rain began. After a few minutes it had become a downpour. The fire barely held a flame, and soon they were all huddled together under the tarp trying to stay warm and chewing on what food they had been able to cook. No one spoke much, and Eden wondered whether they had it in them to make it in the outer limits if this was already so difficult. One by one they fell asleep, agreeing to rotate who was on guard throughout the night.

Nasah was the last shift, but she didn't have to wake her team. Well before Laud all of them were awake and groaning from the poor sleep. The rain continued to fall making it impossible to start a fire, so they pulled some bread and jam from their bags and satisfied their hunger with a cold breakfast. Just as they had each put up camp, they each took it down. Eden fed the horses, making sure all of them were ready for another long day's ride.

"At least you don't need to water them, they should be thoroughly hydrated by the rain," Sela laughed as he came over with the tarps and stored them in his saddle bags, water running off his shaved head into his eyes.

Eden nodded, cracking a grin. "They couldn't have picked the dry season to send us out in?" Although still not fully acclimated to the weather in Kaleo, through this year she had figured out that this was indeed the rainy season. "Going south should mean we're getting warmer in my books," she tried to laugh.

Parzel threw her own saddle bags over her horse, patting the mare's nose as she did so. "I'm thinking we might get a couple warm days, but once we hit the outer limits we'll be lucky for sunshine for several months," she grunted, wiping the rain from her face and trying to pull the hood of her cloak tighter.

"At least we're together," Shephel said, eyeing his horse warily. "You going to let me get on you today?" he asked the horse, who turned away and stomped a hoof.

"You seem to be getting along," Nasah laughed, easily swinging up onto her own. "What did you name him anyway?"

"I didn't," Shephel continued to look at his horse. "The groom said they call him Brick," he paused, "I think it's for his stubbornness. I should have known he was a bad pick," he tried to get his foot into the stirrup awkwardly.

"I'd say it's because he's a brick in battle," Sela said, taking the horse's reins to help steady him as Shephel finally was able to swing his leg up. "He looks pretty solid, be his friend and I bet he won't let you down." Sela blew in the horse's nose making him snort and slipped him half an apple.

"Alright everyone, let's get moving, at least that will warm the horses up," Parzel instructed, and within a few minutes they were all trotting along the road southbound.

They occasionally passed a few travelers, not many were in the near vicinity of Shammah though. Most of the farms that were attached to the capital were self-sufficient, it was the odd merchant or countryman looking for work that was on the road here. It wasn't an easy path by any means as it weaved around the southern foothills of the Addir mountain range, making the terrain as varied as the many twists and turns the path followed. The unforgiving rain didn't help matters. The horses and riders were soaked through well before lunch and the clouds didn't seem to offer much hope of relenting at this point.

Eden glanced overhead, 'it seems they have settled on the foothills just waiting for us to walk through,' she thought. If anything, it kept them all quiet and, at least Eden, contemplative. Training had been so hard in recent months with exams that she felt she had barely had time to reflect on all that the King had told her about her own family history. She wished she could talk to her parents, get their views on life here, on life back home, wherever that was anymore? This caused her to think about Ian and Heather. She really hadn't given them much thought. She was so excited and overwhelmed by finally fitting in somewhere, feeling at home and like she had a family and purpose, that she'd barely given the place that was home for most of her life any consideration.

"I wonder what they thought when I never came back from my ride?" she muttered. That had never occurred to her before. Heather probably freaked out. They would have had the sheriff out and a search party before night fall. It must have broken their hearts. She was the only piece of their best friends' left. "I never thought how they must have felt," she mused. "If I lost any of these guys I'd want whatever I could around me to remind me of them. To be asked to raise their only daughter, that must have been such a blessing and here I treated them so ungratefully," she chastised herself.

"Maybe they know." That was a new idea too. "Maybe my parents told them about Kaleo, maybe they understood their mission and why they took care of me. Maybe someone told them I'm here and not just missing. It's possible." She determined to write a letter to Moreh as soon as they reached the outpost and ask. At least maybe the

King would let her contact them now and try and explain - or something, she thought to herself.

Funny how it's so easy to get caught up in the joy of your situation and changes, achieving dreams of your own, and forget the people who love you and are losing something, or even that they did so much to get you to the point you're at. Eden made a mental note to try and be more observant about things like that. Not so selfish that she only considered her own perspective and expected others to ignore their own feelings to be happy for her. Why is it that focusing on yourself is just so much easier? She wondered.

"I know I read the King's words somewhere that talk about putting others ahead of ourselves, that being the highest goal, but I can't believe how anyone can do it? We all care about ourselves more than anyone, how do you teach yourself to deny what you want for someone else's good?"

"You're awfully quiet," Parzel said, pulling her horse alongside Eden and interrupting her thoughts. "What are you thinking about?"

"Besides how cold I am?" the two laughed together. "Actually, I was just thinking about my old home and what it's like now that I'm gone."

"I never really asked you about where you came from, you were always so interested in learning about Kaleo," Parzel nodded. "What was it like?"

"Well, I don't even know where to begin," she paused, trying to figure out how to explain her world. "The weather wasn't much different than here," she thought aloud, "at least where I lived." She started to try and explain what life was like back home. It was good for her to go through so much, it reminded her of the blessings she had experienced, and how she was loved, even if she never really appreciated it before.

They spent most of the day with Parzel asking questions and Eden trying to explain. The others caught bits of the conversation too. Cars and planes seemed to be the most confusing to all of them.

"I don't know how it is possible to put two hundred people in a metal bird and it stay in the air. It's too heavy," Sela shook his head.

Eden laughed, "Well, they'd say the same thing about a pala stone," trying to imagine showing that to Ian or Heather. Real magic, that would set her world on its head.

Finally, as the day drew to an end so did the rain. "Here is as good a spot to stop as any," Parzel pointed to an outcropping in the rocks on their right-hand side, the river Sheni was just behind them. "Those rocks should give us some shelter from the wind in case the rain starts up again, and we can definitely get a fire going in there and some warm food in us finally." Everyone quickly agreed.

"And I think that tomorrow we'll be able to reach this small town on the map, we could actually stay at an inn for the night," Nasah had been studying their route, pointing to a small village.

"Sounds good to me, but I'm just as happy to roast some of that chicken we brought before it goes bad tonight," Sela smiled, already tying up his horse and starting to gather fire wood.

The others quickly joined in and as they lay down to sleep, with warm food in their stomachs, Eden was able to smile and finally appreciate the journey she had been on all her life and seemed to have missed up until now.

Nasah was right, they were able to make a small rural town the next night. They rode up to the Green Pony Inn just after sunset. The groom hurried to stable their horses, bowing awkwardly and stumbling over his words. "Sorry." he muttered, "we don't get Chayil staying here often," he offered his excuse and then called inside. "Carla. Get these fine folks some warm food and beds."

"Don't be shouting at me boy," the reply came back from the kitchen door before a young girl emerged who seemed quite capable of handling herself with just about any sort. "Well, come on then," she waved them in. They nodded their thanks and headed inside.

Each of them stowed their things in their rooms and then came down to the great room for some dinner. For a small town the Inn was packed. None of them knew how many were strangers or just towns folk, but the room was a buzz. Girls hurried between tables with plates of food, the bartender was sliding ale down the bar top almost faster than he could pour it, and a minstrel was singing some ballad about a great battle for the eastern shore.

Eden sat down on a bench beside Shephel and tried to take it all in. She had gone into town in Shammah but had never actually gone into an inn or pub. This was exactly like she might have imagined from watching medieval movies. The hearth glowed brightly, people were laughing and singing, some had had a few too many, others were playing cards, and there was just the right amount of men frowning and looking disgruntled with life. She breathed it in, enjoying all of it.

"Why are you looking so happy?" Parzel asked, grabbing a chicken leg as the serving girl dropped the plates on the table.

"No reason, just enjoying the adventure," she laughed, as a large man slipped off his stool at the bar and lay confused on the floor until someone dragged him out.

"Seriously, no one should be smiling with the amount of riding we've been doing. I still can't feel my butt," Sela was stretching awkwardly.

"No one wants to see that," Nasah cringed, pushing him off the end of the bench. The others laughed, as did Sela until two heavy boots suddenly stomped up beside him. Sela pulled himself up to face the man. A grizzled beard and missing teeth glared back at him. "You all part of the King's guard?" he snarled.

"What's it to you?" Sela asked in return.

The man took a step closer to him, so that his beard was almost brushing Sela's chin. "Just had a few other lug heads of your type in here, wanted to make sure you weren't going to be causing a raucous like them is all," he turned towards the rest of them. "Y'all always come in here from the outer limits expecting some kind of hero's welcome and getting upset when people go about their lives. Well, we got life to be doing here, not fawning over you types, so just mind yourselves," he growled.

"We are just coming down from Migdal, heading to the outer limits, all we'd like is a warm meal and bed," Parzel tried to ease the man's tension. He grunted in return, eyeing them up and down.

"I suppose you don't look quite troubled enough to be like those outer limit guards yet," he sniffed, "but it won't take long, not sure what happens out there, but it's never good."

"What do you mean?" Nasah asked.

"I mean all you Chayil change, get angry or bitter or something. Something changes you out there. And that commander, Allon, he's not all there anymore. Something's got him all messed up. Scares just about everyone when he comes up here," his expression had softened. "My advice, keep your heads down and get transferred as soon as you can. I don't know what you did to deserve this post but work to fix it," he turned back to the bar and disappeared in the crowd.

"Well, I'm looking forward to getting there now," Shephel leaned over to Eden who laughed in spite of herself. "Warming right up to this outer limits idea. I mean, what's a few months in a place that apparently sucks the life out of you?" he shoved half a potato in his mouth.

No one said much after that, not sure what to expect now. Even Eden's mood was dampened by the conversation.

"What do we have like just under five hundred kilometres to go?" Shephel finally broke their silence and looked at his sister.

"Um, yeah I think that's about right," she nodded, "so I'd say probably another four days, I don't think we hit any more towns the way we are going, just trails, part way through tomorrow we are off the main road so riding is going to be a bit rougher on us and the horses," she explained.

"Can't wait," Sela rubbed his back again.

"Well, then I'm going to bed," Parzel stated, standing. "Back down here for what sunrise?" she looked for agreement before heading upstairs.

"I think that's probably a good idea," Eden nodded, following Parzel's lead. "Night guys." Nasah stood with her.

"I'm downing one more if this is the last night of comfort we get," Sela raised his pint. "You stay with me Shephel?"

"Sure, why sleep?" he laughed, and waved for another ale.

Eden walked into their room just moments after Parzel who glanced up from her bag. "Thought you had a good idea," Eden nodded to her.

"Yeah, I'm pretty sore, I'm not used to all this riding either, but I didn't want to let the guys see that," Parzel admitted, pulling off her jacket and boots. "Guess we all could have spent some more time down in the stables like you."

"I'm hurting too," Eden grimaced. "Riding around the fields is a lot different than two hundred kilometres in three days," she collapsed on her bed without removing any of her clothes.

"Well, I am going to take a hot bath before bed," Nasah smiled at her friends whose heads both popped up.

"How are you doing that?" Parzel asked.

"Well, while you all were wolfing your food down I asked one of the girls to draw a hot bath up here..." she paused seeing the clear envy in their eyes. "Actually, I asked for three."

"You - are - the - best," Eden accented every word as she jumped up from her bed.

"Don't tell the guys, thought they can suffer some more in their stench, that last glass of ale will help them forget it," she grabbed a towel from the rack by the door. "Come on, the bath room is down here."

18

"But you are Eklektos, a royal priesthood,
holy, a nation for his own possession that
you may proclaim the excellencies of him who
called you out of darkness into his marvelous light."

For all the storms the days before, the beautiful sunrise made up for it. The clouds gave the sun the perfect canvas to paint its reds and yellows, oranges and purples hues. Eden was standing with the reins to Ruach in her hands watching as the day moon Hora rose and Alcor beside it, reflecting the sun as it crested the treetops outside of town.

"Hey, what's that smell?" Shephel asked, coming up behind her sniffing as he passed the girls and their horses.

"All I smell is horse," Parzel smiled as she mounted.

"No," Shephel said, "It's different," he sniffed again, "it's like soap or something... clean," he had a puzzled look on his face. "Guess we just smell so bad that everything else smells clean, even a stable," he shrugged, tentatively getting on his horse's back.

Eden grinned at Nasah. "Yeah, something like that I guess," she agreed, then she gave Ruach a little nudge and trotted out of the stables and onto the street.

The day remained more pleasant than previously. The clouds didn't look as sinister, but the weather was definitely cooler. Each wrapped their cloaks tight around them to try and stay warm, grateful that they were dry at least. The terrain, however, did get worse. The road became a trail, and then barely a track through some deeply rutted mud. The horses stumbled often, causing Shephel to panic and grip the life out of his pommel.

"Good thing these saddles come with a handle like that for you Shephel," Nasah laughed. He glared at her. "Could you at least try and look like you're a Chayil?" she rolled her eyes in return.

"Shut up," he growled, "not my specialty alright!," continuing to mutter under his breath.

"You weren't kidding about the road getting rough out here Nasah," Eden pulled Ruach up at the front of their line. They were now forced to ride in single file.

"What's the hold up?" Parzel asked, not being able to see around the bend in the trail.

"Tree," Eden replied over her shoulder, "we're going to have to move it I think," she slipped out of her saddle and let the reins hang. "How anyone travels these roads is beyond me," she said, kicking at some brush.

Sela and Shephel jumped down and let Nasah and Parzel keep watch and hold their horses. They ended up having to actually cut the tree into two pieces to move it before continuing their journey. Up ahead they still ended up having to get off and walk their horses over some treacherous ground to prevent them from injuring themselves. "So," Parzel called ahead as she led her horse from the rear, "Sela, what are you thinking about how you want to study for your re-test?"

"I don't know exactly." he said somewhat timidly, carefully stepping over some loose shale, "I have some ideas, I just feel bad, 'cause they all involve you guys having to do extra work for me."

Nasah laughed, "Stop that right now," she said. "If we didn't all want to do that then we wouldn't be here would we?" she asked.

"We clearly chose this team over anything else, and you are part of that team," Shephel agreed, "Argh," crying out as he slid a few feet towards the side of the trail they were walking on. "I'm okay, I'm okay," he called out once he regained his footing and the others laughed.

"Okay," Sela smiled, obviously touched that they were on his side. "Well, I was thinking, maybe when we aren't on duty that Eden and Parzel can work with me on swordsmanship and hand to hand combat?"

"For sure Sela, we will just figure out schedules once we get there," Eden nodded.

"And then Nasah, you're so great with geography and the King's words, I thought maybe you could come up with some way to tutor me in those?" he asked her.

"Yeah, I'll give it some thought while we are still travelling and work something out."

"And Shephel," he reached a hand out to again steady his friend who had just stumbled looking back when Sela had said his name. "Would you help me with some of the class work stuff? I just need help remembering things."

Shephel gratefully held his arm for a moment to balance, then sighed in relief. "Of course, I'd love to help with that."

Sela was beaming, "Great. Well, here's to hoping that our commander is understanding and will let us work around with our schedules," he said.

"There will be no special treatment, no go easy on the new guys, no preferential schedules, nothing." The old man's voice boomed at them as they all stood at attention. "You are the lowest of the low here on the outer bounds, you will have the worst time of your life until you can prove you deserve anything better. We fight battles others in this kingdom can't even dream about in their worst nightmare. Gaavah stretches in front of us and no one is letting that curse into Kaleo on my watch. My expectations are higher than any you will ever face," by now he was about an inch away from Shephel's face, the spit as he spoke hung off of Shephel's unshaven chin. "Do you understand chayil?"

"Yes sir," Shephel replied, not making eye contact and desperately restraining himself from wiping his face in disgust.

The man who had introduced himself as First Lieutenant Allon, their commanding officer at the outpost, was as rugged as they come. He was wearing a fur lined cloak, a uniform so worn that you could barely see the rank bars on the arms, his sword clearly had several notches knocked out of it from battles, his face was scarred, and a grey beard fought the cold to stick out in patches along his chin. But his eyes, they were the thing that had frozen all of them in place. There was something just not quite right there, a strange fire, maybe insanity that lay behind them, as if he'd seen too much, looked too deeply into the darkness.

"Good," he stepped back about five feet from them. Looked around as if surprised at where he was. "Your dinner is shortly, barracks are over there, and report to your lead guard Holmeman at dawn for your assignment," he turned, paused to light a cigar, and walked away.

"He'll probably let us rearrange schedules," Eden said sarcastically under her breath, and the others burst out laughing.

"That guy at the inn was right, he is crazy," Shephel took the chance now to wipe his face. "That was disgusting."

"This might be the longest year of our lives," Parzel nodded.

"I'm pretty sure Moreh hates us," Nasah muttered.

"Well, I'm getting the best bunk in there," Eden slung her saddle bags over her shoulder and pushed past them all to the barracks. She kicked open the door to find a relatively empty room. A few Chayil were still hanging around their bunks, but it seemed most had been already out heading to the mess hall, or were still on duty. One older Chayil nodded a greeting, "Women's bunks are down there, past that wall."

She nodded thanks and headed down the hall, at the end she turned past the wall referred to and found a set of ten bunk beds, most seemed taken, but in the back there were two empty racks, she flung her stuff on the top bunk just as Parzel and Nasah rounded the corner and took the bottom beds. They unpacked their stuff, stowed most of it in the footlockers at the ends of their beds, and headed back around to the mens area.

"You boys ready to try and find the mess hall?" Parzel asked, sticking her head into one of the rooms. Each room off the hallway had about twelve bunks in it, there were no doors and the walls were only three quarters high, so just enough privacy that whoever was in charge could hear what was going on everywhere.

Sela looked up from where he was putting his stuff away. "Yeah, I think so," he was on the bottom bunk, an older Chayil who didn't look impressed with the interruption was trying to sleep above him. Shephel was on the bottom bunk across from him and he quickly grabbed his cloak to follow the girls outside. "Man, you'd think we were all on a different side the way they growled at us when we came in," he pulled the cloak tight around his neck as a biting wind caught him as they left the barracks.

"There weren't any women in our room when we went in, but I can only imagine what they will be like if the guys are like that," Nasah nodded, also wrapping her cloak closer.

Together they crossed the outpost to what smelled like the mess hall. As they pushed open the doors all eyes turned to look at them. It was as if everyone froze, noises stopped and the whole room started to examine the new young Chayil.

Eden looked back awkwardly until she finally had to drop her eyes to the ground, she felt like she was back at the first day of training, getting sized up again.

Finally, everyone seemed to make their assumptions and resumed their own conversations and dinners. As eyes turned away, all five of them breathed a collective sigh.

"Really, I'm loving it here already," Parzel groaned, picking up a wooden tray and heading to the back of the food line.

Dawn found the group shivering in front of their barracks watching as their commanding officer seemed to be memorizing a clipboard of papers. The night had been relatively uneventful, in fact no one spoke to any of them. The men glared and grunted at Sela and Shephel who decided they too should be quiet and went to bed early. The girls faired little better, the other women in the barracks whispered behind their backs as they changed and pulled themselves into bed. No one offered their names or even a nod to acknowledge them. Eden hoped it was simply a sort of rookie initiation, but she wasn't sure, no one seemed quite right here.

Holmeman finally looked up from his clipboard. "Okay, you are all a part of second platoon, we are a small company out here, only three platoons, but we have several squads. Sela and Shephel," he looked, waiting for them to acknowledge him.

Both stepped forward with a "Yes sir."

"You'll be with the first squad. There are fifteen of you and you'll be heading out on morning patrol this week. You are so lucky as to have me as your Sergeant. We leave at a third of Laud today because we were waiting on you two. Get your cloak, sword, canteen and any other hand to hand weapon you might have. We will be doing exploratory sorties into the enemy territory to get as much information as we can on their movements." When the two didn't move he stepped up to Sela's face. "Did you not hear me?" he barked. "We are already waiting on you, move Chayil move," and the two sprinted back to the barracks to retrieve the items he listed.

"As for you three, you'll be up top of the wall with the third squad. Sergeant Gande will be your commanding officer. The squads switch up normally on half day shifts. We are still waiting on more replacements so we can put that down to thirds, but for now that's where we sit. Listen to Gande, he's been here forever and knows what he's talking about. You do what he says, no matter what you think," he paused and zoned in on Eden. "Do you hear me Chayil?" he barked, his dark eyes squinting into a glare as if he knew something about her already.

"Yes sir," she spouted.

"Good," he mumbled, still staring at Eden. "Go to the armoury and pick up your bows, and quivers then meet Gande on the South East parapet," he made a note on his paper, finally looking away from Eden, and turned and headed towards the command post behind them.

Eden let her shoulders droop.

"What's that for?" Nasah asked her as all three of them started towards the armory.

"Guard duty?" Eden asked incredulously, "that's all we get to do?" She threw up her hands. "Those two goofs get to go out and engage the enemy, do something while the three of us, who could run circles around them in a fight, get to stand still for half a day on a wall?" she shook her head.

"I didn't think about it like that," Parzel said slowly, contemplating Eden's words.

"It's a waste," she spat. "If this is some stupid, 'we're men and you're women' thing I'm going to pick a fight with one of them just to prove I can take them all."

"I don't think it is," Nasah argued. "We've never seen that in anything in training."

"Yeah, but did you notice, out of this whole company there's like what? Ten women? What's that about? Think they can't handle the outer limits?"

"I'm sure there's a million reasons why there aren't more women," Nasah said, "I mean, clearly anyone with brains wouldn't take this placement," and all three of them started laughing.

Eden sighed and pushed open the door to the armoury. They were met with the sound of blacksmiths pounding out steel, fires roaring as the metal smelted and racks upon racks of swords, arrows, shields, spears and bucklers. They moved through the rows a bit in awe of the amount of weaponry hanging here until they found someone who looked like he was in charge.

"Hey new recruits," he smiled, the first smile they'd received from anyone here. "Welcome to Gehenna," he spread his arms and pointed towards the fires behind him. He laughed at his own joke. "What? You guys have no humour?" he looked offended.

"To be honest, no one has even smiled at us since we've gotten here, so not sure how to take you," Parzel admitted.

"Oh, yeah, they are all pretty rough on newbies," he stuck out his hand. "They call me Coal."

Eden took his hand and introduced herself, Parzel and Nasah. "We just got here from Migdal. Just graduated."

"And hence the reason no one has smiled at you," he laughed.

"Why is that?" Parzel asked puzzled.

"Honestly? I probably shouldn't tell you," he took a second to pause. "We lose more new grads than anyone. It's not an easy placement out here and usually the ones we lose are the ones who haven't been here more than a week," he shrugged, "no one wants to get attached, it's too hard." He nodded towards a pile of damaged armour. "That was our last two new grads'. Didn't make it three days, it's hard on the heart and mind to get attached. But if you make it, these guys will be yours for life. They'd do anything for each other."

The girls simply stared open mouthed, until Eden finally got her voice back. "But come on, they put us up on the wall. How dangerous can that be? We haven't had an incursion at a guard post in years," she was quoting her history.

"Not that you've heard of," Coal snorted. "They've never got more than hundred steps, but they've gotten inside, lots of times," he started pulling some quivers out for them and making notes in his log book. "Serving on the wall seems safest but it's in the perceived safety that is the greatest danger. The guys out in the sorties, they're the safest I say. Can see the enemy, know the battle. It's not like that on the wall. You'll learn," he handed each of them a quiver. "Now, on that back wall is a bunch of arrows, I'd like to say they are all straight and true, but a few misfits slip through so pick yours carefully. Then the bows are near the door, feel free to try them out, make sure you have a good feel," he waved them away, "Oh wait," he tossed each of them a finger tab. "Fingers get pretty sore when you're holding your bow string for so long."

"Can I use my own bow?" Eden asked.

"No, these are specially fitted for distance and weight. Only real use is up on the wall, when you're out on other duty use your own," he instructed.

Parzel thanked Coal and they made their way to the arrows and bows. After each choosing fifteen arrows they felt comfortable with, they spent some time going through and trying the bows. Checking the fistmele, trying different weights, different woods. Eventually each of them found one they were satisfied with. "Woah, it's almost a third past Laud, we had better get up on the wall and find this Gande guy," Nasah pointed out.

They rushed from the armoury, calling a goodbye to Coal and were hit with an icy blast of wind. They wrapped their cloaks tightly around themselves, and found their way to the southeast section of the wall. They trudged up the five flights of stairs and were met by the oldest Chayil any of them had ever seen. He glanced up at them from where he had been leaning on the wall staring into the grey. He had a rugged old bow slung across his back, a looking glass, like a sailor might have, hanging from his neck, and when he straightened up, which was with much difficulty, they saw that he had a staff to hold himself up with. He turned towards them.

Eden could see about ten other Chayil spread out along the wall at what was about fifty step intervals. Each one was staring out into the grey that was surrounding the wall. Some had their bow in hand, but most had it on their back. But every single one was staring as if he could see something out there. Eden turned her head and could barely see the tops of the trees ten feet from the wall, she couldn't imagine what they were all focused on. Not one turned towards them, just Sgt Gande.

"'Bout time you all got here," he rumbled from lungs that sounded like they might breathe their last at any moment. "You all suited up? Bow, quivers, canteens?" They nodded. "Good," he leaned behind the door and pulled out three looking glasses, and small leather pouches. "You'll need these," he nodded to the scopes, "it'll take some time to adjust your eyes to the grey, so I'm posting you between seasoned Chayil. The bag has some beef jerky in it. My wife makes it, keeps us all on our toes for the shift. Has a bit of a kick, just to warn you," he laughed at what he clearly felt was his own joke.

"Alright," he hobbled on his staff and waved for them to follow him. "You clearly made enough of an impression in Migdal to get sent here. They only give us the ones they think can do this and survive, and they aren't always right," he sniffed. "So prove 'em right," he said it as a command that he expected them to follow, "but some ground rules they don't teach you in the academy," he pointed with his right hand towards the grey, exposing a similar ring as Moreh's on his index finger. "You shoot at nothing. I don't care what you see, you don't shoot."

"What?" Parzel said, taking her eyes off his ring, "that makes no sense."

"You listen to me Chayil. The only time you shoot that bow is if you see the enemy actually attacking," he turned to face her, an inch from her nose. "You do not give away our positions for any reason," he turned and kept walking. "The enemy is scouting, they can't see the wall, or our armaments, but they know it's here, they feel the arrows, but they are always trying to figure it out. We are sheltered by the King, but if we give them an opening they will flood that hole with all they've got. You shoot an arrow because you see something, then they know where you are, they know your position … our position and they might not be able to breach the wall itself, but they can take us down if they can find us."

He stopped beside a Chayil, "Brant, move down I'm putting one of the newbies in here," the Chayil nodded, grabbed his stuff and jogged to the end of the line. "You, Eden?" he asked, and continued when she nodded "You stay here."

"So, what exactly are we doing if we aren't to shoot anything?" Nasah asked.

"We have to know the enemy's strategies if we are to defeat them. They show themselves as they try to find us and our weaknesses. Our sorties have brought back tonnes of information for the King, we even do undercover missions into some of the neighbouring towns. And as a last resort, if one of our squads comes under attack out there, they know they just have to run to the wall and then and only then, you take down the enemy," he glared at them. "Do I make myself clear?"

"Yes sir," all three replied in unison.

"Good, you two follow me," he left Eden there, and Parzel and Nasah gave her a shrug. As Eden watched them walk away from her she tried to sum up her courage and at least look like she had a clue what was happening. She took her bow off her back, fit the finger tab on and then stared out into the grey. After ten minutes of literally seeing nothing, she glanced at the Chayil closest to her out of the corner of her eye. He had his bow on his back, looking glass in hand and his brow was in a little furrow, as if he was watching something. Eden tried to follow his gaze but shook her head to herself, it was just grey, like a pea soup thick fog.

Just then the Chayil she had been watching turned to her with a crooked smile. "Name's Lucky," he said.

"Eden" she replied, somewhat embarrassed he obviously saw her watching him.

"Having trouble seeing?" he asked.

She nodded, "Honestly," lowering her voice so the others, especially Sgt Gande wouldn't hear her. "I have no idea what I'm looking for, and if I see something I'm not supposed to do anything?"

"Yeah, Sarge isn't the best at explaining things, but as you get more time up here with him, just listen, he is a fountain of wise information. Taught me everything I know, just took a while, and me listening carefully, especially when he's not talking to you," he laughed, then stepped closer to Eden. "Let me help," he said, coming right beside her and focusing out past the wall. "Okay, so about a hundred feet from the wall is the start of the forest. It's not thick there, just a few trees, and takes about another hundred feet to fill in. If you can approximate that distance you'll be able to start focusing and seeing the base of the tree trunks, about, right there," he pointed and pulled Eden's head down to his arm so she could follow his finger. "Can you see it?"

Eden squinted, then did again, and finally pulled the looking glass out. "Yes," she exclaimed suddenly. "I can see it."

"Now put the glass down and see it with just your eye," Lucky instructed.

Eden did, and after a few more minutes she could actually make out the trunks of the first few scattered trees.

"You just focus on learning to see," Lucky smiled, giving her a pat on the shoulder. "I'll keep my eyes open for both of us but if you see anything else, just shout and I'll come over. It takes time for your eyes to learn to see again out here. The light is different, the grey is different, you have to learn to discern the grey and eventually you'll know what's actually black and white," he sauntered back over to his guard post, pulled a bit of jerky from a pouch and settled back into his surveillance.

Eden didn't see Nasah and Parzel the rest of their shift, but she definitely felt like this was the longest half day of her life. Sgt Gande would wander by on occasion, checking each Chayil in the squad, making sure everyone had water and jerky still. He relieved each in turn so they could sit and eat some lunch, use the latrine and he was always muttering some sort of instruction, word of wisdom or proverbs as he walked by. "A clear eye makes the whole body light," he said once as he passed Eden, "but if the light is darkness, how great is that darkness." She didn't feel like she fully understood most of them, but like Lucky said, she tried to pay attention and planned on writing them down when she got back to her room. "I'll bring my journal with me next time," she promised herself.

Finally, she heard boots on the stairs and squad four tumbled out onto the wall to relieve them. Eden had never been so glad of anything in all her life. She nodded to the man who took her spot and then slung her glass and bow over her back and started for the stairs.

"Same time tomorrow Chayil," Gande called to them, "and leave your bags so my wife can fill them up." Eden had noticed each man was dropping his little bag of jerky beside the Sarge as he passed, she quickly pulled the last piece of hers out and deposited the bag too.

"Good work Eden, seems like you were getting the hang of it," he nodded. "Now I hear you all have some work to do in off hours eh?" When she looked puzzled at him he continued. "Your fellow Chayil, Sela?"

"Oh, yes sir. We are working with him," she was surprised he knew.

"So I heard, so get to it. I expect a lot," he grumbled.

As Eden hit the bottom stair Parzel came up behind her, then Nasah. "Did he just tell you to get working with Sela?" Parzel asked.

"Yeah he did." Eden nodded. "Weird, that he'd know that."

"I don't know, he had something about him that reminded me of Moreh," Nasah said, dropping her glass into her backpack.

"Really?" Eden was surprised.

"Yeah, maybe it was just the grumpy disposition and lack of information with the expectation that we'd know what to do," Nasah laughed at her own joke, and the others joined in. "No, but for real, not sure what it was."

"Huh," Parzel mumbled. "Well, I guess we should find Sela and Shephel and see if they managed to live through their first day or not," she stretched her back. "Even though all I want to do is sleep. How do you get so tired doing nothing but staring into fog?"

Together they made their way back to the barracks hoping to find their friends.

19

"As you come to him, a living stone rejected by many
but in the sight of the king eklektos and precious,
like living stones built up as a powerful house,
a holy priesthood to offer sacrifices acceptable to the king."

When the girls came into the barracks they realized right away that Sela and Shephel weren't back yet. Their bunks sat empty, so they decided to get their own supper and wait for them. As the evening got later they started to get worried.

"It's past Vesper now, they've been gone for five watches!"

"Thanks for the update," Parzel raised her eyebrows, "can you stop with the count downs?" Nasah had been checking the sentinel since they had sat down to eat.

"I'm worried," she mumbled.

"We all are," Eden agreed and glared at Parzel.

"It's just, what you said Eden," she looked up, "that we could run circles around them, they aren't the best yet and now they've been gone so long. I mean, my brother can be smart, but not all the time."

Parzel stood up. "Hey, look," she pointed through the tarped doorway of the dining tent, "I can see some Chayil coming in the gate." Sure enough, the others saw boots clumping past the doorway headed to the barracks.

Eden jogged over to the door. "Hey!" she yelled when she spotted Sela's massive back and bald head. He turned and smiled a tired grin.

"We'll be in there soon," he waved and dragged his feet into the barracks.

After the guys had thrown on some clean clothes they joined the girls in the dining tent and wolfed down their supper like they had never eaten.

As they were finishing up, Nasah finally asked. "So? What was it like? Why were you so late getting back? Was it dangerous?"

"Woah, sis," Shephel put up his hand and wiped his mouth with his shirt sleeve. "Let's go for one question at a time."

"It wasn't really hard," Sela jumped in. "We were scouting, so we were pretty much in silence most of the time. You follow in a single line, you can see a bit better down on the ground in the grey, at least a bit further, but it's cold and wet, worse than here on the edge. Someone is on point, and we just keep our eyes open for the enemy."

Shephel took up the story. "The guys with us are alright, though still haven't talked much. But they told us what to do and kept their eyes on us. After we had stopped for a quick lunch of bread and cheese our guy on point suddenly signaled for all of us to be quiet. We were just about twenty feet off a trail, and as we crouched and got into cover all of a sudden a bunch of Nachash's soldiers start filing past. They seemed in a hurry and were completely unaware of us, so we decided to follow behind and see what the rush was. We are being all stealthy and keeping behind them, when we break out of the trees, and below us is this town, and it's not covered in grey. That was the weirdest part, everything seemed totally normal, like any town we would have passed through."

"Turns out the grey is only like a band dividing Kaleo from Gavaah, you can pass through it. No one seemed to know if it was put there by the King or Nachash. But as soon as you're out of it the weather changes. It's hot and dry, pretty barren for the most part."

Shephel swallowed his drink and went on in his best storyteller voice. "So we spread out along the tree line, because obviously we don't have cover without the grey in the middle of the day. Sgt Holmeman wants to investigate, not sure why he was so interested but he was. He sent two guys down through the fields to see if they could hear any conversations and see what's happening. Problem was, when they got down, they found a spot off an alley where they could overhear some of the people, but then this huge crowd came down the street and it was like they were holding a meeting or something and the guys couldn't get out. It lasted for hours and I guess Sarge had some way of communicating with them, cause he knew they were okay and just waiting it out, but it meant we had to just sit and stay. Nothing else happened, no one else came by, and it wasn't till the sun went down that the street cleared enough for them to get out and get back to us. Then we still had to hike it all the way back here. Hence, we were late."

"That's interesting," Eden said, mulling things over in her head. "Did you hear what the scouts heard or saw?"

"Nope, they huddled up with Holmeman but no one thought the rest of us should hear anything, we just tried to double time it back here," Sela shrugged. "But I'm so tired, I don't think I have anything left in me to study any more tonight," he looked uncomfortable.

"Yeah, that's going to be a problem," Parzel nodded. "We're pretty exhausted too, so not sure how we're going to be able to make this work out here, it's not like we got some simple duty."

"Tell us about your day," Shephel asked, after going to get another cup of hot qahua.

The girls started telling them about Coal, the armoury and the wall duty. Trying to explain the bits and pieces of information that they managed to get.

"In truth, we still don't know exactly what we are doing or what we are looking for," Parzel admitted.

"Yeah, I saw trees, that's it," Eden shrugged.

"According to Holmeman we switch up to wall duty next week, I assume you guys would be out on the scouting missions then," Sela replied

"I don't know, I mean, you need two squads to fill the wall duty for half the day, we might end up being on nights," Nasah said thoughtfully, "in which case tutoring is going to be even more of a challenge," she looked at Sela.

"Okay, we have to make a plan," Eden finally said. "If we don't none of us will want to work after hours."

"Right," Parzel agreed and reached to pull a piece of parchment from her coat pocket along with a piece of charcoal. "So, tonight, we won't train - but tomorrow we do, and hope you guys don't get stuck anywhere. Let's start with some hand to hand combat stuff, since you guys will possibly need it, and we will need to do something so our minds don't go crazy staring at nothing all day," she sketched a little chart out. "We will rotate, in pairs. Sorry Sela, you'll have to be there every day."

"Yeah," he grinned. "I figured that."

"Eden and I will start tomorrow, then Nasah and Shephel the next. We will meet in the training ring after supper."

Everyone nodded, then they slowly gathered up their dishes to deposit them in the wash barrels and headed back to their bunks to try and rest.

The following day found them all working hard in their respective squads. Eden felt like she was starting to see more in the grey, either that or her mind was playing tricks on her now. Lucky was beside her, and seemed to have decided he was going to help her learn. He'd give her little ideas, point out things like animals passing by, which helped a lot in distinguishing things in the grey, to actually see something moving. Gande handed out his wife's beef jerky again and they wrapped up their watch heading to the dining tent.

Thankfully, this time Sela and Shephel were back earlier, and were already eating by the time the girls arrived. "Hey," Sela mumbled between bites.

"Anything exciting today?" Parzel asked, dropping her plate down beside them.

Sela shook his head and Shephel answered, "Nah, we double timed it through the grey to the town and sat there watching it all day. Seemed pretty normal, we didn't even send scouts down, but Holmeman was writing a tonne of notes," he shrugged. "Don't know about what."

"I saw a rabbit today," Nasah smiled, proud of herself.

Sela snorted. "Who'd have thought that'd be our big accomplishment eh?" and the others laughed.

"Alright," Eden smiled. "As soon as we are done eating we are hitting the training yard," Sela wiped his face and nodded.

Eden and Parzel went back and forth for two thirds of a watch with Sela, going over all sorts of fighting techniques, using weapons, without them, finding what's around you to make use of them. Sela seemed to be doing well. Finally after taking down Parzel using a nice leg sweep, he stood there panting.

"I wish I was this good with all the maps and stuff," he wiped the sweat dripping from his head and helped Parzel up. "I feel like that's what I failed during the testing."

Eden high fived him. "That might be true, but improving everything isn't going to hurt, and it's going to be good for all of us here. Let's call it a night, I need to shower," she picked up her cloak and tossed Parzel and Sela theirs.

"Wait, can you throw the knife?" Sela grinned, "Just once?" he looked like a little kid wanting a treat.

Eden slid her knife out of its sheath on her belt and let her hand feel the weight of it. "What if it doesn't work if I'm just playing with it?" she asked him, with a sideways grin on her face.

"Well, guess you can stop training me then," he laughed, confident it'd work and all of a sudden there was a blur past his face and Eden's knife was embedded in the beam beside him! "No fair, I didn't even see! You could have just missed and not even aimed at me!"

Eden laughed, "Ha, like I could miss that big body," and Parzel started to laugh too. "Only a miracle of the King can make me do that!" she retrieved the knife. "Okay fine," she agreed again, secretly as fascinated at how the knife worked as the others. She'd often tried throwing it at her own foot to see it move, but she never told anyone. "Parzel, stand still."

She took a stance against another beam and spread her arms out. "I'm trying to give you as big a target as Sela."

"Hey!" he cried but laughed all the same.

"Okay, let's see if we are still friends," Eden smiled mischievously. She took careful aim at her friend's head and threw with all her might. All three watched the knife instead sink deeply into the beam above Parzel's hair.

"You know, maybe you should play this game by throwing at a less critical part of my body!" she exclaimed, stepping away and looking at the knife, just a sliver above where she stood.

"Yeah, I guess there's no telling when you might turn on me," Eden laughed and again retrieved the knife, pausing to consider the gravity of what she'd said.

Just then Lucky came into the training yard. "What the heck was that about?" he exclaimed, walking quickly up to Eden to examine the knife in her hand.

"Oh," she said, surprised and embarrassed. She didn't actually want news of any "eklektos" stuff getting out here, it wasn't the type of crowd that would handle that well she thought. "We were just playing around. Lucky this is Sela," she tried to change the conversation.

"No, you weren't! The first time I thought you aimed beside him, but that time I saw the whole thing. You threw right at her and yet it moved!"

"Really?" Parzel tried to help Eden, "I just thought she had bad aim."

"What's the deal?" he asked again. "Come on, what have you got here," he extended his hand to see it.

Eden sighed. "Fine," she placed it in his palm. "I was given this at Migdal, it's got special properties, if I throw it can distinguish between friend and enemy. It will never hit a friend, no matter how close I am or how well I throw."

He was rolling the knife over in his hand and tracing the inscription. "Do you know what this is?" he exclaimed. "I mean, do you know what this means?" he clearly knew his history. "I guess you do," he looked up at Eden suddenly and handed the knife back. "Sorry, I'm just..." he actually looked nervous. "I'm going to go now," and he turned to exit the yard.

"Lucky, it's not a big deal. Really, nothing special!" she tried calling after him, but he just sort of waved and slipped around the corner.

Parzel stepped up beside Eden. "Don't worry about it. I'm sure he won't say anything, and even if he does, it doesn't change anything. I mean, what the heck do we do here? Watch rabbits! Can't be using any special 'eklektosness' here I'm thinking." Eden smacked her on the arm.

"Thanks" she mumbled, "Come on, let's head back," and the three walked back to the barracks in silence.

The next morning they discovered how "few" people Lucky had talked to. As soon as Eden and Parzel walked into the dining hall every head turned to stare at them. "What did you say last night?" Eden muttered out of the side of her mouth.

"Maybe it's me," Parzel tried to lighten the tension. "I mean, I am rocking this whole outfit today," she attempted a laugh but Eden just walked away.

As they sat eating their breakfast Parzel mumbled between bites of toast, "this is ridiculous. No one has given us the time of day before now, and now they can't stop talking about us."

"Me," Eden corrected her

"What?" Parzel looked up.

"Me, they are talking about me," Eden grumbled.

"Well, la ti dah little Miss special. I forgot this was all about you," Parzel dropped her toast on her plate and pushed her chair back, obviously annoyed.

"What? I didn't ask for this, I don't do anything differently and yet I'm the one who has to deal with... with whatever this is. You don't, so stop acting like you do," she snarled angrily.

"Right, I forgot, nothing you do affects anyone else!" Parzel slapped herself in the forehead. "My mistake," she stood. "Fine, wave to your fans all by yourself then," and she grabbed her qahua and walked out.

Eden sighed and looked miserably into her own drink.

"Where did Parzel stalk off to?" Nasah asked dropping her plate beside Eden's.

"I kind of ticked her off," Eden admitted.

"Intentionally?" Nasah tilted her head at Eden, glancing at the other Chayil who kept stealing looks and then whispering.

"Yeah, I wanted to be mad and a donkey and I guess I accomplished it," she sighed again.

"Because Lucky clearly told everyone you're the eklektos?" Nasah asked, not even glancing up from her breakfast.

"You noticed?" Eden snorted.

Just then Sargent Gande burst into the dining hall. "Is no one in this place on duty anymore?" he bellowed. "You're all late!" Fire seemed to burn in his eyes. "Get your sorry boots out of here before I throw you all out in the grey!" Everyone started to rush at the same moment for the door. "Goes for you too Nasah and Eden, no special eklektos rules," his comment earning him some laughs.

'Great," Eden rolled her eyes and shoved the last of her bread in her mouth. At the end of their shift on the wall, during which everyone avoided speaking to Eden, even Gande seemed to ignore her, she was finally able to get a hold of Parzel.

"Zel," Eden grabbed her shoulder before she could get across the courtyard.

"What your highness?" Parzel mocked.

"I deserved that," Eden dropped her eyes. "Listen, I'm sorry. I know all this affects all of you too, I just don't know what to do or how to deal with it. It was the same when I got to Migdal the first time. You guys treated me like this," she pleaded. "I just don't know if I can deal with it again, I felt so alone then."

Parzel softened instantly, looking at Eden's tormented expression. "Yeah, I was a donkey, or a jerk as you like to say, wasn't I?" she laughed and got a smile out of her friend. "I know, I'm sorry I got so angry," she pulled her into a hug. "But it's different this time," she pushed Eden to arm's length and gripped both her shoulders. "You have a team who knows that you're nothing special!"

Eden punched her in the gut. "Still a jerk," but laughing she started to tear up. "You're right, I know."

"So you – we - do what you did when you arrived in training. We kick everyone's butt at everything and act like it's nothing unusual. They have to respect that at least, I know we did." She put her arm around her friend and they started towards the barracks.

Just then Nasah ran up on Eden's other side. "Hey, would you guys help me today with Sela's training? I need some ideas how to test his geography and memory skills."

Parzel looked at Eden and both smiled. "Let's do it," Eden agreed, and all three headed off to meet the guys patrol coming back in.

The rest of the week went about the same. People whispered and talked behind their backs. Sometimes they could catch a few words and phrases. It mostly consisted of doubt as to whether this girl could possibly be the eklektos the prophecies had talked about. Sometimes there seemed to be a bit of hope in the conversations that there might come a grand victory soon, and not a few seemed slightly in awe of Eden and her team. But they did what Parzel suggested. They worked so hard at each of their duties, no matter how difficult or painful. After the first week they switched up so that the girls squad was also out on patrol, this made training more difficult because they were scheduled opposite each other, but they made it work sometimes with Sela practicing and studying alone, other times working together when they should have been sleeping or eating. Their work ethic was duly noted and their commanding officers soon stopped any jokes or comments about the eklektos and had even begun chastising other Chayil who commented or treated any of them differently.

Although the attitudes were getting easier to deal with the work wasn't. All of them agreed this was one of the hardest jobs. The hours of monotony, and then the need to be sharp for the rare but dangerous moments when the enemy came close to the walls. It was a nightmare on the senses. Shephel joked he was going to have a permanent nervous twitch soon, they all laughed but agreed it really could happen. Some of the oldest Chayil there seemed to be a bit - unhinged. But they were getting used to it, and Sela was improving, and soon the weeks slipped into months, and his re-tests were looming.

20

"Well, this has been a rare blessing," Parzel remarked, half way into their shift on the top of the wall. She looked down the wall at her four friends who were spaced apart from her.

"Yeah," Eden nodded, still squinting at the grey. "I never thought they'd let us serve together. And it couldn't have been better timing, with Sela's re-test next week, we will all be on the same schedule to train."

Lucky was next to Eden, he never quite got back to his friendly self since he made the connection with her knife. She thought that he was always sort of looking out the corner of his eye at her, but at least he was willing to serve beside her now. He had spent a few weeks being as far from her as he could get in the squad. "You guys are pretty good friends to work so hard with him," he commented, having overheard them.

"Well, we kind of banked all our futures on him passing, so we are sort of invested," Eden smiled.

"What do you mean?" he turned, a puzzled look on his face.

"Well, the four of us got offered spots to go into Gibbor training, but he failed. We had worked so close as a team and knew his heart, and honestly I don't think any of us would rather serve with someone else, so we said we wouldn't move on without him," Parzel explained, leaning on her bow.

"You're kidding right?" Lucky asked, looking back and forth between the two of them. "You didn't seriously say that to the King?"

Eden turned sheepishly back towards the grey. "Yeah - we did."

Parzel smiled."Presumptuous beggars eh?" laughing at their own audacity.

"I can't believe it. And he didn't kick you all out on the spot?" Lucky leaned on his bow as well.

"Yeah, we kind of all expected that, but apparently he values teams and individuals over test scores, so he sent us all out here and set up Sela's re-test and if he passes, then we all move on to Gibbor training," Eden shrugged. "I mean, it sort of makes sense now that I think about it. So much of the King's words are about supporting each other, putting others first, and they spent so much time on making us a team. Of course, at the time I didn't think about any of those things when I opened my mouth," she smiled again, remembering her own shock as the words left her lips.

"Well, you must have some kind of courage to speak up to the King like that at least," Lucky shook his head in disbelief.

At the same moment, all three of their heads spun around as they heard the sound of a bow twang and an arrow flew out into the grey.

"What are you doing?" Lucky shouted at Sela who was on his right side with bow in hand.

"There!" Sela pointed. "A scout was right on the base of the wall!"

They followed his finger to the body that lay crumpled at the base of the wall directly below them.

All of a sudden ten more enemy soldiers appeared and made a bee line for the downed man. Within seconds they had shot grappling hooks up and were already scaling the wall by the time Sargent Gande could give the warning.

"Look to the hooks!" he pointed. "We have to release the hooks! Get them off the wall!"

Their squads scrambled, several further down the line started shooting at the enemies climbing the ropes, but their angle was difficult and they seemed to climb like ants so only one arrow found its mark, thankfully taking another enemy out as the first fell.

Sela started immediately in on the first grappling hook. With his brute strength he managed to muscle the claws from the wall and fling it over the side, sending five others to their doom in the fall. But no one else could get the hooks off and in what seemed like a breath, three of the enemy had made the top of the wall.

Parzel engaged the first with her sword, Gande had moved so quickly, his staff left behind, that as the next man who gained the top and had straightened, he planted a swift round house kick to his midsection and sent him off the battlements. Lucky was fighting hand to hand with another man. Eden didn't dare try and get into the fight with Lucky, afraid that she might send both he and the enemy to their deaths as they were intertwined. He would have to battle this out on his own for now, but as Parzel had her back to her and was straining against her opponent, Eden drew her knife and without a second thought hurled it at the man. It sunk deep into his throat just as he was about to bring down his blade on Parzel again. He froze and gasped, his eyes wide. Then his sword dropped from his hand and his eyes glazed over and he toppled backwards into the outpost and lay still.

At that moment Lucky managed to get in a solid punch to his opponents kidney, crumpling the man at which point Sela grabbed him from behind and pinned his arms behind him in an awkward headlock. The man stopped struggling and glared at Lucky.

"All clear Sarge!" Shephel called from down the line. They could still see the forms of the bodies lying immobile at the base of the wall, but no other movement seemed to come from the grey.

"Everyone okay?" Gande asked, looking at Lucky and Parzel.

"Yes sir," both responded, swords still at the ready and looking at the man who seemed resigned to his fate in Sela's grip.

"Sela and Lucky, take this one to the cells then meet back here. Parzel and Eden, go clean up this one," he pointed to the man inside the wall. "And you two tell Allon what happened then get a team to clear the base of the walls," he pointed at two other men. "And quick about it, we don't need to give anything else away for Nachash."

Everyone sprang into action. As Parzel and Eden turned the man over they both paused. "Doesn't get easier does it?" Eden asked, looking at the man and thinking he could be any of them.

"Nope, but by the grace of the King it's not us," Parzel nodded, sharing Eden's thoughts. "And I've never been happier for your 'party trick' with that knife!" she patted her friend on the back. "Felt it fly right by my ear and was glad we are friends!"

"Yeah, me too." Eden bent down frowning as she pulled the knife out of the man. She stabbed it into the ground to clean off the blood then slipped it back into her belt. Together they went through the man's pockets, and finding nothing but a couple of knives, took his body to the medical clinic to be removed and buried.

They finished just as Sela was returning to the wall and they walked up together. Gande stopped them at the top. "I want to talk to you all," he handed each a piece of his wife's jerky. "You're still new, so I want to explain this situation." He turned to Sela. "You all reacted well, fought well, but the whole thing shouldn't have happened."

Sela frowned. "What do you mean sir? That man was on the wall, he had a hand on it."

Gande nodded. "Yes he did. But if you'd left him alone, he'd have wandered back into the grey with his troop. Just because he felt something doesn't mean he's going to attack it. All it says to him is there's an obstacle. But as soon as you engaged, you showed his troop where we were, you exposed us and what Nachash knows and teaches his men is that where there are men there are flaws. There is always a chance that one of us will fall, or fail as a squad, the wall can't be beaten but man can be."

"So he would never have tried to scale it without me shooting at him?" Sela's face was concerned.

"No, because he has no idea how tall it is. Is there a top, can it be accessed? And the way the King has made this wall, although it never moves, the grey makes it appear to be in different locations each time to them. Their eyes are veiled."

"So, I messed this whole thing up?" Sela's eyes dropped to the ground.

"No, not really," Gande assured him. "We fought well, no one was injured, it was a good test, and I liked seeing Eden's little weapon there," he glanced over at her and she unconsciously put her hand on her knife. "And we captured one, that's rare, they usually kill themselves first, so hopefully we can get some sort of information out of him," he paused. "But I want you to understand our strategy, at this point we are not on the offensive here. Our job is to protect the people behind us. We don't need to go looking for a fight, because the more info we give to Nachash the better prepared he is. He is a master strategist, I have to give him that. We lose our people because he outsmarts us," he paused again, thinking about something else. "One day we will go on the offensive, and then we will see who has learned more." He took a step back to allow them room to pass. "Back to your posts," he barked, and they hurried back.

As they walked off the wall later Eden caught Sela's arm, "You ready to practice?" she asked as she slung her bow over her shoulder.

"Yeah, I guess," he replied. Eden watched him walk towards the barracks, uncharacteristically quiet. She assumed he was still thinking about the shift and all that Gande had said. She knew she was. It still seemed so counter-intuitive to let the enemy walk right up to the wall and not do anything about it. And yet, what happened today clearly demonstrated the problem. She had seen other days when the enemy had walked close and all they did was alert each other and watch them and like Sarge said, they just left. She had always thought that was an odd plan, in her mind it made sense to get rid of as many of the enemy as you could, when you could. But then again, looking at that soldier as she pulled the knife out of him she couldn't help but think there wasn't much difference. Change one thing in her life and she could be him, doing her best for the wrong side. So maybe there was a chance that the King could save those who served Nachash? She shook her head, having reached her bunk she dropped her bag and changed into more comfortable clothes. Thinking too much about this hurt her brain, she trusted the King so she was going to do what He said, and that was all she needed to know right now. At least now she knew he had put the Grey there as a protection. She grabbed her sword and knife and headed back out to the training yard.

By the time she reached it everyone was already there.

"Great, so now that we're all here, I thought we could go over a plan for this week," Nasah started. "I think that we should spend today and tomorrow on the fitness test portion, then the following two days you should study all the geography and medical topics and then I'll give you an exam that I wrote. We can mark it and then the next day you actually go to the re-test." She looked for everyone's agreement. They all nodded, Nasah was always the best planner, so it made sense to do what she came up with, plus it meant that the rest of them had the last three days off from training.

"Alright,"s he looked at Eden. "Can you set up some test components for him to run through?"

Eden twirled her sword in her hand, "Sounds good." She glanced around the training field. "Let's start with a little interval set."

She went about setting each of them into different positions, sword fighting, archery, hand to hand, balance and explained the runs between each for Sela to do. "Generally they would time you, but I don't have a standard time to run you against, so we will just see if you can improve on it by tomorrow. It's not just better training, but it's using your mind to do things faster, more efficiently and still win," she explained.

Sela nodded to her. "Yeah, I think I'm starting to get that concept."

"And you're in your best shape ever," Nasah encouraged him.

"Let's get started." Eden looked at her personal sentinel she had bought before they left and then shouted, "go!"

Sela fought Parzel with the short sword and when he finally disarmed her he sprinted to the gateway and rushed to face Shephel in hand to hand. This was always his strongest skill and he bested him quickly and set off on another sprint. He came back to face Eden with a broad sword. He always tended to use his brute strength which usually allowed Eden to take advantage of an opening when he would be unprotected from the follow through of a giant swing but this time he kept his swings tighter, didn't over extend, and when she did, in an attempt to draw him out, he countered on her weak side and pinned her sword to the ground.

Eden smiled as he dropped his sword and ran for another sprint, she was surprised and pleased. He quickly shot ten targets that Nasah had set before running his last sprint and pulled up in front of Eden. He was breathing heavily but not badly out of breath.

"Wow Sela," Parzel glanced at the dial. "I'm so proud of you. That was really fast and the first time you have ever beaten Eden!"

Sela smiled at her and beamed to see them all looking so proudly at him. "I tried what Sarge said, don't let them see you fight. I didn't let her see my strength so that I could use it at the right moment."

"Huh," Eden grunted. "That's a really great application of that Sela. I never thought of it like that, makes total sense," she nodded.

"Thanks, I guess," he mumbled, embarrassed by the praise.

"Well, I'd say that's going to be hard to beat tomorrow," Parzel smiled at his awkward shyness, "but even if you don't, that was a great time." She punched him playfully in the arm, trying to get him to look up.

"I am all for dinner then," Shephel said. "If we are done embarrassing the poor guy. You're going to make him too shy to even go to the test the way you guys are going on," he laughed and grabbed him by the shoulder. "Come on big guy, the gross stuff they call qahua here is on me."

The team continued to grill Sela. Although he didn't beat his time from the first day, he did tie it and seemed a lot more confident in his skills now. The next two days were definitely not his favourites though the rest of the team enjoyed the time off. He spent his off hours with Nasah going over his geography and medical skills. At one point they asked Eden to come in as a victim and she spent the next two hours wrapped up into some creepy version of a mummy with every extremity bandaged or taped to fix one ailment or another. When Sela started to recite poisons and their antidotes she quickly excused herself, trying to tear the bandages so she could get out before he started practicing those on her.

After two days of review, Nasah gave him her exam and he spent three hours pouring over the pages. Eden and Parzel were playing dice outside the little library that was in their outpost when they heard the heavy door swing open behind them. They looked up to see a frazzled looking Sela gripping the exam in his fist.

"There!" he exclaimed and handed it to them. "That was like ten times harder than the one we wrote with Moreh," he wiped his forehead. "Let me know what I get on it, I need a break." Without another word he turned and headed to his bed.

Eden smiled at Parzel. "Ready to practice being a master?" she joked.

"Only if I can be Petros," Parzel frowned at the paper in front of them. "What is this rubbish?" she quipped in her best Master Petros voice.

Eden almost fell off her chair with laughter. "That was perfect! You should go on the road doing impersonations if this Chayil thing doesn't work out."

Parzel laughed. "Okay, where is Nasah's answer sheet, we probably don't know these either," she pulled the sheets from her bag, pushing the dice aside. They spent the next third going over Sela's test and surprised themselves at some of the questions and answers. Once they finished, they called the whole team together.

Sela was standing awkwardly just behind everyone else. "Do we all have to be here to get my scores?" he muttered.

"I think it's a good idea, I mean we stuck our necks out for you, you know," Parzel shamed him.

"Yeah, and it's a good thing we did," Eden continued. "You scored a ninety-five percent on this!" she exclaimed, waving the paper in her hand.

"I did what?" Sela looked dumbfounded.

"He got what?" Nasah exclaimed. "Did you mark it right?"

"Yep!" Parzel pulled the exam from Eden and thrust it at Nasah. "We didn't even know half the answers. He nailed it!"

Nasah opened the exam and went over it in her hand, her face breaking into a smile. "Well, unless you are the best cheater in the world... this is incredible!" she threw her arms around Sela and hugged the big man. He gently squeezed her back, not sure what to do with this kind of show of emotion.

"You're going to rock tomorrow," Shephel slapped him on the back.

Just then another Chayil came into the practice area. "Hey Sela," he held out a piece of paper. "Letter came from Migdal for you." He handed it to him.

Sela pulled the seal off and opened it. "Says I'm supposed to use your pala stone Eden, and be at Migdal for Terce," he looked up at each of them. "Thanks so much for your help you guys, I'd never be here without you."

"Great. So don't mess up," Parzel joked, laughing with the others. "You are clearly ready for this. Let's get dinner and you go to bed early so that you're ready for tomorrow," she turned and started towards the dining tent.

"Yeah, that's if I can sleep at all," Sela replied, but shrugged, stuffing the letter in his pocket and following.

21

"But the king said to him,
"Go for you are my Eklektos weapon,
to carry my name before the peoples
and the rulers and the children of Kaleo."

The team spent a restless day without Sela. They tried to busy themselves with work, the girls had been out on patrol but none of them seemed very focused. Eden was startled several times by a rabbit that seemed unhappy they had invaded its space, while Parzel, who was on point, managed to stop the squad's progress five times for what turned out to be the wind.

"For Migdal's sake!" Gande exploded after the fifth stop. "Would you get your mind back here before we get killed!" he chastised her.

"Or we get blown away," Lucky mumbled to Nasah beside him who stifled a laugh.

"We are just on edge for Sela, our futures kind of rest on how he does today."

"I know, I heard," Lucky nodded. "I'm just kidding, but come on, it's kind of funny."

Nasah shoved him forward and they kept moving.

Shephel's day was even more painful. On guard duty on the wall, staring off into the grey for half the day all his mind could do was wander. He had worked up every worst case scenario possible and by the time he was off the wall he was convinced he was going to be a farmer in the outlands and die alone.

The girls met up with Shephel in the dining tent for supper and they all sat miserably, trying to find something else to occupy their minds.

Finally Parzel stood. "I'm going to clean my weapons," she stated and promptly left the tent. The others stared at her back as she went, no one said a word. Eden swirled the qahua in her mug.

"Remind me to try and explain coffee to you guys sometime," she mumbled, then said louder, "I cleaned mine last night when I couldn't sleep." Causing Shephel and Nasah to both laugh. She looked up and smiled. "Like either of you slept?"

"Actually, I did," Shephel admitted. "A whole watch before I started my worstcase scenario plans that have continued throughout the day, do you think farming is hard?" he raised an eyebrow.

"Oh man, I just wish he'd get back here," Nasah said in exasperation. "What could be taking them so long?"

"Maybe he was given a few hours of leave after he mastered all the tasks to celebrate, he probably won't be back till tomorrow." Eden smiled, hoping she was right. But just then they heard a scream that sounded remarkably like Parzel.

All three of them jumped up from their seats and ran outside to see Parzel in a bear hug with Sela. He looked up to them and smiled, "So, guess who killed it at the re-test?" he puffed out his chest.

They cheered and ran over to envelope he and Parzel in a group hug.

"What?"

"Tell us all about it."

"What did you have to do?"

"What did Moreh say?"

"Did you see the King?"

"What did he say?" They peppered him with questions.

"Woah, slow down, I might have aced the tests but I'm still not that quick," he laughed, putting his hands up to try and get them to stop talking.

They wandered over to the barracks and grabbed some chairs in the common room and Sela started. "There were actually a few people there getting re-tested," he went on, "so I guess it's something they do more than just with me. But we basically started off the way we did before, did the physical testing stuff, and at the end of that Moreh said she could see a huge improvement, even though that wasn't the area they were concerned about for me," he smiled timidly. "So that was encouraging. Then I had to do the tests. Moreh sat and quizzed me verbally for a watch. It was kind of brutal, I didn't feel like I had a lot of time to think like you do when you write your answers out, but she kept nodding and never corrected me. Then the last thing was the medical stuff, I had to actually treat a bunch of the other students for different injuries, kind'a like we did that last day here Nasah, that helped a lot."

"No poisons?" Eden asked with a smirk on her face.

"No poisons," he laughed

"At the end of it, Moreh came over to me and said I'd passed and that she was proud of me, and then get this..." he paused for dramatic effect, "she said she'd been getting good reports about us from her brother!"

"Wait, what?" Nasah asked, her brow furrowed trying to understand.

"What brother? Here?" Shephel asked, also looking confused.

"I knew it!" Eden exclaimed, "Gande! He's her brother!" she slapped Parzel on the back. "That's why he reminds us of her and her ways and things he says and he has an identical ring to hers."

"He does - " Parzel sounded unsure.

"Well, who else could it be?" Eden asked, "Lucky? Allon?"

"Holmeman has the same ring too," Shephel pointed out.

"Well, maybe Allon," Nasah nodded. "They are both a bit off," she chuckled.

"No, maybe you're right Eden," Parzel finally agreed. "But seems strange that Moreh would be Gibbor Chayil protecting the King and her brother would end up here, in the outer limits in what seems to be a punishment sort of placement."

"Yeah, that's weird," Nasah said. "Maybe they had a falling out, no, then he wouldn't be in touch with her about us. I don't get it."

"Well, I'm not about to ask him," Sela stated. "But Eden is apparently pen pals with Moreh so she could write her and ask," he looked at Eden with a mischievous smile.

"What?" she asked, cocking her head to the side.

"Moreh gave me this for you," he handed her a letter. "Said she didn't have time to reply to you before, and said to make sure you got it," he didn't let go of the letter as Eden took it. "So, what are you writing about?"

Eden snatched it away from him. "That's none of your business," she suddenly got upset, then seeing all of their faces she realized how snappy she sounded. "Sorry, it's just... personal, something about my past I thought she might know. Not something I want to talk about right now if that's okay?" she looked at Parzel for help.

"So you're saying you won't ask her about Gande?" Parzel tried to lighten the moment, and it worked, they all laughed. "That's okay, just don't forget we're a team if we need to know anything okay?" she raised an eyebrow.

"Yeah, for sure," Eden was relieved.

"Oh, and your necklace," Sela pulled the pala stone from his shirt and put it over Eden's neck. "Pretty cool toy."

"Yeah, apparently not a toy," Eden held the stone out and looked at it for a moment.

"What do you mean?" Nasah asked at Eden's odd answer.

"Oh, well, remember when I was an idiot?"

"Which time?" Shephel asked and got knocked to the ground for his joke. "Hey!"

"The time I got hurt and stuck in the pit," she glared at him, but smiled. "When I was serving the King I asked Moreh why the stone didn't work when I tried to escape and come back to Migdal and she said 'it's not a toy' and that it won't do anything that is not in the King's will."

"That's interesting," Nasah reached out and looked at the stone. "I should study this more, since it seems to be a part of our team with you, we should know what it can and can't do." She let it fall back onto Eden's shirt.

"That's a good idea Nasah," Parzel agreed.

"So, that's all interesting and stuff, but I kind of want to celebrate if you know what I mean, I realize we all have duty in the morning, but anyone down for a ride to that pub just back up the road and have some celebratory drinks?" Sela changed the subject.

All of them looked at each other, at the time and they quickly agreed and made a run for the stables.

When they arrived at the little pub about a ten kilometre ride Northwest from the outpost, they found several other Chayil already enjoying a night's relaxation. The common room was busy with music and drinks, hot food and a warm fire. The noise helped the team feel the spirit of celebration. All Eden really wanted to do was get back to her bunk and read the letter from Moreh, but she knew this moment was important for all of them and she sure wasn't going to read it with them here and have to answer a million questions, so she tried to put it out of her mind. She raised her glass just then. "To Sela!" and with agreement the whole team crashed their glasses together, spilling more ale than not and shouted, "Sela!"

In the next few hours several other Chayil came over to offer their congratulations to the big man, news seemed to have spread quickly. Sela took the back slaps and handshakes with continued enthusiasm, enjoying positive attention for once in his life. The last man to come over was

Lucky, he held out his hand to him. "I hear congratulations are in order," he smiled.

"Thanks Lucky," Sela grinned.

"So does this mean we lose all of you now?" he asked, taking a swig of his own pint.

"What do you mean?" Eden asked him.

"Well, you all said that you were here till he passed then you were getting to be Gibbor Chayil," Lucky explained. "I assumed that would mean you leave now to go back to training," he glanced from each face to the next, finding no answer. Then his eyebrows raised. "Oh, so they didn't tell you that eh?" he laughed. "Leave the eklektos in exile out here!" he took a big drink then set his glass down with a crash on the table. "Maybe you should have clarified that before you came to this King forsaken place," he turned to leave, still laughing.

Parzel and Eden turned to face each other. No one wanted to agree, but Lucky actually made a good point. None of them knew what happens next, nine months was up but they hadn't heard any news about going back to training.

"Did Moreh say anything to you Sela?" Nasah asked hopefully.

"Not about that specifically," he tried to recall everything she said. "She did say she would see us soon. Maybe she's going to come get us?"

"I'm sure they haven't forgotten us," Shephel said with a roll of his eyes. "Don't let Lucky get under your skin, he's still freaked out about you being the eklektos, and then using that knife the other day Eden," he shook his head. "He's afraid he's not so important." He waved his hand at the waiter to get another drink. "You can tell he wants to get back to the top, I heard him asking Gande to question the prisoner yesterday and then couldn't wait to report back to him what he thought he'd found," he snorted. "It was so obvious he was trying to worm his way into his favour, Gande totally dismissed him, said he's never heard of a drawing rod." Shephel thanked the waiter for the drink.

"Wait, what did you just say?" Eden asked, her mug suspended halfway to her mouth.

"I said Lucky is trying to get in Gande's good books," he repeated himself.

"No, about the questioning and the drawing rod." Eden waved her hand trying to get him to the point.

"What? Oh, well, he went in yesterday and was questioning the guy Sela caught. But they've been doing that every day since we caught him," he shrugged.

"Yes, but you said he said something about the drawing rod., Eden was getting exasperated now.

"Yeah, why? Have you heard of it?" Shephel suddenly started actually listening to Eden.

"Yes!" she exclaimed, then lowered her voice. "The King told me about it, it was stolen from him ages ago and it's the thing that Nachash uses to enslave people from my world here. From what I understood most of his followers are slaves because of it, it's only supposed to be used by the King. He's been looking for it I think since Nachash first rebelled," she explained.

"Well, why wouldn't Gande know about it?" Parzel asked, leaning in so their conversation wouldn't be overheard now.

"I don't know, that is weird," Eden agreed, "but we need to question that guy again."

"Or at least find out what Lucky learned," Sela agreed. "Shephel, you don't remember exactly what he told Gande?"

"No, I only heard the end of the conversation where Gande said he was being deceived and to forget it," he shook his head. "But I'll ask him when we get back."

"Okay, you ask him and then maybe we can convince Gande to let us question the guy too if everyone else seems to have had a shot," Nasah said.

They all sat quietly, their celebration of Sela forgotten. Eden looked up, "I think I'm going to head back, I want to think about this more," she explained. "Anyone else coming?"

"I just want to finish my drink."

"My food should be here soon, then I'll head back."

"You want someone to ride back with you?" Parzel asked, clearly thinking she probably wanted to be alone to read that letter but offered her company anyway.

"No, no, I'm fine, you guys enjoy still. I'll see you at the barracks. Congrats again Sela!" she leaned over and gave him a kiss on his head that caused him to blush. She gave Parzel a grateful look of understanding and headed out the door.

She mounted Ruach and kicked her into a gallop. She flew down the road towards the stronghold, but pulled up about a kilometre away. She led Ruach off the main road and up a rough trail that some of the local farmers used to move their animals and slipped off her back to let her graze. She found a spot at the bottom of a tree, made sure Ruach was munching happily and pulled out her letter.

She used her knife to slit the seal and unfolded the paper. She took a deep breath and began to read.

Eden;

I wondered if you might be asking some of these questions soon, and I hope I can tell you what you need to know to be at peace.

The simple answer is 'yes' your guardians in your other home know where you are. I'm not sure they understand exactly, but they know you are safe and have gone to your home, where your parents were from. They did not know the whole situation with your parents as far as I know.

I suppose there is a chance your parents tried to explain things to them, they were very close friends from what I understand, they did seem a little more understanding of the story we told them than I would have thought if they had never heard of Kaleo, but I guess that is only a question they can answer.

So I think what you needed to hear was that they were not devastated by losing you after losing your parents as well. Unfortunately, that is something I cannot tell you. They know you are safe but were terribly disappointed to have lost you. They clearly loved you and your parents and I'm afraid there is a hole left in their lives now.

I'm not sure how comforting any of this is but at least know that they are not worrying and even seem to know that there is a greater purpose for you.

Now, I should offer you no special treatment, but I have to admit, you all mean more to me than you should, so if you need anything, talk to my brother, Gande, if you haven't figured that out yet. He is on direct order of the King and is one of the best Gibbor Chayil and men you could ever learn from.

Listen to him.

I look forward to continuing your training in the new year.

Until then, as Master Petros would say, 'don't die'.

Moreh

"Ha! I knew it!" she laughed, "Gande," then she reread the letter several more times. The thought that Ian and Heather missed her that much broke her heart. Partly out of guilt, partly out of her own sorrow, they were her only family. "I wonder if I'll ever get the chance to go back? To talk to them, maybe bring them all here?" she thought out loud, Ruach looking up at her voice. She sighed, she wasn't sure what answer she had hoped to get from Moreh, but she certainly didn't feel at peace with this one.

"Not much I can do about it though is there girl?" She stood up and went over to her horse. She tucked the letter back inside her jacket. "At least I can tell the team who her brother is," she pat her neck. "Let's get back," she whispered in her ear as she mounted and kicked her into a trot.

22

*"What then? Kaleo failed to obtain what it was seeking.
The Eklektos obtained it, but the rest were hardened."*

The next morning Shephel pulled them all aside as they came off their shifts. He hustled them down the corridor beside the dining tent.

"What's up Shephel?" Nasah asked, finally getting his hand off her back.

"Okay," he glanced around them nervously, which made them all start looking around suspiciously. "I was talking to some of the other guys, friends of Lucky, and apparently it's true. He went in to question him the other day and came out with some information about the drawing rod. They seem to all think it's nothing though. Gande has convinced them it's a trick."

"I don't understand, Moreh said we can trust him. He has to have heard about the rod before, even from her," Eden shook her head. "I just don't get it."

"Maybe he knows it's a lie," Parzel suggested. "Maybe he knows that it's somewhere else?"

"I'd think if the King has been looking for it all these years and someone knew where it was he'd be moving the kingdom to get there," Nasah shook her head.

"So - " Shephel interrupted them, looking annoyed at not being able to finish his story. "I talked to Gande to see if Nasah and I could question the guy. I said we wanted to learn more about interrogation," he smiled at his clearly perceived genius.

"What? Why you two?" Eden asked.

"Because they will cause way less eyes to be raised than if you asked," Parzel pointed out. "That was a good call Shephel," she agreed.

"Oh, I can't wait," Nasah clapped her hands. "I have always wanted to try this!"

"Well, get yourself ready," Shephel looked up at the sun. "We have about a third to get some questions together, then we are in. We have to go now, the prisoner is being transferred tonight."

"That's interesting timing," Eden mused again.

"Everything isn't a conspiracy," Parzel rolled her eyes and laughed. "Come on, let's get dinner and help these guys think of some questions," she pushed them all back out towards the doorway.

As they stuffed their mouths with fresh bread they debated what approach to take with the prisoner. Sela seemed to think the good cop bad cop idea was best, though when Eden laughed and called it that, they all just stared at her.

"What's a cop?" Nasah finally asked. Eden's smile faded as she tried to think of an explanation, but then waved her hand as if throwing it away,

"Never mind, doesn't matter."

They threw questions out, argued with each other and finally came to no decisions at all when Shephel stood up.

"Well, doesn't matter now, we have to go," he looked at Nasah. "Guess we are winging this."

No one else said a word, mostly because they didn't know what to say. They simply watched the two leave the room and then silently finished their meals.

The two siblings looked at each other as they stood outside the cell. The guard there had his hand on the door. "Are you ready?" he asked. "He's a mean one so be careful," he looked at the two.

"Guess we will follow each other's leads and hope to the King that we get somewhere," Shephel nodded to the guard, and they walked into the room.

It took a moment for their eyes to adjust to the dark cell. Without any windows and only one lamp burning on the wall it cast the room in deep shadow. That made the captive look even more intimidating. He sat on a chair on the far side of the room with his hands chained to his feet, forcing him to be bent over slightly. Despite what had to be discomfort, his black eyes stared straight ahead, and his face was set like flint. He made no movement that acknowledged their entrance. Both Shephel and Nasah automatically straightened their backs and tried to look as intimidating as they could, hoping the shadows worked in their favour as well.

Nasah silently walked closer to the prisoner until she was standing about two feet in front of him. He had been stripped of his armor leaving him only in a pair of dark linen pants. He was even barefoot. As Nasah looked at him she could see a tattoo on his arm. She was pretty sure it was an old spelling of Nachash. She glanced up from the tattoo to see the prisoner now staring at her face.

"You like it," he spoke in a thick accented voice. It wasn't a question but a statement.

Nasah caught her breath for a moment, then decided not to answer. Shephel stepped up beside her.

"We show our true colours," he said, his eyes never leaving Nasah's. "You were one of the ones we fought on the wall. You were with the one with the knife," he smiled, showing a set of grey and broken teeth. "That was a fun trick, I wonder how she was able to do that. I have only heard of one blade that can work like that," he paused, his gaze still staring into Nasah's eyes. "But surely a Chayil on the outer limits wouldn't have such a weapon, unless..." he let the word hang in the air.

Nasah's eyes flashed unintentionally. Was he saying he knew that Eden was the eklektos? That she was there? Would that information already be back to Nachash? Was this all a trap? But still she didn't speak, and clearly Shephel had decided this was the best strategy as well and stood stoically beside her.

The man continued, his eyes narrowing as he seemed to be trying to read Nasah's face. He hadn't even once looked at her brother. "I suppose that's why that other pawn was so excited about the drawing rod. The eklektos near the drawing rod, that's a coincidence isn't it? A game of chess then. Moves and countermoves. Who moves first? Who sacrifices the pawns? Who are the pawns? What will tip the balance and will it be in time? It's exciting to watch from the sidelines isn't it?" he stopped and with no more emotion turned his eyes back to the far wall and didn't glance at them again.

They stood there examining him awhile longer. Nasah wanted to get the tattoo firmly in her mind, but they still didn't speak. After some time, she turned to look at Shephel and nodded towards the door. He turned and banged on it for the guard and with a click that sounded much louder than it was in the silent cell, they slipped back out into the hallway.

The guard who let them out seemed to be looking for some information from them, but the two just turned and walked away.

Once outside Shephel grabbed her arm. "What was that?" he asked, his voice cracking, clearly disturbed by the encounter.

"I don't know, but he recognized us, he seems to have known who Eden is and I can't help but wonder if he's planting information. Maybe he is trying to mislead us and that's why Gande said it's nothing and they are transferring him out of here," she mused.

"Well, the guy is creepy beyond anything I've ever seen, well except that ebed guy in that village," Shephel shivered at the memory.

"Exactly, and with that tattoo on his arm, I think he is more than just a 'pawn' as he called them. There has to be a deeper strategy here. But I don't know what?" They started out towards the barracks. "Does he really have the rod somewhere close? Is it a trap, or does he think it's safely out of reach already?"

"I don't know, but he seemed to be trying to mess with us with all that gibberish about chess and moves. He definitely had an agenda," he nodded as they entered the barracks and found the others sitting in the common room anxiously waiting for them.

"So?" Eden asked. When Nasah's eyes darted down the hall towards the rooms she continued. "No one else is here, the rest of the squad's headed out to the tavern for the night, and Allon doubled up the patrol so we can talk here."

Shephel dropped into a comfortable chair while Nasah started pacing. They recounted their story asking the same questions again.

"I just don't get it."

"But he didn't give you any more information like where the rod was exactly? When it might move?" Eden asked.

"No, just all this conversation making a point of recognizing us and then hints at something. But it doesn't make sense, why say anything?" she replied.

"It would have to be in that town we found," Sela mumbled as he chewed on an extra piece of jerky that he'd found in his pocket. "We've been out scouting for weeks now and there hasn't been a sighting of any other town or even campsite anywhere in a two day march in Gaavah."

"It has to be a trap," Parzel stated. "He'd never give up so much information otherwise."

"But maybe he didn't mean to and now he's just trying to cover it up," Eden disagreed, "to make us suspect something so we don't go find it."

"It's true, there's no way he could have gotten a message out since that skirmish, so he could never warn them, and they can't have known Eden would be here or Nachash would have sent a lot more troops to try and breach the wall I'd think," Shephel agreed.

Just then a few Chayil came back in, waved to the group and continued on towards their beds.

Nasah sat down and leaned in towards everyone, lowering her voice. "Well, I suppose we will see what Allon orders for tomorrow. If they take his intel seriously they'll be moving a squad out to that town tomorrow."

"Maybe that's why they want to get the guy out of here so soon, to prevent any secrets getting out or any more of the enemy coming to rescue him, before they make their moves," Sela suggested.

"Possibly," Nasah mulled the idea over.

"But...?" Parzel asked, seeing she clearly was having other thoughts.

"Well, what if they are moving him so he can't spread misinformation?" she asked.

"Now who's talking conspiracies?" Eden laughed. "They wouldn't have allowed two first year Chayil to interview him if they were worried about that."

"Shhhh, lower you voice," Parzel hushed her.

"I think this is awesome news, and I just hope we are the squad who gets a crack at this," Eden whispered, her eyes dancing with the anticipation. Perhaps this was the thing she was chosen for, the eklektos purpose, she thought to herself.

"Speak for yourself, one time with that creepy guy was enough for me, I'd prefer not to run into his little gang again if I can help it," Shephel shivered again.

"And I was just starting to think of you as an equal with you asking to question the guy," Eden shook her head, her words meant to sound like a joke, yet they bore the truth of her thoughts. Shephel's countenance dropped, clearly hearing the rebuke in it, but Eden didn't notice. "Well, I'm going to bed, I have never been so excited to get up and get our orders for the day tomorrow." She got up and headed to their room.

Parzel watched her leave, "I don't know what I want to hear tomorrow," she admitted. "But something doesn't feel right to me," she looked at Nasah who nodded, then got up to follow Eden.

23

"On that day declares Melek,
I will take you, O servant, declares Melek,
and make you like a signet ring
for you are my Eklektos declares Melek the Elyon."

"What time is it?" Parzel growled, glaring at Eden who was rifling through her footlocker not very quietly. She rolled over to look out the window where it was still pitch black. "It can't be even close to dawn yet," she threw her pillow at her.

Eden glanced up as the pillow hit her in the back. "Oh, sorry, I just can't sleep," she apologized. "I'm going to get some qahua, it's almost Laud we have to be ready in a third anyway."

"Yeah, a third, before a long half day shift. Why would I want as much sleep as possible? No idea," Parzel snapped sarcastically and rolled back over, pulling the blanket up over her head.

A third later they were all lined up in front of Gande awaiting their assignments. Parzel yawned and kicked Eden in the shin.

"Hey," she whispered back.

"That's for making me tired," she glared at her again.

"Are you two done?" Gande asked, his glare overpowering anything Parzel could have shot.

"Yes sir," Eden nodded, lowering her eyes, but unable to stop grinning.

"Well, I don't know what you look so happy about on this wet and cold morning Chayil, but since you seem thrilled to be here you can lead your squad up on to the wall for the long shift today," Gande looked at his clipboard. "Squad one you're on patrol, and two and three, looks like you're up on the wall this week," he flipped the paper over and looked at Eden again. "Well, not happy with your assignment now?" he raised an eyebrow at her dumb struck face.

"Um, well," Eden was so confused she couldn't find the words. "Sort of," she glanced at Parzel and Nasah. "I mean, why aren't we going to get the drawing rod? If we know it's here, why would we wait till Nachash moves it?" she asked. The rest of the squads all looked at her as if she was crazy.

Gande stalked over to Eden and stood alarmingly close to her. "Where did you hear such - nonsense?" he barked at her.

Lucky dipped his head and turned so there was no chance he could make eye contact. Eden looked at Nasah and Shephel for help, but none was offered.

"I overheard it from interrogations with the prisoner," Eden said, refusing to throw anyone else under the bus.

Gande stood even straighter and seemed to tower over her. "Chayil, there are so many things wrong with that statement I don't know where to start," he took a deep breath and then spoke even louder so the entire company could hear him. "First, eavesdropping on interrogations is not even close to your pay grade, second thinking that a servant of Nachash is telling you the truth about anything is downright stupid and third thinking that you, a newbie, has the gall to suggest what your squad's assignment might be on any given day is ludicrous."

Everyone was shifting uncomfortably in line now, feeling awkward for Eden, as if they were intruding but also, now nodding in agreement with their Sargent. "If you don't get your sorry looking examples of Chayil up on that wall in one minute you will wish you never got deployed to my command."

Eden furrowed her brow and turned sharply on her heal, leading the squad over to the wall. "I wished I never got deployed here a long time ago," she mumbled to herself as she stomped up the stairs.

"Wait, we don't get breakfast?" Parzel asked, just loud enough to be overheard by Gande. "I'm going to kill you today Eden," she growled.

"Parzel?"

"What?" she turned to see Nasah standing beside her with a plate of warm biscuits and a steaming mug of qahua awhile later.

"I said, Gande relented a bit." and she put the dishes in front of her on the wall. "Where were you?" she asked, commenting on Parzel's lack of attention.

"I was trying to figure out what was going on with that tirade by Gande. There really was no reason for it. He seemed to be going out of his way to make a point to Eden and the entire company. He had to know if he let you and Shephel in to interrogate the prisoner you would tell us. He didn't say you couldn't. And clearly he already knew what the prisoner had said. Why would he make such a show that he didn't believe it?" shoving a biscuit in her mouth.

Nasah nodded, "I don't know what to make of it," she shrugged. "It doesn't make sense."

"I don't know either," Parzel glanced over at Eden who was further down the wall and clearly not watching anything in front of her. You could almost see the steam coming from her brain while she was thinking. "But he practically pushed Eden out the door to do something on her own," she nodded towards her.

"I was thinking the same thing," Nasah agreed. "Do you think that's what he wants? And just can't say it?" she wondered.

"I thought that too, but again it doesn't make sense because he is right, why would we ever believe the enemy, he always lies and seems to have chosen the exact one that would set Eden off," Parzel picked up the qahua for a drink. "I must be having a bad day, I actually think this tastes good," she glanced in the mug.

Nasah grinned. "Well, with the long shift up here, that might be the best part of your day, especially after Eden has had that long to plan something that I'm sure we will all regret," she turned and went to hand out more food and drinks to the squad.

The day dragged on, how half a day could seem like forever never ceased to amaze them, but finally they could hear the sweet sound of the boots on the stairs, as the next squad came to relieve them. They silently hustled down to the mess hall and piled their plates full. The biscuits just didn't cut it for a whole day, and Gande was conspicuously absent from the wall, which meant there was no jerky to tide them over.

Sela dropped into a chair already with a leg of chicken in his mouth. "I'm starving," he moaned. "If you ever get us in trouble again so we miss breakfast I'll kill you myself Eden," he grumbled.

"Stop whining, you could stand to lose a few pounds," Eden glared at him. "Like that was my fault, Gande was going to say something any way, I just gave him an easy target," she stirred her food around her plate with a fork while she thought.

"Yeah, you think that's it?" Shephel asked, his tone obviously unbelieving.

"What's that supposed to mean?" Eden asked.

"He clearly picked you out, he wouldn't have said all that to anyone else, he pointedly addressed you," he shrugged. "The question is why?"

"You think that was all said to me for a purpose?" she asked, looking from face to face of her friends.

"It seemed like it, but it makes no sense at all," Nasah agreed.

"I can't decide if it was a warning not to listen to the enemy, so you wouldn't do something stupid, or a challenge because he can't actually assign you to do this but he wants you to," Parzel took a big forkful of food. "But I agree with Sela, if I miss another meal for you I'll help him," her words muffled by her food and she high fived the big man with a smile.

Eden continued to stir her food. In all her anger that day she hadn't actually thought to objectively consider Gande's words. She was mad and thought they were being obtuse, failing to see what was right in front of them, the fact that he might have been trying to send her on a secret mission never crossed her mind. She started going over every word he said to her.

After they had all finished, and Eden had even managed to take a few bites she put her fork down with authority. "That's got to be it," she stated. "He wants me to go try and find it."

"Woah friend," Parzel raised her hand. "Or he is trying to keep you from killing yourself which seems much more likely," she shook her head. "Why wouldn't he just say that?"

Eden paused, then squinted her eyes a bit. "It can't be a regular mission, can't let the squad know, it's my task, why I was picked in the first place," she said matter of factly.

Everyone else stopped chewing and just looked at her in silence.

"You know I'm right," she stated.

Nasah nodded ever so slightly. "Maybe," she admitted hesitantly. "I mean, the prophecies do call you the eklektos which begs for something to be chosen for, you've been given your sword and dagger that have powers for you alone, and the King gave you the pala stone. Everything points towards some special mission," she listed the facts.

"And that would make sense why Nachash is trying to stop me, if I'm the only one who can get that rod back," Eden continued.

Again, they all sat in silence, thinking about what Nasah said and trying to figure out what that meant. Eden was starting to get agitated waiting.

Finally she burst out, "Say something! I have to do something."

Shephel hushed her. "Well, I'm not letting you run out there half cocked with no plan. I don't care if it has to wait a day, we plan what you're going to do," his tone made it clear he wouldn't take any objections.

"And you don't go alone," Parzel stated, looking down at her food, then finally lifting her eyes to meet Eden's. "That's stupid."

"I can't ask you all to go, it's me that has to," she shook her head.

"No, there is nothing that says the eklektos is a lone servant running off on her own," Nasah agreed. "If we have learned anything this year it's that we are a team and the King honours a team."

"But..." Eden began.

"Are you that slow of a learner?" Sela asked putting his big hand on her shoulder. "We come whether you okay it or not."

Eden sighed and honestly relaxed a bit. There was nothing she wanted more than her whole team with her, though deep down there was a dark fear that was lurking, but she pushed it aside. "Fine," she said shortly, but her eyes betrayed her gratitude and love of her friends.

"Do we tell Gande?" Shephel asked.

"No, he'll figure it out when we don't show for roll call tomorrow," Parzel said.

"Tomorrow?" Eden raised an eyebrow.

"Well, knowing how slow you are at running it'll take us forever to get to this town so we'd better head out tonight," she smirked, then ducked the punch she had anticipated.

"That gives us a couple hours to plan, figure a way out the main gate and out into the grey," Nasah calculated. "So, Sela, Shephel, tell us everything you can remember about that town."

24

"I am not speaking of all of you,
I know whom I have as the Eklektos
but the prophecies will be fulfilled."

A third later the five of them were slipping their backpacks and weapons under their cloaks. "Are you sure about this?" Eden asked Nasah again, with a skeptical tone.

"Of course I am," Nasah threw her backpack down in disgust. "Did none of you actually read your maps in Geography?"

The rest of them looked away a bit ashamed. "Not my strong suit," Parzel said quietly.

Nasah sighed. "The wall doesn't cover the entire space between Kaleo and Gaavah, that'd be ridiculous to build an entire wall the size of the whole country. It just covers the main populated areas and roads, where the enemy would need to travel to move large weapons and an army if he were to attack. It leaves forest, some pastures, and rough terrain vulnerable to small attacks, knowing that we should be able to discover and defeat the enemy when faced within Kaleo. If we just head back to the pub like we are going for a drink tonight, then cut off the road about a kilometre from here and strike cross country. It'll take us about two thirds to swing back around where the wall ends and return to the grey, but the advantage is that we will already be to the west, so if Sela and Shephel are right in their directions to this town, we will be only add a third to the hike than if we left by the gate." She had picked her bag back up and pulled her cloak over top while she was talking.

Eden secured her sword to her belt, then felt for her knife as well. Finally she let her hand rub the pala stone and said a silent prayer.

"You're all sure you want to come?" she asked them again, fingering her father's ring.

"Well, no, I'd rather stay here safely, but since I'm pretty sure you're going to go run off like you did in Migdal, I don't have a choice do I?" Parzel raised an eyebrow. "Of course we are coming and if you bring it up again we will leave you here and go on our own," she pushed past her and started to leave the outpost towards town.

"Hey," Lucky called out to them from the mess tent. "You guys going to town?" he asked. "Walking?"

"Oh boy," Nasah muttered.

"Yeah, after a day standing still we felt like we needed the walk," Eden replied, praying he didn't ask to join them.

He looked for a minute like he was going to walk over, then seemed to change his mind. "It's a bit late to head out I'd think, remember we have another half tomorrow," he waved and ducked back inside, clearly unimpressed at their decision making. All of them sighed when they saw his back, and kept walking.

"And someone tell me why we aren't taking the horses?" Parzel asked.

"We don't know what's out there, I'd hate to leave them in danger while we go inside the town. This way we don't have to worry about anyone except ourselves," Eden replied, secretly wishing she could bring Ruach but too afraid for her horse.

"Well, I hope we get enough of a head start before they come looking for us," Sela whispered as they passed through the gate and out to the road.

"At least this way they will start looking in the wrong direction, that will help too," Shephel said.

They walked the road in silence for a while, then when they made a turn that had them well out of eyesight of the outpost and unable to be seen from up ahead in the pub, they followed Nasah off the trail to their left, and started cross country to the southwest. There wasn't a trail or track so they were bush whacking through shrubs and over rocky ground. Thankful for the darkness as there was little cover here, Parzel walked at the back of the group trying to keep their trail to a minimum, wiping foot prints when they couldn't stay on the rocks, and trying to fix branches that bent or broke as they passed.

Finally, about a third later they came to what would have been parallel to their outpost. Nasah stopped here for a minute to consult her map.

"So probably about five kilometres to our left is the wall," she glanced up in front of them then at the grey that stretched out endlessly. "And according to you guys this town is approximately, what a watch and a half hike in front of us?" she asked.

Sela and Shephel nodded. "I went over it all in my head again, it's got to be," Shephel agreed.

"Okay, then let's go," Eden took the first step forward into the grey and drew her sword as she did so. She was determined to walk point now to try and protect the others as best she could. They each pulled a weapon out and followed behind her as they disappeared into the grey. Parzel stopped trying to hide their trail as she couldn't even see Eden four people ahead of her, she figured it didn't matter any longer.

It didn't take them long to get through the grey and everyone was able to breathe a bit easier when they could actually see several feet in front of themselves now, even in the dark. This was working to their advantage moving at night, there wasn't much tree coverage here so they would have been easily seen by anyone tracking them or the enemy ahead, but with their cloaks and the moonless sky tonight they were able to move swiftly and stealthily.

Eden held up her hand to stop them suddenly as they were walking through a denser forest area. To their right was a twenty foot cliff, easily climbable and with lots of tree coverage. In front of them you could see that the trees were thinning. She waved the team up to her. "Is that the town?" she asked the guys, pointing through the trees to what appeared to be several fires spaced perfectly apart.

"Think so," Shephel nodded. "They had watch towers at each of the corners of the town, looks like those fires would be at each of them," he yawned as he finished his sentence and shook his head to try and wake up.

Eden nodded, then started to move forward but Parzel grabbed her arm.

"Wait," she said. "We have to rest, we came off a half day shift and have been hiking for two watches. The sun is going to be up soon, this is the best place we are going to get to camp, rest and then scout out the town, there's no cover out of those trees," she pointed ahead.

"But they'll be coming after us. And that rod might be moving!" Eden argued.

"Parzel is right," Nasah shook her head. "We are going to make bad decisions if we don't stop soon. We will set a guard, they can watch for any large movement from the town. We should be able to see everything from that ridge beside us, and even if our squads are looking for us, that won't be for another two thirds at least, and then they'll have to head to the pub and determine we aren't there... by the time they get here it'll be dark again and we will be in the town," she saw Eden's disappointed face. "We have to be smart or we are going to be dead."

Eden looked between them, knowing they were right but hating it at the same time. "Fine," she muttered, then walked towards the ridge. "I'll take the first watch," she said.

They found a small grotto under the rocky edge that was partially covered with shrubs, and in a few minutes they had completely concealed it. Parzel did make sure they left no tracks outside leading to their camp, and Eden climbed quickly to the top of the ridge and found a tree with a perfect blind to be able to keep watch on her team and survey the town.

Eden pulled her sword out and ran her fingers over the inscription again, then her hand went to the pala stone. This had to be her quest, the King told her she was the eklektos didn't he? He told her what her parents had done to save her, he gave her the sword and the knife and the stone. Why else would he have done all that except for this moment, this chance to stop Nachash in his tracks, if not to defeat him to strip his powers. Yet, in her mind that fear lurked. She didn't understand it, but something felt wrong. Could it all be a trap? But how? No one knew where she was, until that attack...which wouldn't have happened if Sela hadn't shot... she shook her head. She couldn't make sense of it, logically it all seemed to fit, even Gande almost challenging her to defy him and go. But what if she was wrong? What if he was commanding her not to, just like he said? She pulled her cloak tighter around her neck to block the wind out, it had a bite to it tonight. She flexed her fingers and toes to stay warm when she saw Shephel slip out of their cover and start towards her. She smiled, looking forward to a bit of rest, even though part of her just wanted to run into town. She slid down the tree to meet him.

"I half expected to find you gone," he smiled, stretching. "Seemed like something ridiculous you would do."

"Thought about it," she acknowledged. "Then Nasah's angry voice cut through my thoughts and I was too afraid to go," she laughed.

"Good choice," he nodded. "Get some sleep if you can," he grabbed the tree trunk and started to climb up as Eden carefully headed down the rocks to their grotto. She slid in quietly and pulled her bag under her head and surprisingly fell right to sleep.

When she awoke she noticed that Nasah must be on duty, as the others were still sleeping. The sun was up and it must have been close to Sext as her stomach rumbled angrily. Not wanting to wake the others by pulling food out of her bag, she slipped back out and climbed up to see Nasah. She moved more carefully in the sunlight, checking to make sure nothing else was moving. She heard a whistle above her, and knew she was safe to climb.

"Can you climb up here too?" Nasah asked, "I want to show you something."

Eden quickly scurried up the tree to stand on a branch just below her friend. Nasah handed her the looking glass.

"This was a brilliant idea," Eden smiled, taking the glass.

"Someone has to plan ahead," Nasah smirked. "It's not your strong suit," she laughed. "But look at the town walls and tell me what you see."

Eden pulled the glass up and started at the corner closest to them, which was just like Shephel had said, a watchtower, then she followed the wall along to the next watchtower. "What am I looking for?" she asked confused. "I see two guards at each post, they don't look like our prisoner, they look like regular foot soldiers."

"The walls," Nasah admonished her. "Look closely."

"Okay, okay, the walls," Eden focused on the bricks between the posts, and then suddenly put the looking glass down and looked at Nasah.

"Right?" Nasah's eyes were huge, seeing that Eden saw it too. "A lion and a lamb."

"This was a city of Kaleo at one time," Eden concluded.

"It has to be," Nasah said. "But how the border has moved I don't understand, but it has to make it easier for us knowing the King built that town not Nachash."

"Right!" Eden looked through the glass again, studying the walls closer. "There must be more than one way in, every town he's built has his ways in them according to history, we just have to find them," she was getting more and more excited. "Good idea this sleep thing," she glanced at Nasah humbled.

"Now take my advice and eat something, Sela is taking my spot soon, but you all should eat then we can plan a bit before resting again till nightfall," Nasah gestured for Eden to go back, and as her stomach growled she didn't protest.

As she slid back into their cover she saw Parzel was already up and Sela as well. She nudged Shephel and whispered, "Breakfast." and started to pull some food out of her bags. Parzel was holding up a match at the back of their hideaway, running a hand over the stone.

"What are you doing?" Eden asked, biting into an apple while trying to spread jam on a biscuit.

"Oh, nothing," she blew the match out and walked back over to the rest of them. Shephel grumpily sat up now. "Just thought I saw something," she pulled some jerky out of her bag and started munching on it while Eden told them about the bricks on the town wall.

In a little while Sela headed out to spell off Nasah. When she came in and joined them for lunch she had a smile on her face. "So, here's what I'm thinking," she said between bites. "That town was definitely built by the King, so it must have been lost during a battle before the outposts and the grey was put here, who knows how long ago that was, but in any case," she waved her hand dismissing that information, "...since it had to be on the outskirts of Kaleo, it was probably set up like our outpost, meaning there were secret tunnels and escapes built in..."

"What?" Shephel and the others looked up at her surprised.

"It was built by the King..." Nasah started again.

"No, not that part, the bit about being like our outpost with tunnels and secret exits," he shook his head.

"Yeah," she looked from each of them to the next. "You guys didn't know that?" This time she was the one surprised.

"No," they all said in unison.

"Oh," she nodded understanding now. "Coal told me about them one day. He said you don't get the keys to them unless you're a Sargent or the Lieutenant, someone who would lead others out. He said he only knew where they were because he had to help Gande move some new weapons in secretly a few years back. He wouldn't tell me where they were but he said there were three," she explained.

"So, you're thinking that there would be some in this town? And maybe the enemy wouldn't know?" Parzel asked slowly.

"Exactly," Nasah pointed her biscuit at her. "Especially seeing as the town has open fields all around it, it'd make sense that there'd be a way to get out and to safety or cover. Coal said that it appeared most of the keys to the tunnels were words of the King or some sort of action like it."

Parzel grunted and swallowed her food.

Eden looked at her. "What is it?" she asked.

"Well," she wiped her hands on her pants, stood and made her way to the back of their grotto. "I noticed this carving back here, and I was trying to figure it out," she crouched down and ran her hand over the wall, and as the others crowded in the low space they could see what appeared to be a carving of a winged figure.

"Look there's a second one," Eden pointed about two feet to the right. She reached over Parzel and rubbed the excess dust and dirt off it. "Seems a strange place for such elaborate carvings," she mumbled.

"I wouldn't have noticed except I was trying to stand up this morning and hit my head off the rock and sat down right in front of them," she kept glancing between the two carvings.

"For he will command his servants concerning you to guard you in all your ways, on their wings they will bear you up, lest you strike your foot against a stone," Shephel quoted some words of the King. As he finished Nasah pushed past both Eden and Parzel and put both hands on the inner wings of the two figures. There was a loud crack and the rock above their heads slid forward.

"What!" Eden exclaimed, reaching up she slipped her hand into the crevasse and pushed the stone. It slid easily into a slot in the wall exposing a tunnel above their heads. Eden stood up, her head and shoulders in the space. "Someone give me a torch," she waved her hand until Shephel put a torch in it and pulled out a match to set it a flame. She held it over her head and could see a five rung ladder carved into the wall that led to what appeared to be a tunnel above them. "There's a tunnel up here," she held the torch in one hand and climbed up the rungs, then stretched the torch out into the tunnel. As she swept cobwebs out of the way she could hear the music of Saint-Saens 'Danse macabre' playing in her head as she inspected the creepy passage.

"It looks to be about four feet high, maybe seven feet across. You'd have to crawl, and it seems to slope down from here. But it looks pretty secure, where it's not actual stone that's been carved out, there are wood beams supporting the sides, and they don't look rotten or weak. Creepy but safe." She came back down the ladder to let the others look up.

Once they had all inspected it they moved back to the larger space where they had been eating. "So now what?" Shephel asked.

"We go!" Eden exclaimed. "The King is obviously with us, to have led us to this point."

"That or he trained us well to know where to seek shelter, remember His words and history," Nasah tried to be rational.

"Either way, we don't have to wait till it's dark now to get into the city, no one will know we are coming," she rolled her eyes at Nasah's practicality.

"But, we have no clue where this leads, if the enemy has found it, or if there are guards or a trap on the other side," Parzel pointed out. "But," she put up her hand to stop Eden's argument before it started, "I agree we should go. I think this is the safest bet, and I think there are pretty good odds that the enemy hasn't found it, especially because you have to know the King's words to use it."

"Agreed," Nasah said, "But, I'm pretty sure we will need to watch for other protective things left by the King to make sure only his servants use it. We have to go slow and keep our eyes open. No rash movements," she looked pointedly at Eden.

"I get it!" too excited to be upset by their handling of her. "I'm going to go get Sela, make sure he hasn't seen anything new, then come back here and we can pack up and head out." She crawled out of the grotto

25

*"They will make war on the Lamb
and the Lamb will conquer them, for he is Bara,
Melek of kings, and those with him
are called and eklektos and faithful."*

It didn't take them long to pack up and break camp. Again, Parzel took care of cleaning up their trail and then they crouched beneath the opening.

"I'll lead," Eden volunteered, Re-lighting the torch, she held it up into the opening and stood up.

Parzel shook her head. "You know you don't have to keep protecting us from your decisions, we did all choose to be here," she called up to her.

Eden stuck her head back down. "I know that!" she looked offended. "I'm just obviously better at this than all of you," she replied with a smirk. "But thanks," she added quieter and started up the ladder.

It was a bit more difficult with weapons and packs on to get up and into the tunnel. Once there, they all had to crawl on hands and knees forward. It was quite the accomplishment for Sela, the big man barely fitting. He finally pulled his pack off and tossed it ahead of himself.

"They must have been smaller men who built this tunnel," he muttered.

"I wouldn't doubt they were dwarves," Shephel replied.

"There haven't been dwarves in Kaleo for a thousand years," Sela laughed in return.

"I know, but this stonework is too good for man. You're an artisan, look at it. Have you ever seen anything like this?" he asked as he scraped forward on his knees.

"Only in Migdal," Sela conceded.

"And that, they say, was built by dwarves thousands of years ago," Nasah called back to them. "I wonder what's happened to the dwarves though?" she made a mental note to look that up.

As they turned a corner the tunnel started to feel suffocating. Parzel started to cough from the smoke of the torch. Soon they all were struggling to breathe.

"Eden," Parzel called from the back. "You have to put that torch out. We can't breathe in here."

Eden stopped and glanced behind her seeing the trail of smoke that was filling the tunnel. "How are we going to see?" she asked. Every once in a while here she'd have a moment of wishing for something from home. A flashlight, or better yet a head lamp, would make this so much easier, she thought.

"I don't know, but we're going to die in here soon," Nasah coughed again, shoving her face into her cloak to try and block out the smoke.

Eden realized it was inevitable, so she reached up and snuffed out the torch. The tunnel dropped into sudden blackness, so much so that the darkness itself was suffocating.

"Guess we'll have to feel our way forward," she replied, trying to keep her own fear down.

"Eden, your sword!" Nasah exclaimed pointing to her side.

At first Eden was surprised that she could see Nasah's hand at all, but then she realized that it was the glow of something beside her that was lighting up the tunnel. She glanced down at her belt, and pulled her sword from the scabbard. It shone a brilliant white light, casting more light than a hundred torches could have. The dark was beaten back and they all breathed a sigh of relief.

"Of course, 'Even the darkness is not dark to you, and the night is as bright as the day, darkness and light are alike to you'," Eden quoted the inscription. "So much time standing on a wall doing nothing had made me forget what these weapons are for," she laughed.

Turning, she started forward again, casting quick glances at her blade in front of her as she crawled, still amazed by the gift that it was. Sometimes she felt undeserving. Who was she to be chosen? To be given such a gift? She had to prove her worth, she had to get this drawing rod for the King. She had to fulfill her purpose.

"I think we might be able to stand here," Nasah said from behind her, calling Eden back from her thoughts.

"Yeah," she agreed, glancing above her to where the roof had moved away. "I think you're right," she used her sword to help herself to her feet, her knees aching. "Much better," she stretched, able to just barely touch the roof with her fingertips. "Sela, even you'll be able to walk," she looked at the big man as he ungracefully and clearly in a lot of pain, struggled to get to his feet.

Shephel reached over and helped him stand, and picked up his pack for him. "Better?" he asked, handing the pack over.

"Much," he sighed. "I didn't want to say anything, but I didn't think I could manage that much further," he rubbed his legs and stretched his back before putting the pack back on.

The tunnel had started to descend more rapidly, and they felt they must be rather deep under the fields that they had been watching earlier. Every so often there were small side tunnels that brought fresh air flowing to them.

"Ingenious," Nasah marveled. "They must solely work as the airflow system down here. I bet they simply look like cracks between stones in those fields," she was recalling the landscape of what must be above them. "Amazing that they haven't caved in or been covered all these years."

"Not much about the King's handiwork surprises me anymore," Parzel said "He has thought of everything, even the things we don't realize we need before, like oxygen to walk through this tunnel," she laughed at their own lack of forethought for that.

Not much further along, the tunnel started to rise. "We must be getting close to the town or be under it or something," Nasah surmised. "Keep your eyes open Eden, this would be where they would have built safeties in to protect their escape route, or whatever this was."

Eden nodded, her eyes carefully scanning in front of her. Nothing had changed in the view. It was all the same, mostly rock with a few beams and dirt here and there. Nothing that seemed dangerous, out of the ordinary, or a sign. "The tunnel turns up ahead and seems to level off," she looked at the ground. "How about I just peek around that turn before we go forward?" she suggested.

"Good idea," Nasah agreed. "Although, if anyone is up there they'd have to be blind to not see our light coming," she glanced at the sword that had not stopped glowing brilliantly.

Eden shrugged and moved ahead of them a bit. The floor did level out just before this turn, she paused at the side of the tunnel, then crouched down and cautiously popped her head around the corner. There was another, approximately four feet of tunnel, that ended at a door. She held her sword out to get a better look, thinking it safe she went around and approached the door. She could just hear her team coming up behind her.

The door was small and made of solid wood. It looked like barn board and was secured with large brass fittings and hinges. There was no lock. They all inspected it, but could see no signs of warnings, or traps. Eden even leaned against it with her ear to try and see if there was any noise on the other side. She shook her head. "We open it?" she whispered the question.

All four nodded, drawing their own weapons now. Cautiously, Eden pulled the brass handle towards them and the door, remarkably, made no sound as it slid open easily. All five heads leaned around it to peer through the crack. All they could see was an empty room. It didn't appear to have any particular purpose. There was no furniture, no crates, no people, not even any lighting on the walls. They could see that there were two other doors, one on each side of the room, with the side directly opposite them being slightly smaller than the others. The floor was chiseled stone each block approximately one foot square. On some of the stones were carved a lion and on others a serpent, and still others had a lamb, and an eagle. It seemed a rather unassuming room, certainly not dangerous.

Eden looked at the others. "Seems safe right?" she asked. No one really answered, Nasah was staring at the floor. So Eden turned, and with her sword in front, took a step forward. As soon as she put her foot down the stone beneath it immediately gave way, taking pieces of the ones beside it with it. She started to topple forward, losing her balance. She tried to catch herself with her sword, but where she put the tip to hold herself up, that stone also cracked and gave way, tumbling into some abyss beneath them. She would surely have followed had Sela's big hand not grabbed her backpack and stopped her fall. She sighed, facing the hole where the stone had been seeing nothing but darkness. Sela pulled her back to the door frame.

"Well that didn't work out," she smiled, putting her hand on his shoulder as a thank you. They all turned to look at the room again and the floor.

"What do we do?" Parzel asked. She reached out with her own sword and touched another brick that immediately started to crumble. "There has to be a way across."

"Of course!" Nasah exclaimed. She turned to her brother. "What was that quote from the King you said to find the opening from the angels? There's more to it isn't there?"

He frowned first, trying to remember. "Yeah, I think it goes, 'You will tread on the lion and the adder; the young lion and the serpent you will trample underfoot.'"

"It's the carvings again," Nasah pointed. "We have to only step on the stones that have lions and serpents." She tentatively reached her own sword out and with a stretch tapped the closest lion carving. It appeared solid. "See!"

"But the serpents too?" Sela seemed wary. "That seems like a trick from Nachash."

Nasah was so sure of herself now that without testing she jumped to the next lion, then tapped the serpent tile near her. "I don't think there is anything about Nachash in this room," and she confidently stepped onto the tile.

Everyone cringed slightly but quickly agreed when they saw her standing firmly. "Okay then, only the lions and serpents," Eden jumped to follow Nasah.

They each followed in turn, jumping and trying to keep their balance on the small one foot square stones. Occasionally a bit of an adjoining stone might break off into oblivion, but they made their way across and found that this pathway led them directly to the small door that had faced opposite them. They all stood balanced on stones a few feet apart from each other with Nasah and Eden standing on two stones by the door.

Nasah leaned against the door to listen. "There's noise on that side, not a lot but seems repetitive. It gets closer then fades," she still leaned in.

"Must be a guard," Parzel guessed. "Can you tell when they are furthest away?"

"I'd say right now," she paused, "now it's getting closer." They all counted as they waited. "And farther away again so I can't hear it."

"My guess is that was a count of one hundred and eighty," Eden said.

"And now it's coming back," Nasah was counting as well. After a pause, she said, "Yeah, I'd agree, about one eighty."

"So, one of us has to go through the door in that hundred and eighty count gap and hope there is somewhere to hide in there, then knock here to let us know it's safe for all of us to come in during the next interval and hide, then we can make a plan once we know what's on that side." Eden suggested.

Eden started to pull the door when the others nodded. "Just be ready to come through when I knock okay? Right when I knock you come, don't come before," she explained.

"Clear," Nasah got ready to move, as Eden leaned in to the door again. She waited until she was sure she had the pace down for the guard out there. When she thought they were walking away, she pulled the door open and slipped through.

The rest of them stood there frozen, until Nasah leaned in and put her ear to the door again. She couldn't hear anything.

When Eden slipped out the door she found she was standing in a dungeon chamber. She was surrounded by stone walls, and in front of her was a wooden door with a small opening for someone to look in that was barred. She turned as the other door was closing and was thankful she did because if she hadn't seen it close she would never have been able to find it to knock on. It looked exactly like the stone wall on either side. She could just tell, only because she saw it, the crack that had slightly less dust on it.

Suddenly she realized that the noise she heard was definitely foot steps and they were approaching again. She quickly moved to the door and pressed herself to it so that they would be unable to see her if they happened to glance in the chamber. She listened as the footsteps passed her, her own heart was beating as quickly. Once they had walked by she dared to peek through the bars and saw the back of a solider. He didn't seem overly cautious or even armed to the teeth or anything. He clearly wasn't too worried about whatever he was guarding. She watched as he glanced in the last camber then turned on his heel. Now she had to wait another rotation for him to pass before she could knock to signal Nasah. She hoped she'd wait, even though she'd been longer than the plan.

As he slowly moved past her door, she quietly crept back to the hidden door and knocked. Immediately Nasah was through, and with a quick glance at their surroundings and the hearing the footsteps she too took cover by the door.

As she leaned against the wall and turned back to where she had come from, her face registered shock when she couldn't see the door at all. She glanced quickly at Eden, who saw the surprise and nodded.

Just then, instead of hearing the guard's step turn, they heard a door open and different, heavier steps come into the hallway.

"Just checking on you," a voice spoke deeply.

"Still bored as ever," the other replied. "Why do we have to guard some peasant I'll never understand. You want to trade me for a bit? I'm hungry," the first guard complained.

"No way," the other laughed. "I brought you our leftovers, but you've got another third down here. I ain't coming down till I have to," he laughed again, clapped the other on the back. "Besides, we are actually guarding something of value upstairs. He added another team of us, there's eight now, but don't worry, I'll send one of the new guys down here in a third for you." A door opened again, and the sound of the footsteps faded away as it closed.

"Guard something worthwhile..." the first voice grumbled, "I'll give you something to guard," he muttered to himself and then took a bite of his food and kept pacing.

Nasah and Eden looked at each other. "It's got to be the rod," Eden mouthed to her. Nasah nodded, but clearly didn't look convinced. She shrugged, then pointed to the hidden doorway. Eden's eyes went wide and she nodded, realizing they had kept the others waiting a long time, and they were sure to be worried. As soon as the guard passed again Nasah knocked and Parzel burst through the door, her eyes were on fire and she immediately took her forearm and pinned Eden to the wall in anger.

Eden held up her finger to try and keep Parzel quiet and Nasah tried to pull her off. As Parzel looked to Nasah, then took in the room, the footsteps and the situation, she let go of Eden and followed suit hiding near the door. Two more times they knocked and got all five of them into the prison.

The greatest challenge now was just coming up with a plan without speaking. Eden pointed to the door which was clearly unlocked, then to Nasah. Sela raised his hand, pointed to himself and motioned that he would grab the guard from behind and knock him out.

Parzel nodded, and pointed to herself and Eden to back him up. They waited silently until the guard had moved past them and his back was near the opening of the door, which thankfully opened inside. On Shephel's three count they sprang into motion.

Sela slid out the door and in one quick move had wrapped his arm around the guard's throat and was applying pressure. Eden and Parzel had weapons drawn behind him, but no help was needed. He made no noise, and within a minute his hand that was struggling to pull Sela's arm away went limp, and the big man laid him on the floor quietly.

Nasah gasped as she noticed the tattoo on his arm. "Look," she grabbed Shephel's arm. "It's the tattoo that our prisoner had," and he nodded.

"Just another pawn?" he commented, then took his weapons, and they dragged him into another open cell, but this time locked the door behind him.

Now Parzel turned again to Eden. "What the heck took you so long?" she exclaimed in an animated whisper.

"A second guard came and they were having a discussion just down the hall," Nasah again tried to calm her down. "It wasn't Eden's fault, we just couldn't do anything right then."

Parzel relaxed with that answer and stepped back from Eden.

"But," Eden went on. "The second guard did say that they were guarding something of importance just upstairs and this guy could join them when he's relieved in a third."

"And you think that thing is the rod?" Shephel asked.

"What else could it be?" she asked.

"Well, a lot of things actually, but in this case you might be right," Shephel answered. "But we can't be sure."

"So what do we do?" Sela asked. That was when they heard a noise at the far end of the block of cells. "What was that?" he turned drawing his sword.

"The guard said there was a peasant down here, that's who he was guarding. That must have been him," Nasah explained. Quietly they all walked down the hallway and Eden looked into the bars in the far cell and was shocked at the face that was staring back at her.

"Hello," he said.

"What are you doing here?" she asked dumbfounded. In the cell stood her shepherd friend, dressed just as she'd seen him last on the hill with his sheep. He smiled.

"Oh, well, the King has many flocks, I was down here checking on some in Gaavah and seems I crossed paths with the wrong crowd."

They quickly opened the door for him with the keys that they had taken off the guard. "Thanks. It's a bit musty down here," he smiled again, clearly no worse for wear from being imprisoned.

"Have you been here long?" Eden asked.

"No, not long," he looked at each one. "This is your team that you've told me about?"

Eden nodded and introduced them all.

"Well, if we are leaving I suggest we go soon, they will be switching guard duty soon," he started walking towards the cell they had come from.

"We aren't leaving, we are going to go upstairs to get the drawing rod back," Eden explained, stopping him in his tracks.

"Drawing rod?" he turned. "I've heard of that. I don't think it will be easy to get, did the King send you on this mission?" he asked.

"Well, not explicitly, but we think that he intended it by having us out here, and then we caught a prisoner who told us it was here," Nasah replied.

"Oh," he paused thoughtfully. "So maybe it's not your job to do?" he asked.

"You don't understand," Eden shook her head, thinking how could she explain all this to a shepherd. "I don't have time to explain, but we need to do this. But you can escape through here," she pointed to the cell they came from. "There's a ..."

"Yes, I know how to get out," he smiled, a deep understanding in his eyes.

"You do?" Parzel asked.

"Yes," he nodded to her. "I've been here many times, in better times, I can get out to the hills, but I think that I will wait in here for you," he stepped into the cell and closed the door. He looked out through the bars. "Be sure of what you do."

Eden continued to stand, looking into his eyes, thrown off by finding him here, and by something else. That thing that was nagging at her about this entire excursion.

"Eden, we have to make a plan, they'll be here soon," Parzel touched her arm. She too was looking at the shepherd, not sure what had just happened, but feeling that something of deeper significance was going on.

"Right," Eden turned and had to step away from the door so as to not see him. "A plan..."

"My suggestion," Shephel began, "would be that we wait for the next guard to come down and take him by surprise as we did this guy. Then we go up the stairs to wherever they are guarding this thing and surprise them. They will be expecting to hear someone coming so we don't have to worry about noise, but they will also be down two in numbers so we have surprise on our side and hopefully enough to take however many are there."

"Six, there will be six left," Nasah said. "The last guard said there were eight total, if we can believe that."

"Okay, that's a good plan," Parzel looked at them both. "Same deal, it appears the door opens outward into the hall here," she looked at the hinges. "So Sela, stay behind the door, and we can stay in this cell, closest so we can come out to help if necessary."

They all agreed and moved into their places.

It seemed like an eternity until they heard steps coming closer. Sela stepped back, and everyone held their breath. The door opened quickly and another guard stepped into the hall. He clearly expected to see the guy he was replacing and stood still when he saw the empty hall in front of him. But before he could make a sound Sela had wrapped his arm around his throat and had him on the ground.

"Good work Sela," Eden started taking the man's weapons.

Shephel glanced in to see that the first guard was still unconscious, then unlocked his cell door. "Come on, hurry up," he waved them in.

Sela dragged the guard into the cell and Shephel locked it again. "Gets a lot better than we would if we were captured," he grunted.

"We ready for this?" Parzel asked, standing next to the door. "We have no clue what we are walking into."

"But we know this is my task, the King will be with us," Eden said convincingly. "And I have the best team to go forward with," she smiled at them, wanting to say something about the fact that they could all leave, but knowing that they'd just get mad again. She couldn't believe how much she had come to love them.

"Then let's do it, I can't handle waiting any longer," Shephel took a deep breath, drawing his sword. Each of them stood, weapons in hand, and without complaining, let Eden take the lead.

26

"Put on then as the King's eklektos,
set apart and beloved, compassionate hearts,
kindness, humility, meekness and patience,
bearing with one another and if one has a complaint against another,
forgiving them."

Eden pulled open the door and looked down a dark hallway. There were torches burning on the walls that cast an eerie gloom over everything, but outside of the life-sized carvings of lambs and lions, reassuring them that this was something the King had built, there was no one else. The hall was not long, only about ten feet, with a staircase rising to the next floor with another closed door. Eden, with sword raised, moved down the hallway quietly, Nasah was directly behind her then Shephel, Sela and Parzel at the rear. She took the steps two at a time and stopped to lean against the door and listen.

What she heard were conversations. There were several voices talking all at once and she couldn't make out anything that they were saying.

Nasah tapped her on the shoulder and pointed to the bottom of the door. There was about a centimetre space there that was letting in some light. Nasah stepped back so Eden could crouch down to look.

Eden put her eye to the crack and could see armour clad boots. There seemed to be three near the door and then at least four more in the open space in the room. But she couldn't see the sides and there didn't seem to be any sort of order to them that would suggest where the drawing rod might be. She stood back up and held up her fingers to communicate seven with a shrug, more than they thought. All of them nodded. Parzel held up three fingers and tilted her head towards the door.

Eden nodded in return, counted down on her fingers - three, two, one and burst into the room.

Light flared around them, and the closest soldiers were caught off guard, mouths open in mid-conversation. Eden's sword took two of them down immediately with two swift moves and Nasah slide tackled the third, dropping the butt of her sword into his temple knocking him unconscious. The other three poured into the room as the other guards, recovering from their shock, were drawing weapons and starting to advance.

Eden had counted correctly, four more faced the five of them, but she couldn't see what they were guarding. The four were moving towards them, but she saw a fifth who hung back. He had been out of sight and now stayed near the door on the opposite side of the room. Beside him was a pedestal but nothing appeared to be on top of it.

She had no more time to consider as the soldiers charged, broad swords swinging down on them. Eden raised her own to block and the metal on metal rang out loudly in the room. She heard the others engage but had to focus her attention on the one attacking her.

Parzel who had entered the room last was quick to move around the side of the room and was able to get a better spot to face two of the soldiers, she kept the wall to her back and matched the two blow for blow. As they stepped back to regroup she used the wall and pillar beside her as leverage and bounded up, in order to pounce down on them, as she blocked one swing, her foot caught the shoulder of the other knocking him to the ground. Able to focus on the one, she moved quickly to strike and disable him, kicking his sword across the room. She spun to face the other, who was struggling to get back on his feet, but with another swift kick to the jaw she sent him sprawling backwards unconscious.

Sela and Shephel were each with one and Parzel turned to help Sela while Nasah went to her brother's side. Eden though, turned to the guard who had not joined the fight and saw him flee out the door.

She checked to make sure her team was doing okay, then ran to the door, she could see him already make a turn in the hall, so she took a second to look at the pedestal. She ran her hand over the top and felt nothing but the flat stone. It didn't make sense, to have left a guard to guard nothing and then flee when his fellows were losing the fight. She heard a cry behind her and spun to see Shephel take a blow to his hand and lose his sword, Nasah quickly blocked the next blow that was aimed at his head and then spun to slash the soldier across his chest as he had tried to recover from his own swing. He fell to the floor at the same time that Sela, who had also lost his sword in the fight, landed an incredible punch with his fist, crushing his opponent's helmet into his skull.

"Shephel! You okay?" Eden called.

"I will be," he replied, tearing a piece of his cloak to wrap his hand and try and stop the bleeding.

As Eden turned to start leading them through the next door a burst of fire blew it off its hinges and sent her sprawling across the room. Lights went out and flames encircled them, separating each of them from one another and consuming the soldiers on the floor. All of them shielded their eyes from the flames and faces from the heat. And then just as suddenly, it was gone and two men stood in the doorway. The darkness of their souls reflected in the countenance of their faces. Their arms were outstretched and as Eden looked up she could see that each had the same yellow eyes fixed on them that she had seen before. Nachash's Ebed. She reached for her sword only to realize it lay by the door.

"Looking for this?" the one said, stepping on the blade of her sword. "The eklektos' sword," he sneered. "Not very helpful today was it?" he laughed. His eyes flew to Sela who had reached for his sword. With a flick of his hand a flame of fire shot out and wrapped around his wrist. He cried out with pain and released his sword to have it stripped away from him.

"You are no match of us," the ebed laughed. "I cannot even believe the King would be so foolish to send you here. I thought this plan madness, but here you are," he had a look of mock surprise on his face. "Did you come looking for this?" and with another wave of his hand towards the pedestal a black rod, about a foot long appeared right where Eden had felt the stone.

Her eyes gave her away in that moment. "Didn't see it earlier? Did you think a mere mortal as you could just take such an artifact? Only royalty, and our illustrious leader Nachash have the power to hold such a thing."

Eden was trying desperately to clear her head. She was so confused as to what was happening, why she couldn't have even felt the rod, and then to figure out how to get out of this situation. Her mind tried to find the words of the King that would free them from this - trap. It must have been a trap. She'd led her friends, her team that counted on her, into a trap. Their lives were on the line, because of her. She had to do something.

"Go and get Nacash, he is going to be thrilled with our catch," the one doing all the talking said to the other, who turned and vanished down the hallway.

Eden dropped her head, out of ideas, when she saw the knife at her belt. She looked over at the others who she could see were all within a step of the open door to the prison, the prison where they could escape. She looked Parzel in the eye. Her friend shook her head, not wanting Eden to move, but Eden just smiled, then moving as fast as she could she swept to her feet and let her dagger fly, while sprinting towards the rod.

So much happened in such short a period of time that it was hard to catch it all. As she threw the dagger Eden shouted, "Parzel get them out!"

Parzel immediately started to move, shoving Shephel and Sela who were basically in the doorway, down the stairs backwards as she stepped in with sword drawn and turned to call Nasah to her.

In the same moment, Eden's dagger, true to its nature, found its home in the heart of the ebed. It sank deep and his yellow eyes registered surprise as they followed Eden to the rod.

Just as Eden's hand closed on the rod, what appeared to be a bolt of lightning shot into the room and seized Nasah from where she was one step from the doorway. As she screamed in pain, she managed to kick the door closed in Parzel's face before she was lifted into the air and held there writhing as the electricity wrapped itself around her.

"Nasah!" Eden cried out, seeing the pain gripping her friend's face, now unable to make any noise. Eden turned to see the ebed fall, yellow eyes unseeing now, but the bolt didn't come from him. It was coming from the doorway where another man stepped carefully over the body of his own servant with one hand extended towards Nasah, holding the other end of that electricity like it was a rope.

He didn't look much different than the King. He wore what appeared to be a royal robe, but embroidered with golden serpents, its colour such a deep purple it appeared black. His hair was jet black as well, with a black beard trimmed perfectly. He stood at least six feet tall, and appeared thin underneath the robes, but his arm was steady and hand sure as it held the end of that bolt. He turned his face to look at Eden and she shivered as two black eyes ringed with yellow stared at her. His face broke into a smirk that held malice in its curves. His eyes went from Eden's hand, gripped around the rod, to Nasah writhing in his hold. "Your friend, or the rod?" he asked, his voice deep and grating. "Your choice eklektos."

When the door slammed in Parzel's face her sword was knocked from her hand and down the stairs. She glanced after it, and at Shephel and Sela getting to their feet at the bottom, then turned back to the door and tried to open it again but it wouldn't move. "Nasah!" she screamed, pounding on the door. The last thing she had seen was that terrible blinding light wrapped around Nasah's body lifting her into the air. "Nasah!" she cried again, beating the door in desperation.

"Parzel," a different voice called behind her. "Parzel, come down," it repeated. She turned to see the Shepherd she had just met, standing with Sela and Shephel. His face didn't look very shepherd-like anymore, he had an authoritative look to him now, one that seemed strangely familiar.

"Come down," he said again. And unsure why, other than her heart was drawn to obey his words, she slowly came down the steps leaving her friends behind. At the bottom he held out her sword for her.

"You need to go," he instructed. "She told you to protect them, and you must."

"But Nasah, and Eden," she turned back to look up at the door.

"Are beyond your help," he said sadly. "But not beyond help," he put his hand on her shoulder. "You know the way, tread on the lion and the serpent and get these two back. Shephel will need attention soon, that wound is deeper than it appears," he looked to where Sela was now supporting Shephel, whose hand was dripping blood as the makeshift bandage wasn't doing much. "You know the way, go directly to your outpost. Help will come," he smiled. "I know you are able, and now you are called to it. Go!" his voice took on that authoritative tone again with urgency and Parzel was forced to obey.

"Who are you?" she asked as she gestured for Sela to help Shephel down the hall and started to follow.

"You know me," he replied, putting his foot on the first stair. "And you will know me again. Now go."

She moved to hurry her friends out to safety. Just as they entered the prison she glanced back and saw the shepherd ascend the stairs and lay a hand on the door, then she turned and ran.

"What's your choice?" Nachash's eyes narrowed, the grip on Nasah seemed to intensify and Eden saw silent tears roll down her face.

"Stop it!" she cried, unable to take it. Her hand released the rod, but did not move away from it. "Put her down and you can have the rod."

Nachash laughed, "I've always had it," but he flicked his wrist and the bolt vanished, tossing Nasah aside like a rag doll. Eden sprinted to her side.

"Nasah, can you hear me?" she lifted her friend's face to hers and tried to wake her up. "Nasah, please," she leaned down and could hear shallow breaths rattle out of her lungs. At least she was alive, but she could see the burns from the electricity wrapped all around her body. She was deathly pale, and her one arm hung at an awkward angle at her side.

"What have you done to her?" she cried, glaring at Nachash.

"What have I done?" he laughed again, picking up the rod and slipping it into his cloak. "I think, my dear, you should ask what you have done. I knew that moving the rod around near the limits would tempt the King too much. Some day he would have to send you, I just never expected it so soon," he tilted his head seeming to come to a conclusion and let out another laugh as he gazed at her. "He didn't send you did he? You did this on your own!" The room felt like it was shaking with his laughter. "How incredibly prideful to think you could best me. How ridiculous to not even obey your King. If these are the types of Chayil he is producing now the whole kingdom will fall to me soon. And to have chosen you ... even his own decisions are failing," he bent and picked up Eden's sword. He examined the blade. "It shall be a fitting end to kill you with your own blade. Pity I couldn't have done it so long ago with your family," he turned his malice filled eyes back to see her's burning with anger as she held her friend. A tear fell down Eden's cheek.

"For, behold, your enemies, O Lord, for behold your enemies will perish and all who do iniquity will be scattered," she spat the words of the King at him through gritted teeth, and as she spoke the door behind her flew open again and in walked the shepherd.

Nachash's eyes flashed at the sight of him, he raised Eden's sword and his hand towards him. "You," he hissed.

"I have come as a replacement," he said, not looking at Eden, but directly in Nachash's terrible black and yellow eyes. "Let them live, and you may take me."

"You would trade your life for theirs? You would love them so much?" he asked unbelieving.

"I would, and so would my father. I know you don't understand it, you never will. So have your revenge, have me, willingly," he held out his hands.

Eden shook her head. As she knelt cradling Nasah's head in her lap she was trying to understand what was happening. Why would Nachash trade her, the eklektos, for a shepherd? One he already had in prison? And why was this shepherd suddenly more regal than anyone she knew. What was it that reminded her...

But her thoughts were cut short when Nachash cried out. "So be it." Suddenly a black wind enveloped them like the flames had and a moment later Eden opened her eyes in a different cell than the one they had entered through. She was in the same position on the floor with Nasah, and across from her stood the shepherd, his hands bound.

"What's happening?" she asked. "Who are you?"

"You don't know me yet?" he asked, coming over and kneeling beside her.

"You're his son," she said quietly, suddenly understanding it all. The conversations, the appearances. "All along," she wondered aloud.

"All along," he smiled. Then he turned his face to Nasah and wiped her brow with his tied hands. "You must get her to my father. Only the King can heal this devilry that has wrapped her."

"But how?" Eden shook her head. "We are all trapped here now. It's not the room we can escape from."

"Isn't it?" he asked, glancing around the room.

Eden followed his eyes until they rested on a carving of a great eagle on the wall beside her.

"Wasn't there something my father said?" he asked.

"For it is the King who delivers you from the snare of the trapper, and from the deadly pestilence, he will cover you with his pinions and under his wings you may seek refuge," she quoted, watching him stand and place both his hands under the wings of the eagle. Just as before, the wall gave way and a door opened. Looking in Eden could see the same room they had come through beyond it.

"This didn't used to be a prison, but it is definitely coming in handy as one now," he laughed.

"Let me get those ropes off your hands and we can go," she said, laying Nasah's head down, noting that she had started to sweat.

"Oh no, this is a trip for you two alone," he shook his head.

"But he's going to kill you!" Eden cried.

"I know. I made the trade and I must fulfill it or you will never be safe," he smiled at her again, his eyes so like the King's, Eden couldn't believe she never saw it before.

"But.." she protested again.

"No, you must obey me now or Nasah will die. She has to get to the King."

"But Migdal is so far," she pointed out.

"Where is your horse? Your Ruach?" he asked.

"I left her at the outpost. I thought it'd be safer for both of us," she dropped her eyes, realizing it was the wrong decision.

"Never leave Ruach, always keep her close, but in the meantime..." he stepped up to her, and with his bound hands, he reached to her neck and pulled the chain holding the pala stone. "The King is as close as you need," he let it fall on the outside of her shirt. "Now the power of Nachash prevents this from working in this place so you have to carry her through the tunnel and back to the grotto, then use the stone, fix the throne room in your mind and go," he instructed her.

Tears were streaming down Eden's face now. "I am so sorry," she sobbed.

"Stop Eden. Nasah needs you. Weeping may endure for the night, but joy comes in the morning," he stood next to the doorway. "Now go."

Eden got down on one knee and picked Nasah up onto her shoulders, much like she carried others what seemed ages ago in her fire training, she now carried her friend. With one last tearful look at the shepherd, her shepherd, she stepped through the door and onto a lion carving. She heard the door swing shut behind her and lock into place. With a deep breath of determination she carefully stepped from stone to stone with Nasah on her back. As she walked she could see drops of blood, and assumed the others had gotten out as well. She prayed Parzel could get them to safety. Maybe Gande had figured out where they went by now and met them?

Her heart was wracked with guilt at the failure she was. To fall into a trap, to get two of her friends hurt, maybe killed if she couldn't get to the King fast enough...and his son! Executed in her place? How could she ever face the King? How could she ever face herself? If she didn't have to care for Nasah she probably would have run and hid from the shame and guilt, but for now her focus had to be her friend. She had to get her to help.

The walk was exhausting, carrying Nasah, even as small as she was, so far. Finally, the tunnel started to narrow and she had to take her off her shoulders. She started backing through the tunnel and pulling Nasah behind her. Sweat was pouring off her forehead, but as she looked at Nasah's face getting paler by the minute she pushed on, willing her body to fight for her friend.

After what seemed an eternity she could see the hole they had entered just behind her. She let her legs drop down and find the stone rungs, then pulled Nasah towards her. She wrapped her arms tightly under her arms, pulling her back to her chest, then leaning her own back against the stone she slowly eased Nasah down backwards, on top of herself. She collapsed in a pile on the floor, with Nasah's weakened body resting on her.

She took a couple of deep breaths, while she pulled the pala stone free from under Nasah's back and held it in her fist.

Hugging her friend fiercely Eden closed her eyes and spoke as loudly as she could. "Open to me the gates of righteousness; I shall enter through them, this is the gate of the King," with her heart willing them into his throne room.

She felt the temperature change and the cool of stone against her back. Opening her eyes she saw the two thrones in front of her and sighed with relief. Everything else tumbled into her vision.

"We're here now, Nasah, It's going to be okay," she whispered in her ear. Looking up for help she saw Moreh and Petros running towards her. In the same moment she felt a hand she knew all too well on her shoulder.

His voice sounded like she was underwater. "Let her go Eden, I need to help her." The King gently moved her away and knelt beside Nasah, pressing his hands to her forehead.

Eden knelt feeling disoriented, she just stared at him. Not sure what to do, what he would think of her once he knows? Then two other hands dropped a blanket onto her shoulders, helping her to her feet and turned her to face them.

Moreh stood there with such compassion on her face that Eden collapsed into her teacher's arms and started sobbing. "I'm so sorry, so sorry."

Moreh held her tight, shushing her and slowly leading her out of the room. When Eden looked up she saw she was in the King's sitting room. "Oh I can't be in here," she said, shaking her head and looking at Moreh's face with fear in her eyes.

"He asked for you to come here, he said he would need to talk to you," she explained, gently directing her to the couch.

"You don't understand, I can't, he won't," she sobbed again. "I'm so sorry."

Moreh held her head for a moment, then sat down beside her and looked in her reddened eyes. "I don't know what you are sorry for, or what has happened, but he definitely does and he will alwyas desire to sit with you. Remember who he is, even when we are not who we want to be," she consoled her.

They sat side by each for a long time in silence.

Finally, the King entered the room, he looked at the two of them on the couch and nodded for Moreh to leave. Eden watched her go in the grips of fear, then looked down at herself covered in dirt and sweat, without sword or dagger, helpless and useless in his presence.

"Much has happened has it not?" he asked, sitting down beside her.

"Oh I am so sorry, so sorry. Your son, he's dead because of me!" she blurted it all out.

But rather than shock, the King's face registered compassion, even joy Eden thought. She sniffed and stopped crying instantly, confused by his response.

He got up and took what looked to be a journal from his desk and came back to her side. "This is my original copy of, well, my words," he chuckled, "can you read the last lines here?" he pointed to the bottom of a page.

Eden swallowed and read. "He who loses his life will gain it."

"Do you recall the tapestry on the wall you have always loved to look at?" When she nodded he continued. "That's the lamb part of the lion and lamb aspect of this throne. My son has laid down his life for you, and for everyone else in this kingdom, but he has the power to take it back," he smiled as he watched her seek to understand. "Have you ever noticed the sword in the hand of the enemy in the picture? It's yours," he paused, Eden looked shocked, having never noticed it before. "All along," he smiled. "Now my son has freed the slaves by returning this to me," and he lifted the same black rod that Eden's hand had held not long before.

"What? How?" she asked, eyes as wide as saucers.

"I think that's a story for him to explain to you some day. For now, you need to hear these words... 'You sought the king and he answered you, and delivered you from all your fears. You looked to him and were radiant and your face will never be ashamed.'," he put his hand under her chin and lifted her face to his.

"You are eklektos, not to find a rod, but to be saved," he spoke so quietly but Eden's pounding heart almost overpowered his words.

"There is nothing any more special about you than anyone else, you were chosen to be saved, just like everyone else, the eklektos, not just one. Nachash can't understand that and he can't understand love, he made you to be his nemisis by misunderstanding the calling you had... it was always my plan. You have nothing to be ashamed of now, you're a child of the king, safe in my house."

"But I thought that the tapestry was a picture of the past?" she asked, remembering Moreh's words that first day in Kaleo.

"Time does not matter to me in Kaleo," the King smiled. "Just one of many wonders you will come to see but never fully know."

Eden's heart was now full to overflowing. To have gone from certain death, to being saved, to being forgiven and in a way made new and her entire life explained in a moment, it was too much. Too many emotions to consider, too many moments to think about that she just stopped and looked in those familiar eyes of the King and wrapped her arms around him and said, "thank you."

He held her close, his own face glowing with joy. Then he sat back. "Now, you need to go to the hospital wing to be with Nasah when she wakes. I've already talked with her, she's fine, but needs rest to get her strength back, she will want a friend. Tell her the whole story," he grinned. "And don't worry, your other friends will be here in a few days bringing your horse with them," he stood and then turned back to her. "By the way, don't ever leave your Ruach behind. Now go," he shooed her out the door.

Eden ran the whole way to the hospital wing and smiled at Master Rophe as she barged into Nasah's room. Her friend had her colour back and looked like she was asleep, but healthy. Eden could see the scars from where that lightning bolt had wrapped her.

"New tattoos I think," Nasah's voice caused Eden to jump. She smiled. "You were looking at my arms, I think they are nice tattoos, I'll look so much more fierce in training and battle now. Those ebed have got nothing on me with their lame yellow eyes."

"Oh Nasah," Eden threw herself on her and hugged her.

"Easy, I've been wrapped up a bit tight lately," she laughed and hugged her back. "Are you okay?" she asked, pulling back to look Eden in the eye.

"I am now. But I'm sorry to have put you in this position. To have gotten you so hurt," she lowered her eyes and Nasah reached over and took her hand.

"Stop it, the King has the drawing rod, I don't quite understand what I remember about the shepherd guy, but the King told me to ask you. But in any case, you didn't get me hurt, the enemy did. You fought for me, you saved me. I would go into battle with you any day." Her eyes full of more wisdom than her years Eden thought.

"Thank you," she smiled, "I don't deserve any of you as friends, yet I'm so blessed," then she started to recount all that happened and who the shepherd was.

Several watches later Master Rophe came in. "Eden, I think you need to let my patient rest," he said gently. On cue, Nasah yawned.

"What time can I come back?" she asked.

"First thing in the morning, come have breakfast with her," he smiled and ushered her out the door. Standing outside, looking at the practice fields and seeing the sun starting to set she decided to head to the pastures, even if Ruach wasn't here she could still walk out and enjoy the peacefulness, besides, she had so much to think about.

She strolled out, mulling over everything in her mind. She and Nasah had traded thoughts and talked more in depth about what happened. She was still incredibly overwhelmed that he would elect to save her. She got to the edge of the field and climbed up onto the fence to watch as the sun dipped into its hues of red and orange before falling below the horizon. Just then there was a shout from below her.

She glanced down and her mouth dropped. There, coming towards her was her shepherd. She leapt off the fence and ran, or more accurately tumbled, down the slope to him.

"How are you here?" she cried, throwing her arms around him. "I can't believe I didn't know who you were!"

He laughed, that same laugh the King had. "Oh, I like to keep a low profile sometimes, people have to find me when they are supposed to. As for how I'm here," he reached under his cloak and pulled out her sword and lay it in her hands, "the inscription."

"Even the darkness is not dark to you, and the night is as bright as the day..." she quoted.

"Yes, well it seems Nachash doesn't remember his studies as well as he thinks. He used the very sword that would be his undoing. He made the darkest moment into the brightest. He who loses his life will find it," he smiled. "Can't keep me down and even brought my father a present."

"The rod," Eden nodded, "I saw it. But why couldn't I see it in that room?"

"Well, that Nachash was right about, no one can wield it but the King and I and those we entrust its power to. He could only pervert its uses through dark powers, but no mortal could take it, or even see it without it being revealed to them. You could never have completed that mission, like I tried to tell you in the cells."

"And that's another thing, why were you there? How would Nachash imprison you and not know who you were, because he definitely knew you when you came through that door," Eden asked.

"Well, I was waiting for you. I let the guards take me earlier in the day, but Nachash wasn't about to bother with a peasant shepherd causing problems. I had other business to take care of," he started up the hillside with her.

"I just can't believe it, I've never felt so grateful for anything in my life. To be eklektos, to be saved. I thought I was chosen but for such a different thing, and it let me fall into pride. I'm still chosen, but it's not the same, it's nothing of me, and all you. It's humbling," Eden explained some of her thoughts. "And I think I finally figured out the answer to the question the King asked me when I was attending him all those months ago," she smiled, more to herself at the realization. "His words, I always succeeded because of his words, it was never me in any case."

"Good," the shepherd helped her back over the fence, smiling as well. "Now, what are you going to do?" he asked.

"I don't know exactly, I guess..." she turned to look at him, but he was gone. She shook her head. What *was* she going to do with this life now? Later, she fell asleep in her old room with that thought running around in her mind

27

"Behold my servant whom I uphold,
my eklektos, in whom my soul delights."

Several weeks later Eden, Parzel, Nasah, Shephel and Sela all stood shivering in the pouring rain on Migdal's practice field once again. In front of them Master Petros was raving about something, Moreh stood trying to look stern but letting her emotions show every time her eye fell across the five of them, and just to her right stood Sargent Gande - Master Gande they had to call him now. He glared at the five of them the whole time. After the wet lecture was finished and Master Petros had felt he had berated the entire group sufficiently to be soaked to the skin he dismissed them.

"Well, you guys sure you're up for this?" Shephel asked, as they tried to shake out their cloaks in the mess hall. "I mean, I was perfectly happy staring into a grey wall for months on end with grouchy old men yelling at me, did we really need to come here to stand in the rain and have grouchy men and women yell at us again until we can start training?" he laughed.

"You should be happy they even let you into the Gibbor Chayil training," Parzel shoved him and he toppled over while trying to take his boots off. "You're the one who couldn't hold on to his own sword."

He glanced at his hand and the scar that crossed all four of his fingers.

"At least my scar is terrifying," Nasah laughed, flexing her arms and showing off the scar that wrapped itself like a snake up and down her arm.

"Besides, did you see Moreh?" Eden asked. "Every time she looked at us she was trying so hard not to smile. We'll be fine," she moved to get in line for food.

Just then Gande and Moreh burst into the mess hall. "What do you think you're doing? On the field, some of you need a lot more training with your swords if you are going to keep all your limbs once you leave for Gibbor Chayil!"

Eden couldn't help but laugh as they rushed out into the pouring rain again to keep training. 'I was chosen for this,' she thought, but with a whole new understanding.

The Renaissance

Connecting Calling to Culture

The Renaissance is a movement to help people find their calling, form their character and forge a culture of goodness, beauty and truth for the glory of God.

For more information on workshops, mentoring and other resources contact:

info@theren.org

"For the word of God is living and active, sharper than any two-edged sword, piercing to the division of soul and of spirit, of joints and of marrow, and discerning the thoughts and intentions of the heart. And no creature is hidden from his sight, but all are naked and exposed to the eyes of him to whom we must give account."

Hebrews 4:12-13

Eden: The King's Eklektos is the imagination of these verses come to life. The writer of Hebrews gives a vivid metaphor of the power of the Word of God, but what would life be like if the King's words literally did battle for you? What if the King oversaw your growth as a warrior wielding His words against the enemy and within yourself? Kaleo is that place. Follow Eden as she is drawn into this strange world from our own, as she chooses to lay down her life and put on a new one and learns what it truly means to be chosen.

Patti LaRose has served in vocational ministry for over 20 years. Having graduated from Brock University with her B.A. in English Language and Literature and from the University of Western Ontario with her B.Ed. in secondary education, Patti taught high school English before co-founding two charities that address the basic needs of people in the community. Now with her Masters in Counselling Psychology she also works as a therapist helping to meet people's mental health needs. She currently lives in Ontario, Canada with her dogs and their supreme commander – the cat.

She has a passion to see the people of God come back to their Bibles. To stop merely taking what they hear on Sunday and trying to survive on the table scraps, and instead to feast on the Word of God.

Renaissance Publishers